ASHLEY MACK

The Sight of You

CONTENT WARNINGS: *sexual content and sexual situations, blood, violence, infant loss, parent loss, death, kidnapping, suicide, and some scenes involving impact play and restraints.*

First edition

ISBN: 979-8-9865191-0-4

Cover art by Rachel McEwan Designs

This book was professionally typeset on Reedsy.
Find out more at reedsy.com

To my husband, for always saying yes.

Tapping persistently breaks the stone.

- WELSH PROVERB

Contents

1

Them

It starts like a fairy tale, a romance, and it will be - just not yet. It's
going to be bloodshed and heartbreak, and full of doubts and betrayal.
It's going to be more than just their story, but they don't know that
yet. Instead it's a woman and a man who are meant to meet.

She's on vacation. The week she's forced to take twice a year by her
father who is also her boss. A father who looked at her and her sisters
and decided he didn't need princesses. He needed warriors. She's a
soldier with the scars to prove it.

But on vacation, she's someone else. On vacation she's a woman
who lets her hair down and her curves show, who highlights the lines
of her face and the bright golden color of her eyes. The vacation
version of her doesn't like typical locations - she looks for rain. This
time she picked Seattle, sneaking a bit of work in with her relaxation.

She sleeps in late, on the silken sheets of her hotel bed, and eats
breakfast that's for flavor rather than function. She doesn't go to the
gym, or check her email. Aside from texting her sisters, she creates a
bubble of relaxation and nothingness around herself. Tries to turn off
the instincts and vigilance that are a part of her every day and pretend
to be a normal person moving through the world.

This is the reason her father forces her to take the time. She would never choose to take it, but benefits from it nonetheless. Everyone needs to breathe sometimes. Sometimes it feels like she doesn't take a breath for months - always bracing for impact, holding it in, holding herself down.

This is her letting go.

She does all the tourist things during the days - the Public Market, the aquarium, the Chihuly Garden which is probably her favorite part because she's seen his work every chance she gets, and on her last day the Museum of Pop Culture because why not? She spends money at expensive restaurants, she buys her sisters silly souvenirs, and indulges in some shopping. She sits in public places and watches the people, imagining lives unlike hers, and envisioning the dark secrets we all keep.

There's one last thing she does on vacation.

She gets dressed up, she goes out, and she attempts to find satisfaction. At home it doesn't feel safe to put herself out there or let anyone in. The real version of her has to be careful; the vacation version gets to take risks.

Tonight she's in exceptionally fine form. Her long hair, usually pulled back in a restrictive and functional bun, is down and curling, almost to her wide hips. The dress she's wearing is gold and sparkling, clinging to her body in invitation, although the clearly defined lines of her muscles mean she won't be easily handled. She might be beautiful but she will bite.

First, she'll dance. The siren call to find a mate for the night.

That's when he sees her.

The club belongs to him, one of many, but this was his first and it will always be his favorite. It's the one that's built and designed to his personal tastes rather than trends. The colors are subdued, the music deep, and the seating areas and VIP are cozy and lush. It's got

2

an exclusive list, practically members only, unless you're willing to pay the exorbitant cover and even then you might get turned away.

He cultivates the group of people that are let in here - people who will keep with the vibe and not turn it into something it isn't. People who won't let slip that if you can't find him anywhere else, you can find him here. This is a place for secrets. For a certain kind of person to find somewhere to get a little bit loose. It's a place of discretion and decadence, and he works hard to keep it classy.

This is his playground, his restoration place, where he can watch and breathe and not have to deal with sycophants who both want and fear his power. Here, he's not the CEO or the criminal. This is the place where he is most himself, even if those around him don't know it.

He named it Cartref, which most people who come can't pronounce correctly but he doesn't care. He named it to honor his Welsh side which has always been dominant in his heart. To honor that this, if any place, is his sense of home.

When he sees her, it feels like she belongs. More than anyone else. Or maybe it's that the moment he sees her, he knows that she belongs to him.

He comes down to the bar to watch her, waiting to see what she does. What happens. If she'll feel him. He isn't against one night stands although he has to be careful that there isn't an ulterior motive. Greater men than him have fallen to the call of their dicks. He doesn't indulge often outside of his regular mistress. Even with her, it's a biological function he engages in to keep his head clear. There are no emotions or promises, there aren't even dates or dinners. He shows up, he releases, he leaves. There's barely even desire, let alone need to be with another person.

Watching her, this beautiful woman, he feels the need for her down to his bones. Deeper even than that. He needs to touch her. He can imagine being with her so clearly it's like he's had her before.

Their eyes meet, and lock.

She lifts one corner of her mouth in a smirk, and for the first time ever he walks onto the dance floor of his own club. When he puts his hands on her, even though he's behind her, she knows exactly who it is. He can see the apples of her cheeks lift in a smile. She presses her body against him, liking the feeling of this man, sensing the possibility of a very satisfying night in his obvious strength and intensity.

They move together to song after song, their bodies easily matching the rhythm and moving together, sensual without being overly sexual. She loves the way he smells, strong and clean. He loves the sparks he feels when she touches his skin, or runs her fingers through his hair and her nails scrape his scalp. It's intoxicating.

He turns her around, holding her tight to his chest. It's disconcerting how well she fits there. There's power in her body, he can feel her strength, and is very aware that she's allowing him to hold her this way. He likes that she's giving him permission.

She, on the other hand, is not aware of that on a conscious level. She feels weak, unable to break away from him, vulnerable to this man in a way she doesn't understand. He moves, she moves, a conversation without words. He flicks his head toward the VIP area and she nods in agreement. They sit down on a cozy couch. Never once do they stop touching.

"I'm Brody," he offers a hand and she takes it with a small laugh.

"Allie."

Both are true, and both are a lie.

She doesn't usually look for intense, but she's drawn to him. To the tension he's holding in his body like he might take the world out if he lets it go. This man is a ticking bomb, but when he touches her and she becomes the center of his attention - she wants to destroy the world with him. This is something she's never felt before and it terrifies her as much as it intrigues her.

Allie tells herself it will be fine. Anything that happens tonight has a finite timeline. She has a flight to catch in the morning.

Much to their surprise, they talk. They talk for hours. She slides off her heels and curls her feet under her on the soft couch, laughing with him, seeing him, enjoying this conversation more than a quick fuck in her hotel room that leaves her feeling both full and empty. They have a lot in common without actually telling each other anything. They don't know that they live in the same world, not yet. For this time, they're pretending that they are normal people who like normal things.

They don't tell one another they've both had blood on their hands.

Instead they talk about movies and music, about safe memories of childhood, about their secret delight in late night talk shows, old musicals, and that their favorite flavor is cinnamon. They both pretend well that this is who they are, not knowing that they are revealing important parts of themselves to the only other person who will ever understand them. They share that they both grew up without mothers and feel responsible for their siblings. That their favorite places are empty spaces and open air. That they both love the rain, and look forward to overcast skies.

If they notice they aren't mentioning their jobs, they don't point it out. Allie knows what this is and what it can never be. Brody is already trying to find a way to turn it into more. He will abandon his commitments for her because this is something he has to hold onto, and Brody never loses.

"Come to my hotel room," Allie asks.

"Where?" Brody responds.

He waves to the bartender to cover her tab, and gives a subtle nod to his usual security detail that they don't need to follow. She notices, but doesn't say anything. Rich men need protection, that's not abnormal.

They leave the club and his driver takes them to the boutique hotel where she's staying. It tells him that she's careful and she's got money, and it makes him trust this more. That she doesn't know who he is and that she can take care of herself. That this isn't a ploy to get something from him other than his company. That this is by chance rather than on purpose.

She's anxious to touch him, be with him, to take the memory of this night into herself and have when she's frustrated by the life she's committed to lead. She knows already this memory will sustain her for a long time. Allie fears that the next time she goes on a trip, she won't find anyone to spend a night with because tonight will ruin it for her. There will be no one else like this. It doesn't bother her as much as she thinks it should.

When they get to her room, they don't rush.

Brody touches her slowly, with his hands and then his mouth, worshiping her body. He tastes her and she's better than he imagined. The feeling of her skin is like nothing he's ever felt before. Every part of her he touches becomes his new favorite, every sound she makes the best sound he's ever heard. The level of satisfaction he feels when she screams his name and comes on his tongue is infinite.

He wants to keep going but she pushes him away, taking her chance to explore his body in return. It's a surprise to them both when she bites down on his hip, in the deep V from his abs to his groin. It leaves a mark and she loves it. For a few days at least, he'll remember her. When she takes him into her mouth they groan simultaneously, him from the pleasure and her from the masculine flavor of him, strong and salty.

Then she's climbing over him, letting him into her body, bringing them both to the edge as they cling to one another, joined by their mouths and their cores, unable to give each other space. There isn't a breath between them that they don't share.

He doesn't usually kiss the women he has sex with; in the two years he's used his mistress he's never once gotten close to putting his mouth on hers and she learned quickly that the fastest way to shut him down was to try. Kisses mean intimacy and trust. He doesn't think about it because when something feels right, it happens. Kissing her is right.

He can't stop kissing this woman because kissing her makes him feel like he's breathing for the first time. The taste of her drives him insane, both new and familiar, like he's been waiting to have her again even though it's the first time. They never seem to stop, going and going, touching and feeling until the sun is starting to come up over the skyline. They are sunk inside one another's skin, the scent of her living inside of him, the taste of her now the taste of him.

Allie doesn't usually let the men she takes to her hotel stay the night. Doesn't let herself feel what it's like to close her eyes while pressed up against another body. She's never slept with a man.

For an hour, she lets herself sleep with him.

Then she needs to leave.

Brody doesn't stir when she gets up, when she gets dressed, and collects her bag. Everything was packed to go before she left for the night and all she had to was slide in her dress and her shoes. All she had to do was grab and go, and now she doesn't want to leave. Every trip she only hooks up on the last night so there's no temptation to get involved, or no annoyance to get rid of. This is the first time she has regrets.

Regret that she can't spend the day in bed with him. They'd watch an old movie, naked and tangled in those sheets, and talk about the normal things that she never gets to think about in her day to day life. Allie can imagine it all so clearly, the way the day and the time would unfold. She's already attached to him and they haven't even known each other for 12 hours. If she stays, it will only hurt more to leave. She has to leave.

She writes him a note, and leaves it on the pillow where he last saw her. She stares at him for a long time, finding it difficult to breathe. She reminds herself again that they need her at home. That he's probably a completely normal rich guy and wouldn't understand who she was at home, the blood on her hands, the violence that takes her over sometimes. She has to go home.

He feels like home too, but that's an irrational thought, and she has to slip back into being rational again.

Before leaving the hotel, she asks them to give him a wake up call before checkout.

He's not awake yet when she gets on the plane back home. When he left with her he also gave himself a day off, canceling the few obligations he has on Sundays. He was hoping to spend more time with her, to ignore his responsibilities while getting lost in something he's never felt before. To explore this obsession and find out what it means.

When Brody does wake up, it takes him a moment to remember where he is, and to believe that the woman from the night before wasn't a dream. Her absence makes him doubt himself. The room is emptier than he remembers, and there's no sounds of her in the shower or the bathroom.

Then he sees it.

The note next to him in bed causes rage of course, but also something else he hasn't felt in a long time: pain. The loss of her hurts him. It hurts that she's gone, and that he thinks she didn't feel what he did. It feels weak, and that makes him angrier. The content of the note makes him hope that someday he'll get to punish her for it.

> *Brody,*
> *Last night was more than you'll ever know. I hope I find you again.*

XX,
Allie

He has to believe he'll find her again, and this time he'll know what he's found and she won't get away. Business deals and future plans be damned, he wants her.

She goes home.

She puts away the vacation version of herself; she's not Allie anymore. For the first time since she started taking her trips, she doesn't tell her sisters much about it. Doesn't give them the dirty details of her hook up because it was more than that even if she doesn't want it to be.

She's a soldier again. Dangerous, bloody, and alone.

2

Alina

The graveyard is the same as always. I'm the only one who comes every year, marking the day of our mother's death. Today it's been 15 years. She's been gone longer than we ever had her but it doesn't make me miss her any less. The pain faded, the longing didn't.

This time all my sisters agreed to come with me and acknowledge our loss. We stand outside the mausoleum that bears our family name - Sorrelle. The building is stately and gray, carefully maintained ivy growing on the outside. It makes us look like old money but our father had it built just for her.

I can tell that Anora and Aro don't want to be here, and Aster could care less. Our father, who misses her as if it's only been a day since she died, tries not to let his grief show in front of us anymore. It threw our lives into chaos and sometimes it feels like our family barely survived the emotional fallout.

He told me once that the graveyard isn't where he remembers her. I know he's been with other women since her death, but he'll never marry again. Tonight he'll go to dinner at the restaurant where he proposed. It's one of the nights where I am specifically dismissed from his security detail, so that he can grieve and remember her as he wishes. He will always belong to Arianna Sorrelle, and she will always belong to him. One of the deepest secrets in my heart is the reality that I'll never feel a love like that. I will never belong to anyone but myself, and no one will belong to me.

None of his daughters will get a love story like that, but we came to terms with it a long time ago. We knew the lives we chose would be lonely, that more often than not we'd only have each other and sometimes not even that. Even had our mother lived, the reality of who we are and the world we were raised in makes that impossible. Still, if she was here it might have softened the truths we faced.

My mother's death was unexpected; a cancer diagnosis that took her away from us in a year when we thought we'd have more or even a chance to fight. Anora and I, as the oldest, remember her the best - she was 12 and I was 11. I have good, clear memories of spending time with her, and then ones I wish weren't so clear of watching her fade quickly and brutally.

My youngest siblings, Aro and Aster, were 8 and 6. Aro has a few memories but Aster says she has none. Aster being the way she is, I'm not sure she cares. Aster doesn't need anyone, and has no place for sentimentality or grief. All she's got is loyalty to us, and it's the only reason she's here at the cemetery. If I was in a better mood, I would have told her not to come but I've been leaning on them lately.

Our lives were always bound to be chaos, but losing mom made it happen faster.

Don Sorrelle was a computer genius, and took a chance on digital security before people even knew that was a thing that they would need. His best friend, Roman Carver, was the business-minded risk taker that built them an empire. It boomed. Designation Technology created the landscape where none had existed before. A few years after college they went from solidly middle class men to billionaires.

They married, they had children, they created and schemed. They became so staggeringly wealthy that it changed how they had to operate in the world. They needed to protect their legacies and make sure they had heirs and plans and alliances. They knew their were targets on their backs just for having money, and that people would always be coming to them with a hand out or an offer, some of them that they couldn't refuse. Money makes the world different.

Money always breeds corruption, and Roman, who we knew and loved like an uncle, allowed himself to be corrupted. So when his best friend asked, dad created programs that made it easy for someone to hide their tracks, and to clean their money. Roman got in deep with the underworld, making himself and the technology my father created indispensable to anyone who wanted to hide what they were amassing. It opened up whole new avenues of crime. The money was good, but the safety became questionable. When Roman couldn't deliver, when things didn't always go perfectly, there were consequences.

While the Sorrelles are Italian, we aren't mafia, and the Carvers are as lily white as they come before Roman got them dirty. It was a disaster waiting to happen.

When Roman became too big for his role, they took him out. He'd pissed off the wrong man who had no morals, and didn't like that Roman thought he was above the criminal playground he worked in. As if covering up the money from crime didn't make him a criminal.

Roman was out with his wife for their anniversary and they were executed in an alley right next to their car. They left behind their son, Owen, and that's how a surly 16 year old joined a household of girls he barely knew who were only a few years out from the loss of their mother. It should have made us close, but it didn't.

Owen wasn't like a cousin or a brother to us, but a presence in our house that warned us of how fucking dangerous the world we were trapped in was. Dad found his entire world had been rocked between the loss of his life partner, and his business partner.

Dad couldn't pull out from Roman's criminal dealings. It was do what they want or everyone dies, and so he kept doing what they wanted. They had no loyalty to him, and all he had was the skills to provide a unique service to the criminal element. This was the mafia, it was blood or nothing, and it was always going to be dangerous for us.

Where some men would think to raise their daughters to be enticing brides for the mafia to strengthen those ties, my father gave us a choice. Learn to fight, to lead, to protect him and ourselves. To protect what he made and built. Become a force to be feared, a warrior to be reckoned with, and a soldier worth following. It's a choice we all made and found our own paths that suited us while also protecting our family.

So I made my body into a weapon, and I work for my father as his head of security, sometimes his enforcer because people underestimate me time and time again.

I have killed for him. I've been wounded for him. I would take a bullet for him. My father isn't perfect, but he does his best to let us make our own choices in a world that would try and put us in a box.

My sisters and I each have our individual skills that make us useful to him, and provide us purpose for ourselves. It won't be this way forever, it's not sustainable or realistic, but for now we're together, clinging to one another as best we can in a world that's violent and uncertain. In a world that doesn't want to believe that women can be just as devious and dangerous as the men who inhabit it.

I'll kill anyone who ever tries to hurt them. I'll do anything to keep my family alive and breathing. We are bound by our promises to each other as much as by our blood.

It's why Aster came today to stand with me.

It's why Anora is next to me, holding my hand.

It's why Aro made sure we had flowers to leave.

This is something that matters to me, so here they are.

We stand side by side in the bright sun and cold spring air, lost in our own thoughts.

"I made reservations at the Sun Drop for brunch," Anora breaks the silence. Always the planner, the socialite, the one who knows where to go to be seen.

Anora is the most beautiful of us all - petite, proportional, and delicate. People stare at her with her dark hair and pale skin, like Snow White come to life because of her deep pink lips. She's the peacemaker and very typical older sibling in terms of being the one who is the most organized and the most responsible in regard to plans and obligations. Anora knows how we need to look to the world and makes it happen. She's great at observing relationships, interactions, and tensions and figuring out how to use them. Despite her beauty, she can be a master manipulator and so sweet looking they never know they've been played.

I don't want to go to brunch but I will because she's leaving us soon. It was the choice that she made when our father sat us down and told us the reality of the world we were living in.

Anora agreed to be our father's bargaining chip. She agreed to become the perfect mafia-adjacent princess, a refined virgin, and be married off to someone she didn't love to strengthen our ties with either the legitimate or the criminal world. Sometimes I think she agreed to it to punish herself for some unknown and unnamed sin, but she always reassures me that it's fine, and this is what she wants. She was 16 years old when she made that promise. She's known that she would be married for convenience and not for love all of her adult life.

Except now the deal is being struck and she's tentatively engaged to Broderick Clayton. CEO of Venture, a competing technology company with the largest server farm on the West Coast. He also has ties to illicit shipping and money laundering. If she marries someone who plays both sides of the coin like we do, it'll keep all of us safer, including Venture.

He's coming here in a few days to meet her and iron out the details of the contract and for him to formally begin their engagement. I've been working on the security and details of their itinerary since I got back from my vacation a month ago. He's bringing his own staff but I won't let anything happen to him on our turf. I want him to see that we're strong, that we don't need him, and this is just planning ahead. We're fine and strong exactly as we are.

It's been late nights driving routes from the private airfield he'll be coming into, making sure that all of our staff will be well-rested so they are at peak attention, and intimidation, when my future brother-in-law walks onto our compound. I want him to know that we're the bigger player in the room and he's fucking lucky to be breathing our air. I want him to leave with the impression that if he hurts Anora or betrays us in any way, the hammer will fall on him and I'll be the one holding it.

I already hate him because he'll be taking Anora from us. She'll be his family. Run his house, have his children, and I won't be able to see her every day and know if she's truly happy. I won't be able to protect her. Anora is a fantastic liar, and I'll never be able to tell from her voice if she's really okay. It's something I can see in her eyes and body language from a lifetime of knowing her, and knowing her before she learned to lie so well. There are horror stories about arranged marriages, and I refuse to let her become another one of them. He will treat her with respect or I will mangle his testicles.

I take a deep breath, bringing myself back to today, to this place. I don't go inside the mausoleum like usual, feeling suddenly self-conscious. But I do take a step closer and put my hand on the door.

"Bye, mom." The metal door is warm in the spring sunshine and feels oddly reassuring. My soul quiets for a second, it's storm raging even harder than usual since my encounter with Brody while on vacation. It's like I left a part of me in that hotel room and no matter how I claw and scramble and dig, I can't get it back. I want it back.

We trudge through the graveyard and back to the waiting SUV that's going to take us all to brunch. Owen is waiting inside smoking a cigarette, the smoke twirling out the passenger window and being caught in the wind. He's protective of us but distant. I heard my father talking to a colleague once that after losing his mother, Owen didn't talk for a month. Even the first year he lived with us he barely spoke to anyone but dad.

Now his silence is a tactic, rather than a coping mechanism. Owen is the official heir, heir to take over ownership and operation of Designation and the legacy of both our fathers. Surprisingly, none of us are bitter about it. For some reason, it fits Owen, and he will be someone no one wants to fuck with. At 16 he was handsome, but thin. Now, he's shockingly strong with a jawline that would break your hand before it got a bruise. We aren't close, but I respect him.

"Why is Owen here?" Aster grumbles.

"Because I invited him," Aro snarls. She's always had a soft spot for our ward. I think because they're similar - lovely to look at, but inside their own minds. Even though she has good intentions trying to treat him like a brother, I'm not sure how he feels about it. Then again, he's here, waiting in a car in a cemetery.

"It was a nice thing to do, Aro," Anora ignores their childishness.

We've all tried hard to not blame him for the sins of his father, and I probably fail at that the most. None of this would be happening if it wasn't for Roman and his greed, not to this extent. Owen would be at home, both his parents alive and well. We wouldn't need to be marrying off Anora to keep criminals happy because we never would've been involved with them in the first place. We'd still be the children of billionaire tech geniuses. We'd still be children of

16

outrageous and decadent privilege.

Now we're children of privilege yes, but also blood. It's unlikely we'd know the weight of a blade in our hands, the texture of the grip of a gun, the scent of gunpowder, and what it's like when there's so much blood you can taste it in the air. There wouldn't be scars from fights we almost lost. When someone asks me about my body count, I wouldn't have to figure out if they meant lives taken or people bedded. One number is far larger than the other.

The only person in this car who's never taken a life is Anora, as far as I know.

Aro is a dreamer, full of creativity and imagination, and flexible in any situation. She can put on a personality to be who she needs to be to get the information needed. When she's not working she's an introvert, wrapped deep in the privacy of her own mind. Aro isn't afraid to silence someone because to her, death is the best way to keep a secret, secret.

Aster...

Well, Aster is something else and even without the underworld we got pulled into, she would have found her way there. A smart programmer who could be so much more, she has a thirst for violence that scares even me. We all pretend like we don't see it, but for someone so diminutive the fact that she's a predator still radiates from her body. Aster is the nightmare you don't know you've met in a dark alley. You'd be dead before you even realized she had a knife.

Silence descends as we drive through the streets to the restaurant. We're all tense with each other and I wish it was different. We're all in our heads thinking about mom, thinking about Anora leaving and a permanent change to our family, and our own business.

Sometimes I let myself think about Seattle, but then there's a pain in my chest so acute that I can't. I can't think about it.

The car stops to let us out, and we all put on our game faces while

THE SIGHT OF YOU

out in public. Aster and I drop back automatically, scanning our surroundings and assessing for threats. The street is clear, and all of us are armed anyway.

The only fight I ever had with Anora was over her learning to shoot and promising to carry. I won.

Obviously.

It gives me peace of mind to know that worst case scenario, she can shoot her way out.

Anora whispers something to Owen as they sit down. He smiles at her, quick and sharp, and then it drops from his face. He looks even more broody than usual, and that's saying something.

It makes it even more brutally obvious that we will be losing Anora when they sit side by side. The heir and the bargaining chip. Anora will cement our alliance with the Claytons and Venture, binding our fates together. Then when our father dies or retires the businesses - both above and below board - become Owen's.

I wonder if I'll still have a job when that happens. He's aware of how dangerous and effective I am - we've trained together. I've been on his protection detail before. Still, nothing fucks everyone over like change, and I can't imagine he'll want to keep my father's infrastructure in place. He'll want to build his own. This is his legacy too, and it's something I have to remind myself. Owen won't be taking this over because he's the male, he'll be taking it over because of all of the children of Don and Roman, he's the oldest. That was the succession they agreed to before ever having kids. Owen takes it seriously and he'll want to find ways to make it his own.

I can't help but respect that.

If he turns the three of us out, we'll be fine. We have money from our mother's side and millions going to each of us upon my father's death. Maybe it won't be so bad if that happens. It's not that I won't grieve my father, it's the chance that perhaps this violence is temporary for

18

me. Maybe I'll be able to build a normal person kind of life. One where I can be Vacation Alina all the time.

My mind filters back to Seattle, to my night in bed with a stranger.

It's not the stranger part that sticks with me - that's a normal part of my vacations. It's how much he didn't feel like one. Brody. I doubt that was his real name, just like I hadn't given him mine. Which was odd, because previously I had no problem saying I was Alina - but with Brody I'd wanted to be someone else. Someone who could stay with that surprisingly sweet, wild man who hooked me with a look. No one had ever called me Allie in my life. But for Brody, I could pretend I was her.

Breakfast passes in silence and heartbreak, and we return to our family compound in the outer suburbs. We have visitors to prepare for.

3

Derick

I've made a huge fucking mistake coming here. I knew that before I even knocked on the door, but I am a creature of habit and control, and right now I don't feel in control.

Work is busy, I'm wrapping up the details before I head to Chicago to meet with Don Sorrelle and discuss our arrangement, and someone has been trying to hack a very specific server in our farm. I have a headache and I'm restless. In the past when I felt that way, I'd go see Cat. Following routine, I came to Cat's house because sometimes fucking the shit out of her cleared my mind.

The problem is that for the last month, I couldn't even get hard. I hadn't fucked anyone since Allie - and even when I jacked off, I was thinking about her. We had done everything in a night. I'd gotten to know her body as well as I knew my own, and I felt like I'd known her mind as if we'd been connected for years.

I didn't want the mindless fucking, or the false attention and flattery, that came along with being around Cat. She'd been my regular pussy for the last two years. She wasn't my mistress since I wasn't married, but she was the one at my beck and call. It had been convenient because she hadn't been looking for a commitment, but someone to give her a very particular kind of attention.

But after two years, she started to think this was something else. Despite the fact that I'd never kissed her, caressed her, didn't cuddle, and barely spoke to her. There was no pillow talk, and no kind words.

Currently, I was sitting on her couch while she nibbled at my neck and rubbed my soft cock.

Nothing happened. Not a spark, a twitch, not even the uncontrollable biological response of physical stimulation. In fact, it felt like my balls were trying to crawl back inside my body, repulsed by Cat and her neediness.

"Baby, what's the matter?" she whispers huskily.

The baby thing had started a couple months ago - after the chatter had gotten out that I was probably getting married. For some reason, Cat now wanted promises from me and I had no idea where that had come from. We fucked. That was it. Suddenly, Cat was invested in me and wanted me to promise I'd still be with her even after I got married. I had no intention of making that promise to her.

The marriage was a business arrangement - I wasn't going to remain faithful, and honestly, I didn't expect my future wife to either. She could only have babies with me, that was part of the deal, but I wasn't going to isolate her when we would likely never connect. The best I could hope for was that we'd be friends. If she wanted a lover, as long as she was discreet, I would be too.

"I guess I'm not feeling it, Cat." I sigh and stand up, pushing her hands off me as she tries to cling to my leg and arm. Without another word or glance back, I head for the front door. I hear Cat trotting after me, saying something about having a drink but I ignore her.

My driver and bodyguard, Andrew, is waiting at the curb, car still running. He raises his eyebrows at me through the window, but it's not really a surprise. This is the third time I've been here since meeting Allie and every visit gets shorter - as does my patience. This will be the last time I see Cat. I'm done.

Andrew has been with me a long time so most formality is dropped - unless we're in business hours he doesn't get the door for me, and when it's just us he calls me Derick. He's only a few years older than me, but life hasn't been kind to him and working for me is the distraction he needs.

He had a wife and a son and they were killed. It destroyed him. He has no life outside of driving me around and being at hand when I need him, and that was how he survived. Andrew struggles to live for himself so he lives for me. I pay him well for it, and do my best to make him do human being things like take a vacation and go to the dentist. I've suggested he go back to therapy, often, but get a soft rebuff in the form of a tight smile. If I have a friend in this world, it's Andrew. I trust him more than I trust my brother, not that it was difficult to do that.

Speak of the devil - I answer the call from Jack as Andrew pulls onto the road and heads home.

"What."

"Is that any way to greet me when I have good news?"

"What." I prompt again. My brother is enthusiastic but ridiculous. He has eyes and dreams that are bigger than reality, and it gets him into trouble - often. Whether it's trying to get in on illegal business, taking over clubs and shops, or the way he approaches women. He wants the Clayton name to be sacrosanct in both legitimate and underworld affairs.

"The Eastons are willing to sell. They want to divest themselves from West Coast operations - we'd get the clubs and the convenience stores. They keep the restaurants."

That is an interesting development. "What are the terms?"

Jack rattles off a number that we can afford, and a request from the Eastons that we keep certain members of the staff. That will be hard to commit to - they could be people who are just working their jobs, or they could be loyal to the Eastons and looking for a way to betray us for taking over, or betray them for stepping out. Then again, if and when I sell our businesses I would want the same thing. We'll find a way to make it work.

"Start looking into everyone before we sign anything. The higher ups, managers - who has something over their head that we need to take care of - and call Ethan in the morning to get the bankroll going. Nice work, brother."

"Thank you," Jack sounds genuinely pleased and surprised, and it makes me feel like shit - I am not good at showing him appreciation because I'm always waiting for him to fuck up. His track record has been clean the last few years, but I have a lifetime of messes on the other side of the scale. It is my job to be the boss, to be intimidating, to punish anyone that tries to fuck with our empire. I made it Jack's job to make the empire grow, to soften the blow that comes with dealing with me. I'm considered charming but ruthless, while everyone sees him as the pushover.

"Are you coming with me to Chicago?"

There's a beat of silence, and I have no idea what Jack is thinking. "I don't think I should. We've had a few warehouses and shipments hit, and with the hack I think it's better if someone from the family stays here. You need someone you can trust in charge."

"Fair enough. I trust you." To a certain extent.

"Later, bro."

Jack hangs up the phone and I feel slightly better. The business is in good hands between the two of us. He's good at the legitimate business even if I mostly keep him in the underworld. The server farm runs itself - it makes so much fucking money we probably don't need the underworld work, but it's who we were first. The Claytons were criminals - are criminals - and it's hard to extricate yourself from that world entirely. I want to, and I'm trying, but it takes time, money, and patience.

We have contacts overseas and in the port to bring in untraceable phones, sell cheap burners, help people mask their locations. If we get the Eastons holdings we'll be able to increase our money laundering options as well, churning cash through the clubs that comes out clean. We have other businesses that are legit on the surface - clubs, restaurants, stores, car washes - that we use for illegal things as needed.

The people that work for us aren't family, but they stay loyal to us because we pay them a fair cut and try to treat them well. My father always believed that we couldn't keep our money if we didn't keep our people. People are the family business, and the people are who make us money. I try to keep living by that. He might have been a shit father but he was a brilliant boss. I think some of his staff cried more at his funeral than his sons did.

He died when I was 16, and I still hate that this is where I am now, even if I'm good at it. Dad wanted to start working to be completely above board but he didn't get far. Part of me doesn't want to let it go completely - I look the part of the CEO skin but the darkest parts of me and the anger I can't let go of suit the underworld. I have no hesitation to kill, maim, burn, and torture as needed. I am not afraid to protect what's mine - not just the money, but the people too.

A few years ago, someone was using our main club, Violenza, to traffic girls. They were taking our patrons and our staff, and when we found out who was doing it and what exactly they were doing...I took care of it. We'll never be in the skin game, not even strip clubs, because even the best intentions get fucked when greed and sex come together. Those motherfuckers died in pain, and the girls they tried to take were saved.

I know there's more women they took from elsewhere that weren't - more they'd gotten in other places with no way to be set free. I hated the idea of that but I was one man and one family, albeit a powerful one, but I had no leverage in that world.

So I'd clean my cash and the cash of others, I'd give people a playground to take and sell drugs, I'd make sure they could deal and do business with phones that couldn't be traced back to anyone, and I'd keep a fuck ton of data that could be at my fingertips if I wanted it to be. That was the life I'd inherited.

I wonder what Allie does for a living.

God damn.

She'd been strong - her muscles defined from the kind of working out that gave her strength and not just shape - they were earned through work as well as the gym. The feeling of her thighs squeezing my face as she came on my tongue overwhelms me. Her endurance as she rode my cock, bouncing her perfect bubble butt onto my thighs - yeah, she was fucking strong. But soft where it counted. I'd kissed her pillowy lips hundreds of times that night, couldn't get enough of them. Couldn't get enough of tasting her.

And now my cock is hard, I can taste her in my mouth, and I am angry as hell because she left. I can't find her - she'd registered under a fake name and been gone before anyone could trace her. If it wasn't for the fact that we'd savaged each other all night I would almost have thought she drugged me for how deep I slept. So deep I didn't hear her leave.

Whatever.

Tomorrow I'm going to Chicago to meet the woman I'm probably going to marry. The woman who will bear my children, even if I have to think of another woman while I put them inside her.

If I ever find Allie, I am going to punish the fuck out of her, and then never let her leave.

4

Derick

I leave a rainy, misty Seattle for a rainy, misty Chicago.

The stairs of the jet are soaked as we descend, and we rush to the black SUVs waiting to take us to the grand Sorrelle compound. I've seen photos - it really is lovely. It reminded me of the house from Home Alone, only surrounded by acres of private land and gardens and enclosed by an impenetrable fence and armed guards.

The Sorrelles aren't really crime, despite the Italian name, but they had gotten in on something that was lucrative to the underworld. They were more legitimate than the Claytons, but it was the work they did for the bad guys that kept them bound to the darkness. Once the underworld has you, and you have something they want, you give it to them before they kill you to take it over. Everyone in the underworld is dispensable, so every single day is a fight. The Sorrelles learned to fight, and that's why I'm willing to work with Don and Designation Tech.

It isn't long before the skyline of Chicago disappears. We drive through sweet, rich suburbs, and then the houses get farther and farther apart.

I'm making this trip alone - no one else in the business is with me. I have my usual security staff, and my assistant Jonah. There are obligations that go along with being CEO of Venture, and Jonah manages them for me. When the deal with Sorrelle and Designation was first offered, Jonah was the one to assess and encourage me to agree to the merger. The whole thing made him excited and that was good enough for me.

I am decisive, but I don't know the ins and outs of the technical work that we do. I have people I trust in place for that, people who know what would happen to them if they fucked with me or my family. As long as they don't do that, I make sure they feel like goddamn kings.

The lead car stops at the manned gate onto the Sorrelle property - a man checks all three cars before going back and pressing the button to open the gate. It surprises me that Don Sorrelle is this paranoid, but maybe it shouldn't. My people had done their research, I knew their history was dark and there's no lack of threats and violence. I knew what had happened to his partner, and knew plenty of rich families who'd had their children kidnapped for ransom. Don was handling it alone.

Arianna Sorrelle had died quickly of cancer, sending the man into a tailspin. I heard he trained his daughters like soldiers, although I'd only seen them in blurry surveillance photos because they were extremely careful about social media. Given their digital power, it makes sense that they keep a low profile. Information is dangerous.

It was only 10 years ago, Don's business partner ran his mouth and been killed for it - one shot in the head, another in his wife. Don agreed to the terms pretty quickly to keep everyone else alive. It was the only reason his partner's son Owen was still breathing. He would take over the company someday on this end, so this visit was also a chance for me to meet my future partner. I'd heard mixed things about Owen - broody and reserved, but smart. He'd gotten a computer science degree and then stepped into his place by Don's side.

Owen had been with Don for years - it would be interesting to see their relationship, as well as the relationship Owen had with the Sorrelle sisters, if at all. Proximity did not breed fondness, in my experience.

The huge brick mansion comes into view, lit up and cozy looking in the gray, hazy day. Don is standing at the door, holding it open with a big smile on his face. The man is so soft it's hard to believe how he's fought to keep what he has. He isn't overly tall, less than six feet, with a body gone slightly soft, gray hair, and a salt and pepper mustache. It's his dark brown eyes and their odd twinkle that make you think you were interacting with Italian Santa Claus - he could give you a gift, he could read your mind to know if you've been naughty or nice, and when he laughs his paunch jiggles like a bowl full of jelly.

"Derick!" he calls as I exit the SUV. "Right on time."

Our staffs size each other up as I walk into the house, and look around at the plush interior. Its a little dated and a little busy, but the house is made for warmth and comfort. Its meant to soothe you with it's coziness, trick you into relaxing.

"Come, we'll have a drink and the girls will join us shortly." He leads me into a parlor at the front of the house that has a full wet bar. Drinks are already made on a tray, whiskey neat, and I grab one but don't take a sip.

I look around at the security staff near him. "Your daughters aren't working tonight?"

Don chuckles. Who the fuck chuckles?

"You might be family someday - I gave them the night to meet you properly."

He gestures to some well-loved leather armchairs next to the fireplace and I sit down across from him. Right away he dives into asking me questions about the business, displaying a large amount of knowledge about exactly what we do. The models of our servers,

28

the specifics of our web services, and more details about our finances than I feel an outsider should have. It makes me both suspicious and impressed. Someone on the inside told him things, but if it works out to our benefit, I won't hunt them down for their betrayal. Yet.

Over my shoulder, one of Don's staff signals to him, and a moment later I hear soft footsteps. Don rises from his chair and holds out his arm towards the door.

"Come, meet my girls."

I stand up and follow him, surprisingly anxious. I know their names and aside from Anora, vaguely what they look like. I've also heard a lot of things about what exactly they were trained to do. Alina, the second oldest, the enforcer. She's already taken a knife for her father when a disgruntled employee tried to stab him. As a result, she broke the man's arm and jaw and had to be pulled off him by other security staff before she killed him. All while bleeding from a wound that resulted in the removal of her spleen. Even I have to admit she sounds like a bad ass I wouldn't want to mess with.

The middle child, and the most mysterious, is Aro. She's about to finish college with a general studies degree. Her only social media is with a platform that tracks her reading, which is constant and varied.

Then there's Aster. I haven't even met her yet and she gives me the creeps. Anyone who has anything to say about her says that something is wrong with her - she's smart, started college at 16 and finished her master's degree at 21. Aster went straight to work at Designation as a programmer. She also works in the darkest part of Don's criminal work, the most traditionally underworld. Aster likes to cut and ask questions, and she is very, very good at getting answers.

All this is in my mind as I turn and watch them enter the room.

Anora enters first, wearing a soft feminine dress of white and gold. Very bridal, which makes me feel like I can't breathe. She's lovely, of course, but I feel like if I push too hard she'll break. She's the skin of a

29

peach and bruises easily.

Then Aro, wearing pink, looking deceptively girly and sweet with a white satin bow in her hair. The smile on her face doesn't reach her eyes, eyes that are observant and calculating and as she rakes them over me I feel like I've undergone a detailed physical examination with no idea of the results. Interesting.

Then Aster, in black yoga pants and an oversize black hoodie with a skeleton hand giving the finger, her curly hair reaching her chin and somehow flying in all directions. Our eyes meet and she gives me a raised eyebrow, and I know in her assessment I have definitely been found wanting. Aster pulls her phone out of her hoodie pocket and starts playing a game with the volume on. Clearly a psychopath, who doesn't have their phone on silent at all times?

That means the footsteps coming quickly down the hall belong to Alina.

She's wearing a black pantsuit that fits her, but also hides her curves as well as it hides the holster strapped across her chest. When I look into her face, she's wearing no makeup and her hair is back in a severe bun. I'm struck immediately with a sense of familiarity and it takes a minute for my brain to catch up with what's happening right now.

There's a look of panic and horror on her face as we lock eyes.

"Allie?" My voice feels like it's coming out of someone else's body.

Fury and relief roar through me in equal measure. I've found her, and she's my future fucking sister-in-law.

5

Alina

I'm arguing with Alonzo in the kitchen trying to get him to tell me where Owen is. Alonzo is his main security staffer and always knows where his charge is, even when he's off duty.

"He has to be here, Lonzo. Dad is going to be furious otherwise. It looks bad."

Alonzo shakes his head at me, some expression on his face I don't understand. "Not today. He said he'll meet the man another time."

It reminds me that Owen and the staff never refer to Derick Clayton by name. Just - the man. Which is a little funny because he and Owen are both 30 - there was nothing about Derick that is elder to Owen, so maybe it's a way to distance himself. It's not like Owen is really attached to any of us, but maybe he doesn't like the idea of sharing power and profits in the future. He'd gone to school and gone straight to work for Designation under my father - maybe he's bitter that expansion also means sharing power.

"The next chance to meet him will be at the wedding and that is not appropriate. He's not answering my calls."

Ignoring me, Alonzo turns his back on me and leaves the room. I yell after him but then check my watch and see that I'm already off schedule and Owen and Alonzo are to blame. We will be having words about this.

Now I'm running late to meet Derick, and I shuffle walk as fast as I can down the hallway to the front parlor. I step into the room, fake polite smile plastered on my face, and look into the face of my future brother-in-law who I will pretend I like for Anora's sake. Except that's not how I feel when I look at him at all. I think my heart stops.

This can't be happening.

The look on his face is fury and heat that makes shivers overtake my body in seconds. I'd worked so hard not to look into Broderick Clayton because Anora asked me not to - she wanted to learn about him organically, and our father had other people who were vetting him. By honoring my sister, I have completely fucked myself over.

If I'd known - if I'd known who Derick was - then he never would have had the chance to be Brody. I never would have gone near him because I would've recognized him as hands off, no matter how my type he might be. That night...that night that I can't get over has been ruined forever.

Brody - standing in front of me, his jaw dropped, looking even sexier than I remember in a black suit and a crisp white shirt. We're close enough that I can catch a whiff of his cologne in the air. The smell that's haunted me since I left my hotel room, leaving him in my bed.

"Allie?" His voice is an angry rumble.

My mouth opens and closes but nothing comes out. When I'd entered the room I'd been prepared to introduce myself, so my brain decided it was a good idea to go with: "I'm Alina."

"Alina. Alina Sorrelle." His voice is full of confusion and disdain.

"Yes." It finally comes to my attention that everyone in the room is looking between us, confused and in Anora's case, flustered. She has a hand pressed to her chest and is looking to our father to sort out whatever is happening. It sends a bolt of frustration through me because Anora isn't weak, but she's bought into her role as a tool too deeply when men are in the room. How she has sisters like us and still cow-tows to men I will never understand. Aro and Aster are both looking distinctly entertained at the turn our evening has taken.

Even though my eyes keep bouncing around the room, shame and fear and anxiety coursing through me, they always get drawn back to Derick.

"Did you know - who I was?" His voice is strangled with fury.

"No," I answer swiftly and with pain in my voice. The pain seems to speak the truth to him because some of the rage calms. Now he isn't angry because he thinks it was a setup, he's angry because I left. I know, because I am still angry at myself.

"What's going on here?" Dad finally steps in, putting himself between me and Derick and making me take a few steps back.

My arm presses up against Aster and she leans over. "What the fuck did you do?" she whispers.

"Slept with her future brother-in-law, duh," Aro hisses from her other side. Anora flinches and pales and I feel like an asshole.

At least I can reassure her that he's an excellent lover and she'll get lots of orgasms on her journey toward motherhood.

That thought fills me with a sharp and brutal agony and has my shoulders hunching inward. I connected with Brody - with Derick - and based on his anger I'm guessing it had been a real night for him too. It's hard to think of him with someone else, let alone knowing that for as long as their married I'll know he's with Anora.

Fate really loves to fuck me over. Take my mother, take my will, and now take the first time I've ever felt connected to another human being and make it a punishment. This is why emotions other than loyalty are a waste of time. I've shut myself up so tightly I can't even tell you if I love my sisters, or I am so fucking attached to the concept of loyalty that I would do anything for them if it meant protecting them.

I'd rip out my heart for Anora, and it kind of feels like I'm doing that. It's not like I can step in and fight for Derick. That's not my role, and it was only one night. One night that I wanted to cherish as a best memory, a comfort memory, that now I'll have to find a way to forget. Anora is going to marry Derick and we have to figure out how to live with that. All of us.

"I met All-Alina when she came to Seattle last month." Derick answers my father but doesn't take his eyes off me. I don't think he has since I entered the room.

"Alina?" my father turns to me and I know what he's asking. It's not like it's a secret that I hook up on those trips because it doesn't feel safe to meet anyone in Chicago. I feel too known, too vulnerable, and so I leave the whole damn state just to get some ass.

"Yes," I answer him, my eyes dropping to my feet and my cheeks heating in embarrassment.

Father turns to my sister. "Anora?"

"It's fine," she reassures him. As if she'd say anything else.

"What are you all talking about?" Derick growls and steps in.

"Anora will move forward with the engagement," my father says like that's no big deal. "It's what we agreed on, and it's not like we're making a love match here. Anora agreed to this, she knows what's getting into."

"No," Derick steps back. "I no longer agree."

The whole room freezes and the tension turns from confused to angry. My father frowns. Crap. Derick is free to back out - they haven't signed anything yet, that's what this trip was for. Everything has been tentative and verbal until the details could be worked out face to face. This could all be over before anything begins. There has to be a way to salvage this.

I can talk a big game that we don't need Venture, but the truth is -

we do. We need to be bigger and badder to keep criminals and rivals off our backs.

"I marry Alina, or this is over."

Someone gasps and I'm not sure if it's me or Anora.

My vision gets a little blurry and I sway. Aster grabs my hand and pinches hard at the space between my thumb and first finger, the pain causing my head to clear. She doesn't let go of my hand though, and I'm surprised by the gesture of comfort.

"Excuse me?" My father turns to face Derick, blocking him from us again. He might use us as security but I know he'd never hesitate to take a hit for us in return. "My daughters are not a menu for you to peruse."

Derick sneers at him. "You offered Anora up easily."

It's clear her doesn't understand the dynamic of our family and honestly it's kind of hard to explain. Dad's always been transparent with us about the business, about the kinds of deals we might need to make to guarantee our future. We were all given choices, and Anora was the only one who took the route of potential marriage. She learned to be a socialite, albeit an incredibly observant one, and the rest of us learned to kill and protect. Dad didn't offer Anora up - not the way Derick thinks he did.

"If Anora hadn't agreed to this, it wouldn't be happening," my father snarls back. "The deal is clearly off."

A ripple goes through the room because no one planned for this to happen. The deal secures a huge amount of security for us, and this is all my fault.

I never planned on getting married or having children; I was going to serve my father and potentially Owen until the day it kills me or I die of old age. That was the path I'd always seen in front of me and I was fine with it. I was confident and unafraid because I knew I was powerful and lethal, and that if someone took me down it would be with a hell of a fight.

Derick demanding to marry me terrifies the fuck out of me because I don't know how to be that person. I don't know how to be the wife of a CEO. I don't know how to host parties and be delicate, I don't know how to keep a house or make him look good if I'm not keeping him safe. Derick saw a soft and vulnerable side of me but I don't know how to be that person all the time. I don't think I'm capable of it. I'm afraid to be that person because being vulnerable gets you killed.

But I love my family, I love my father, and I know he wants this, maybe even needs it. He would never have offered Anora the possibility of this marriage if he didn't think it would be of great benefit to our family, our business, and our future. I can't let it slip away if it means I can help them.

"I'll do it," I say before I can overthink too much more.

6

Derick

Alina's agreement is music to my ears, but her father spins around and draws her close, whispering into her pale and panicked face. Whatever he's murmuring to her she keeps nodding and agreeing, her eyes flicking back and forth from me to him. I haven't stopped looking at her. I can't.

She looks different, and yet the same. All softness is gone. All the femininity that she so openly displayed that night is gone. Her dark, luscious hair is trapped in a tight bun, her skin uncovered and naturally smooth, but it makes her eyes look dark and heavy rather than bright. The suit she's wearing isn't at all flattering and I'm shocked how well her shirt covers her generous breasts. The woman in front of me is all straight lines and function. In other circumstances, I wouldn't look twice at her. She's trying to be visually unobtrusive and it's working. I see why she's an excellent bodyguard.

Yet I can't look away, and nothing about what I'm seeing makes me want her any less.

I'll own her and she won't ever be able to escape me. Alina Sorrelle, my Allie, will be my wife to do with what I please. I'll be able to punish her for my cock's inaction the last month, for the way my head plays nothing but a reel of her and her body over and over, and I will pound into her and come inside her for every single time I jacked off with her name on my lips. Alina is going to be my pleasure playground. For the rest of her god damn life.

"What's the hold up Don? She agreed." I don't mean to sound like an asshole but I'm impatient. The lust and fury are putting me on edge, and it's making me access a side of myself that I usually keep tightly leashed.

Now that she's agreed I'm itching to get her alone, whether to have a private conversation or to free her breasts from the confines of that shirt and what I'm sure is a sexless and uncomfortable bra. She'll be lucky if I even let her wear clothes when she first gets to my house. If either of us can walk after the next time I get her naked, I'll have failed. I will fuck her into submission, into obedience, so she won't ever even think of leaving me again. After only one night with her my obsession burns this fiercely; I can't imagine after having her whenever I went that it will dim in the slightest. Alina is a drug that I know will make me more addicted with each hit.

"You don't know my daughter, Mr. Clayton. I do." I look away from Alina to focus on Don, and attempt to respect that he cares for her. This is her father. I need to pull it back because the whole point of this arrangement is to build bridges, not burn them.

"I do know her, Don," I keep using his first name because I'm frustrated and can't fuck her in front of her family, and I can't roar like some primal beast and carry her away. That would make the holidays awkward. "I know that she's saying she'll do it out of a sense of duty, because she'd do anything to protect you, the business, and her sisters. I know that she won't regret it if it means the deal goes through and the future is secure."

Don blanches and so does Alina, showing me the resemblance in their looks even if he's gone to fat. I imagine 30, 40 years in the future when Alina is soft and old - I'll still think she's fucking beautiful. I'd get my 70 year old dick up and going for her.

"He's right, dad," her voice is soft and feathery, and I remember hearing it like that when she whispered filthy things in my ear. "This is the right thing to do, and I won't regret it. I know you'll be safe without me," she gives him a small smile and after a moment of silent communication he sighs and nods.

"Fine. Fine." He turns to me, still blocking her with his body as if he's the one that protects her. I have to give him credit for clearly loving his daughters. Aside from the business deal, I don't want to be at odds with this man. We really will be spending holidays together because I have no intention of depriving Alina of her family. There's so little of mine left that it won't be hard to be here.

Pleasure burns through me at the trepidation in her eyes, but I can also see the desire there. The way she looks at me and thinks of that night, the same way that I do. She swallows, slow and unsteady, and it makes me feel powerful to unnerve a woman like her. Alina is strong, mentally as well as physically, and my demand for her is something she's not used to. I smile and I know it isn't friendly. It's pure predator.

"For Anora, I was going to tell you that if you hurt or mistreat her I would make sure you paid. With Alina, if you hurt or mistreat her she'll take care of it herself - don't underestimate her." He pokes me in the chest and I let him get away with it, my gaze leaving Alina to meet his fierce expression.

"Can we have a moment? Alone?" I ask him, and then shift my gaze to her.

"No," Alina answers and my fury starts building again. "Not now. I need to talk to my sister."

She looks at Anora, who looks shell-shocked. I do feel bad about that. Hopefully, in the future, she and I will have an opportunity to repair the harm done of such a public and dramatic rejection.

It's funny though - I was prepared to marry a wife I didn't want and not have fidelity be a part of our marriage vows. Now, if Alina so much as looks at another man, if another man even thinks that he could touch her, I would kill him. Our bodies belong together. She will vow to be faithful to me, and I'll make sure she never breaks it.

Alina goes to Anora, and the sisters leave the room. I can hear their high, soft voices going up the stairs and then fading into silence.

I turn to Don. "The business agreement stands as written, but changes need to be made to the marriage contract."

Don turns his back on me and goes to sit in the armchair he had been occupying. He picks up his tumbler of whiskey and downs it, glaring at the empty crystal bottom when he finishes. I take his silence as an invitation to continue.

"I'm marrying Alina before I leave. She'll be coming home with me."

"I was afraid you'd say that." Don takes my tumbler, which I hadn't drank from, and downs it as well. "If she agrees, I'll agree."

"Fine." I move to sit back in the other armchair.

"She didn't raise herself to be a wife, Derick," he warns me. "She's a warrior. Every time you try and take away her choices, she will fight you or shut down. Alina is softer than she accepts about herself and the easiest way to hurt her is to leash her."

"I'll keep that in mind."

One of the staff brings over two new tumblers of whiskey. I take mine and hold it up to toast.

"To family."

Don frowns but lifts his own glass and touches it to mine. "To family."

7

Alina

We make our way up the stairs and all the way down the hall. Anora's room is on the farthest end away from the stairs, right across from Owen's. None of us say much until we get inside and close the door. Anora drifts toward her closet and starts changing her dress. Aro flops down on Anora's bed and Aster slides down onto the floor next to it.

"Holy shit Lina!" Aro cries into the ceiling. "That is the craziest thing I have ever witnessed." She sits up and fixes me with the eye. "He's hot though. Was he good in bed?"

"I'm not answering that." I turn away from her and go to Anora, who is now sitting at her vanity and brushing out her hair. I take the brush from her and start combing it through her soft brown waves. It's something I've done a thousand times, that soothes me as much as it does her.

"Are we okay?" I am honestly afraid of the answer. This was her moment, and I took it out from under her. Anora has told me before she feels like she doesn't contribute the way the rest of us do because her purpose is limited. I've reassured her a hundred times it isn't true. She's the head of the household. Anora keeps us functioning, makes sure we meet our obligations, and that we outclass anyone who might try and snub us. Anora made the Sorrelle name mean something to the bougie bitches we have to deal with in the world of the rich. We'd all have lost our minds without her trying to deal with it. Anora can eviscerate a bitchy socialite with a well-worded, soft-spoken phrase.

She meets my eyes in the mirror, and I see relief in them. It almost takes me out at the knees to see it. Anora repeatedly told us that she was fine with this, that she didn't mind, that it wouldn't be so bad. Her reassurances were the only reason none of us interfered. Now I can see that it was a very well done act because she's glad.

"Of course we are. But are you okay, Lina? Really?"

My siblings and I are all close, but Anora and I are the closest. I know her secret hopes and dreams and she knows mine. I've never hid my ambitions from Anora, and being a wife wasn't one of them. I wanted to go out guns blazing. Now I'd probably die a soft chubby old lady who couldn't recall the last time she'd shot a gun or held a knife. It was some people's dream, but not mine. There had to be a way to meld the two, but the only way to figure out what Derick expects of me is to live it.

"It's the right thing to do."

"Alina," her voice is extra soft because she doesn't want Aro and Aster to hear. Aro is on her phone and Aster has put in her airpods, probably blasting some obscure band that's clashing guitars and bagpipes and screaming. "You have feelings for him."

"No. I'm attracted to him. It's not the same." Feelings is too easy of a word.

Anora shakes her head. "I read between the lines when you told me about Seattle. You snuck away that morning because he rattled your heart, not just your body."

"I have a heart of stone, dearest sister," I shake my head at her and withdraw into teasing so I don't have to confront if she's right or not. It makes me feel weak to think that maybe I ran away, instead of simply following my itinerary.

"Whatever you say. Call me when you fall." Her phone buzzes on the vanity, and we both look at it. It's Owen. Before she can stop me, I swipe the phone and answer it. My earlier anger at him comes roaring to the surface.

"Where the fuck are you?"

"Alina?" he slurs. "I must be more fucked up than I thought, I meant to call Anora."

"You did call Anora, but I saw and took her phone. You're drunk?"

"Yes ma'am." He knows I hate it when he calls me that.

"Why are you drunk?"

"None of your business. Let me talk to Anora. Is she okay after meeting the hubby?"

"He's not her hubby, he's mine, butt wipe."

There's a long silence. "Am I dead, Lina?"

"If you don't tell me where you are so I can get you home, I'll make sure you are."

Owen rattles off the name of a bar and I hang up on him before giving Anora her phone back. Why Owen called her is beyond me, and why he'd feel the need to get drunk today of all days is also unexpected. Owen is moody and kind of an asshole but he's not big on substances. I can recall on one hand the number of times I've seen him under the influence before today. I text Alonzo and another guard telling them to go pick up Owen, sober him up, and bring his ass to me before dinner with Derick and his entourage tonight.

"You're really going to marry him?" Aro asks from behind me. "You're going to leave?" She looks uncertain, and even Aster has a hint of emotion on her face as they both look up at me.

"I'm doing it for us. For you. This will be good for the business and give you more opportunities to do whatever you want."

"What I want to do is illegal so your decision is irrelevant to me,"

Aster drawls, now playing a game on her phone that involves shooting zombies. "However, I'll be happy to disappear him if he fucks up." That's basically a declaration of love from her.

"It's going to be fine. I won't be leaving until after the wedding anyway, so we have time."

"Group hug?" Aro stands up and holds out her arms. Anora and I go in easily, embracing each other. After a few seconds of concentrated staring at her and a lot of grumbling, Aster joins too.

"I love you. Nothing will change that," I mumble into the circle of their heads, because I'm the tallest. We stand like that for a long time, still confronted with a major change and the loss of one of us - even if it's not who we expected.

8

Alina

As I walk down to dinner, Derick is waiting outside the dining room door. I told him I'd give him his moment alone later, and I guess later is now. He stares at me intently, and Aro taps the back of my hand twice, a silent way of asking if I'm good. I tap back once, and she keeps going into the dining room with everyone else.

Derick follows me into my father's office, which is also the library of sorts in the house. It's a cozy room and the shelves are messy and overflowing with every kind of book imaginable. It's Aro's favorite place and when I can't find her, most of the time this is the best place to look. There's a plush green velvet chair near the window that we all know is hers. Sometimes she'll sit in here for an entire day, silent and lost in a book while my father works.

Derick closes the door, and I feel claustrophobic. I stare out the window at the back garden and brace myself.

I'm not prepared for him to come up behind me, splay a possessive hand across my stomach, and pull me back into his strong, warm body. The scent of him wraps around me, sharp and clean, and my eyes flutter shut against my will.

"You left, Allie."

"It was a one night stand, Brody." I put sarcasm into my voice even though it's not what I feel.

Derick grips me tighter, almost painfully. "Do you always sneak out like a thief?"

I sigh. "No."

"It hurt, you know, to wake up alone to a note on an empty pillow. After a night like we had." His cock is hard and he rolls his hips, pressing it into my ass. As soon as he touched me I got wet, but now is not the time. It might never be the time. Giving myself to him the way I did was easy when there was no future to be concerned about. I can't hand myself over to him like that when he's my husband. It's too much.

The idea that he'll fuck me, own me, pull emotions out of me that I don't want to feel, and then get bored of me and fuck someone else causes fear to wrap around my hard heart. That's the way these marriages work, hell that's the way most marriages in our world work. It's a business alliance. If I let him have any of my emotions, I'll end up loving him - Anora is right. And when he breaks me, I don't know what pieces of myself will be left to rebuild.

I spin around in his hold and go on the defensive. "Do you think you know me because of that night, Derick? That what we had was something special?"

It was. It was special. I hate that it was special, and I hate that he's acting like it was special to him too. He might want me at the moment because I'm the one who left him, but rich men, criminal men, get bored. I'll take him while I have him and while I have to, but I have no delusions that he'll love me. The idea hurts so much more than I want it to, so I have to start exposing myself to that reality now. I have to put distance between us.

I closed off my heart so well that I never built up any emotional callouses. I can't let him get close enough to damage me. There has

46

to be a way for me to give him my body without giving him my heart and soul.

"Do you think you know me?" He shoots back.

"I don't know," I answer honestly.

Derick doesn't say anything, and after a moment and a blaze of heated fury in his eyes he swoops down and takes my mouth. It's not a soft kiss, or like any of the kisses we've shared before. It's harsh and violent. He bites at my lips, demanding entrance, and taking me over with his tongue when I open for him. I let him kiss me, and let myself be punished.

When he breaks off the kiss we're both breathing hard, and there's a slight tang of blood in my mouth from him biting my lip. I don't mind.

"You will know me, Allie. And I'll know you."

The words send a shiver down my back. When he cups my jaw in his hand I freeze up, stiff and unyielding. His eyes narrow slightly when he notices but he doesn't say anything.

"You got away once, I'm not letting it happen again. We're getting married tomorrow."

Panic swoops through my stomach and I'm immediately nauseated. "What?"

"I've extended my trip. My brother is flying in. You, me, our families, and a justice of the peace in the back garden. Then you'll pack your things and come home with me."

"That's - I - what about - Derick." My voice is fluttery and I hate it, but it's better than giving in to the urge to cry. My entire reality has been upended in a day, my future plans blown to bits, and my heart at risk of being destroyed. I thought I'd have a few months to wrap things up and plan, to say extended goodbyes to my sisters.

"Your father told me that it's up to you, but I can't accept that, *lleidr bach*. Tomorrow." He captures my bottom lip between his teeth and bites, then soothes with his tongue. "And then, forever."

I don't say anything. I might as well be a statue in his arms for all that I am capable of right now. All he notices is that while I'm not saying yes, I'm not saying no either. There isn't a choice, and I know it. I am leaving all that I know.

Maybe it will be easier this way - ripping off the band-aid rather than a long drawn out goodbye. There won't be time to stress and plan, and then hate that plan and make another plan, to go round and round trying to find all the angles and make sure that everything is as covered as possible. Sometimes I plan myself into paralysis, afraid that if I miss one thing someone will end up dead. If I haven't overthought it to the point of insomnia then I haven't thought about it at all.

I won't have time for that. This is forcing me to take a leap without the luxury of time to think about it. Derick and I will get married tomorrow, standing up with our families, and then I'll move to Seattle. Nothing will be the same.

The capacity for words is beyond me, so I nod.

"Good." Derick smiles and it's almost Brody's smile. They're the same person, but they're not. Like I'm Allie, but I'm not. This is the weirdest thing that's ever happened to me, and that's including all of the weird shit I've seen the guards do to prank each other. This is surreal.

I extricate myself from his hold and leave the library, leading the way back to the dining room where we take our seats. Everyone stops talking when we enter the room, staring at us and waiting for... something.

My father is looking at me expectantly, so I know he knows. I take a sip of water and clear my throat.

"We're getting married tomorrow."

"WHAT?!" Aro screeches, and even Aster looks perturbed. Anora looks over at me concerned, and reaches over under the table to take my hand.

"Are you sure?" she asks, her gaze searching me as if looking for a wound.

"It'll be fine," I assure them all, making eye contact with each of them, as well as my father. They need to believe me and not press this, or I'll fall apart.

"Do you want to go dress shopping tomorrow?" There's Anora, trying to salvage the day. I have no vision for my wedding, so having something small and simple is actually appealing.

"Of course," I agree. It will make her feel better because I know that somehow she's going to twist this around and blame herself that I'm the one getting married instead. There's no one to blame but me, and maybe Derick.

Everything is going so fast and so far beyond my control. There's threats everywhere, and I'm good at looking out for them, but I don't know how to avoid a threat that's abstract. How do you protect yourself from emotions? The vision I had of who I am and who I was going to be is rapidly becoming blurry and no new picture is appearing. I don't know who Alina the Wife is - because there's not a lot of room for Every Day Alina, and Vacation Alina is too lazy.

"That's a lovely idea," dad steps in and I'm surprised to see Derick nodding in agreement. "Get some flowers as well. You know the place," he twinkles at her. It will be good for my father that Anora is staying to take care of him and the house. That calms my heart rate somewhat. I don't know that I'd ever describe myself as positive or optimistic, but I am seeking out the silver linings in this situation. Anora belongs here, and I'm glad she gets to stay.

When dinner is over, I excuse myself and run before Derick can corner me again. I hear someone behind me and I'm surprised when it's Aster who followed me upstairs.

"There's enough time for me to make him disappear," her low, throaty voice is soft. "If you don't want this."

I run my hand over her hair, surprised she lets me touch her. "That's a lovely wedding gift, but getting rid of him is more trouble than it's worth. This is for the best."

"If you change your mind. I'll be a flight away."

I laugh, both proud and disturbed because I know she means every word. Aster would kill him without a thought for me, and no one would ever find the body, let alone evidence of the murder.

As I walk back to my room it hits me that my family will be safe without me. I will be removed from the equation but nothing will change. The guards that I've trained, who are loyal to my family, will keep protecting my father and my sisters. Aro and Aster are both dangerous in their own right and can handle whatever comes at them.

It won't matter that I'm gone. Not really. For years, I trained hard, harder than anyone, pushing my body to the limit. I learned how to fight, how to damage, and how to kill. My goal was to be indispensable, to be the person that could be guaranteed to keep my father safe. That was my place and my purpose.

Now that I'm being taken away from it, I see that I had no place at all. There is nothing special about who I am or what I was doing. Even though my father loves me and is proud of me, I was furniture. I was the dark presence in the room that only became visible if there was a problem. It will be easy for someone to take my place.

I am adrift. After I shut off the lights and crawl into my bed, I lift the covers over my head and for the first time in years - I cry.

9

Alina

My sisters are talking around me at breakfast, strategizing and arguing about whether or not this should move forward. The only ones not saying anything are me and Owen. He's staring intently into his bowl of cereal and I pretend to tear apart and eat a croissant.

Derick isn't here. He and his entourage are picking his brother up from the airport and running some last minute errands. It was implied that he was getting us rings, which makes me feel sick. It's happening. I know it's happening, but it still makes me feel out of sorts.

"We can run, Lina," Aro presses. "We don't need this. Dad will cover for us."

"I'll go with you," Anora insists. "Until it passes, you and I can go." Now Owen sits up and takes notice of the conversation, glaring at Anora, and then at all of us.

"You're being childish," he rumbles. "All of you." I'm surprised when he makes eye contact with me. "And frankly, disrespectful. Alina has made her choice, and you can't unmake it for her. What we do now is support her choices."

"Thank you."

He nods, and then resumes his cereal staring. Anora is looking at him aghast, Aro looks properly chastised, and I don't think Aster has heard any of the conversation because she's doing something on her phone.

Then her head pops up. "He bought rings at Tiffany's."

"How do you know that?" We all stare at her.

She points down at her phone like we're all idiots. "I hacked his bank accounts. I've been tracking his spending since the original engagement was announced. I know pretty much everything about him on paper - and the business."

"And you never said anything?" Aro questions.

Aster shrugs. "I told Dad and Owen everything because they asked."

I hate that a flutter of pleasure goes through me, but there's also every chance in the world that I'll hate it. I don't do jewelry because it gets in the way and it can get you hurt in a fight. Don't ever Google ring avulsion - I've seen it in person and it will give you nightmares and you'll never wear a ring again. So whatever he bought me, who knows if I'll even wear it, but the fact that he chose it himself does something to me. Maybe he would've done the same with Anora, maybe not. We'll never know.

"Anything else I need to know?" I ask.

Aster opens her mouth but before she can say anything, the front door opens and voices echo through the house. Derick is back and his brother is here.

Last night I'd dreamed of Derick and I'm mad at myself for it. The thrill that runs through my body remembering the dream as he gets nearer makes me angry all over again.

A moment later, Derick and another man walk into the room. Derick looks almost casual in a white polo shirt and dark jeans, his muscles obvious in the way the shirt contours over his body. He is a specimen to behold. I still think I could take him in a fight, but my traitorous body would wrap around him rather than take him down.

The man next to him is clearly his brother - same height but slimmer, his face sharper, and his eyes full of mischief and humor. When he sees me he smiles, and before I realize it's happening I smile back. Derick frowns, looking between us.

"You're exactly his type you know," Jack's voice is smoother, higher, than his brother's. Derick has a rumble, Jack has a lilt. I'm even more surprised when he pulls me into a hug.

"He has a type?" I take a step back.

"Not that he knows it."

"It's nice to meet you, Jack." The smile is still on my face and the frown is still on Derick's. He can't possibly be jealous of me being friendly with his brother. We're about to be related - he'll have to get over it. Jack already feels like an ally as well, and it will be nice to have someone friendly in the unknown.

"You as well. It'll be nice to have a woman around the house, especially one who can kick his ass." My cheeks pink and he laughs again. "Your reputation precedes you."

Good. I hope it precedes me to their house and their world and that anyone who interacts with them that's heard of me knows not to mess with me. I might be new blood and unfamiliar with the area, but I will never be any less lethal. I will never stop being a warrior because I'm a wife. Derick will not get an opinion on that matter.

"Do you want anything to eat?" Anora stands and comes up next to me. Jack looks her up and down and over her shoulder I see Owen snarl. It's amusing.

"No, thank you. I know you have places to be." Jack takes a step back and I use it as an excuse to leave the room under the guise of getting ready. I don't look at Derick but I can feel him following me as I step out. He doesn't like it when I ignore him and overnight I decided that the best way to keep him at a distance is to piss him off.

In the hall, before I can go upstairs and grab my bag, he stops me.

When I turn to him he maneuvers me until my back is pressed into the wall, and his body is aligned with mine. For some reason my body won't fight him even though my mind thinks I should. He presses, I follow. Like a dance where only we know the steps.

"No good morning for me?" He skims his nose down mine and I have to take shallow breaths not to get lost in him.

"Good morning, Derick." My voice is soft and weak. Fuck.

"Good morning, Allie." He tilts his head and bites lightly on my neck, right over my rapid pulse point, and I gasp. Heat radiates down my body and I clench my thighs slightly to control my reaction.

"I won't kiss you again until we're married," he trails his lips along my jaw as he speaks and I have to close my eyes. "I'll kiss you when you're my wife." Derick kisses one eyelid and then the other before leaning in closer to whisper into my ear. "We're going to make promises today, *lleidr bach*. I intend for us to keep all of them." With a quick bite of my earlobe he steps away and leaves me panting and confused. I run up the stairs.

Anora knows me well because when we head into Chicago to find me a dress, she goes straight to Nordstrom. It'll be off the rack but still designer because I can't muster the energy to care about clothes that much, or who made them. Nordstrom has everything that I'll need and I won't have to stress about details.

When we get there, Aro pushes me into a chair and Aster sits on the floor beside me. Then Aro and Anora attack the racks, pulling dress after dress and piling it into the arms of two sales associates who take turns bringing the stacks to the dressing room. I'm surprised but pleased they aren't only grabbing white - there's gold, champagne, blush, gray, even a very bright pink dress. Although I think Aro grabbed that one just to see if she could get me into it.

We walk back to where the dresses are waiting on a rack, and I start going through them. Some I get rid of immediately without trying them on - no long sleeves because I work hard for the gun show that is my biceps, nothing short, and the pink dress goes right away.

Then I grab a few that I like or that feel like me.

The first dress is lovely but too structured - it's strapless and fitted, traditional white, and has a big bow that runs from my breasts to mid-thigh. It feels stiff and the way that I can't move my thighs apart bothers me. For a second I feel claustrophobic, the pressure keeping my body wrapped like a pretty little sausage and stopping me from being able to fight is too much.

I take the dress off and then go through the rack again, getting rid of anything that's too fitted down the legs. There's a satin dress in a soft blush color that catches my eye, so I grab that next.

As soon as I put it on, I know it's the dress.

It overwhelms me. Aro has made me watch plenty of reality television, including shows about weddings and wedding dresses. A hundred times I've heard these women gush that as soon as they tried on the right dress, they know. It's unexpected to feel that way.

But it is the dress. It's me, but girly. Strapless, fitted at the waste, then a ballgown skirt that gives me room to move. The hemline is short in the front and long in the back. The material feels so good on my skin, and it fits like it was custom made for me. When I look in the mirror my shoulders don't look too broad, my breasts aren't spilling out the top, and it accentuates how tight my waist is before it curves to my hips.

It almost makes me feel delicate, and I've never felt delicate in my life.

When I come out of the dressing room, there's a tentative smile on my face.

"Oh that is the dress," Aro agrees immediately, reading my face in seconds.

Anora tears up and puts her hands to her face. "It's gorgeous," she says before the tears start to fall. "You look beautiful."

Rather than acknowledge any of the emotions going on right now, I look at the sales associate who looks slightly disgruntled at all the dresses that will need to be put away.

"Shoes?"

Aro once again snaps into action after I change back into my street clothes.

She flits through departments, picking two pairs of shoes (heels for pictures, flats for everything else), jewelry, even a clip to go in my hair.

Then I'm dragged to a salon and spa where I feel like my body is put through a more vigorous assault than going a few rounds in the boxing ring with the other guards. By the time we're done, I've been waxed and plucked and all sorts of other unspeakable things I never thought I'd let another person do to me.

Aro and Anora did all the taking and made all the decisions, and I stared off into space.

Every once and awhile Aster and I would make eye contact and she'd keep me grounded by rolling her eyes or making a face.

By the time they stuff me back into the car, hair and makeup done, we only have 2 hours before the ceremony. Dad and Derick have both been texting me updates and giving us a timeline.

The rush kept me from thinking too much. All I can do is get to the next item, the next task, then I'll walk into the back garden and say vows.

I have to remind myself to keep breathing.

10

Them

The small but significant ceremony takes place in the backyard of the Sorrelle compound, inside a bright white gazebo. It's warm for a late spring day, the afternoon sun is bright but not too hot, and the first flowers have started to bloom and scent the air. It's picture perfect.

When Don Sorelle appears from the house without his daughter, a moment of panic seizes Derick's chest. She could back out. She could run. He would chase her but he hates the idea that she's not going to follow through.

Don waves his concern off. "She didn't want me to walk her." The father of the bride is understandably upset by his daughter's decision, but he also knows her well. Her independence, even in this situation, matters to her. Alina is giving them all the message that her father is not giving her away, he is not selling her, exchanging her, or controlling her. It speaks to this being no one's choice but her own.

Alina walks out looking like a grumpy angel. The dress glows in the sunlight, the skirt buoyed softly by her movements. Her hair is up, accentuating the smooth line of her jaw. The makeup on her face is soft and subdued, and the rose color on her lips makes them a temptation that Derick can't wait to sink his teeth into. She's frowning, flustered, and frustrated.

And barefoot.

The heels were too much and she didn't care about pictures, and the flats were incredibly uncomfortable. After a few moments of thinking about it, and realizing she didn't care, Alina said fuck it to shoes and headed downstairs to her wedding.

When Derick sees, he steps back from the judge and removes his shoes, then his socks. He stands in his bare feet now, waiting for her.

Alina's frown deepens when she sees because it's cute and she doesn't want him to do things that are cute. She doesn't want Derick to notice things about her, or mirror her. She doesn't want him to pull her in when he's going to let her down later.

Instead of relaxing, she stomps across the yard and up the steps into the gazebo. Their families surround the judge, who stands in the center. She's a pleasant, short woman with salt and pepper hair, glasses on the end her nose, and a voice that resonates across the yard as she asks if everyone is ready.

Derick holds his hands out to Alina, and after a deep, calming breath, she takes them.

Everything inside of Derick loosens. Even though they haven't made any vows yet, that was her moment of surrender. That was the last moment to make a choice. She chose him.

The judge talks about commitment, promises, and permanence.

She talks about building foundations that will grow into a future.

She doesn't talk about love.

Then it's time for their vows.

Derick goes first.

"Alina, I promise to honor you, protect you, treasure you, and be faithful to you until the end of my days."

He means every word. It will be years before he tells Alina that he wrote these vows and gave them to the judge.

Derick isn't sure that he believes in love, he's never felt it for someone who wasn't his own flesh and blood. What he doesn't realize is that if you asked him to define love and tell you what it entailed - his vows described it. Honor, protect, treasure, and be loyal.

After a moment, she starts her vows.

"Broderick," he winces at her use of his full name and it's the first time there's even a hint of a smile on her face. She starts again.

"Derick. I promise to honor you, protect you, treasure you, and be faithful to you until the end of my days."

Alina knows she will keep her vows because above everything else, her word has to have value. She is giving Derick her word that she will be his wife, and she will do all these things. A person is only as good as their word, and her word is impeccable.

Derick lets go of one of her hands and reaches out to Jack.

Jack gives him a black velvet box. There are two rings inside.

Alina is surprised by their simplicity when she sees them. Platinum bands, no engagement ring with a big obnoxious diamond. Hers is thinner, with a constellation of small stones all around it. They catch the light and her face softens. The band that Derick got for himself is thick and plain.

When she takes the band from him before placing it on his finger, she sees that "Allie" has been etched on the inside. He'll wear her name against his skin. That name. The name she gave him when she was someone else, a realer, but still a fantasy, version of herself. The version of herself she's not sure she'll ever be able to show him again, and it hurts to know he's still clinging to the imaginary her.

She assumes his name is on the inside of hers as well. When she's feeling strong enough, days later, she'll see that he had "Brody" engraved rather than Derick. Maybe he thinks it'll grow into a private joke between them, instead of an ache for what can never be and never really was.

She takes his hand, and repeats after the judge.

"This ring is a symbol of my promises to you, a circle that never ends."

Derick repeats the same words as he slides the band on her finger.

The judge pronounces them husband and wife, and after a moment of hesitation because she knows where she is and what this is, says that the groom may kiss the bride.

Alina swallows and looks at Derick, remembering his whispered words in the hallway this morning. Remembering the way he kissed her in the library. Remembering the way he kissed her during their night together. She wonders what kind of kiss this one will be.

It isn't anything like she expected.

Derick takes her face in his hands like he is holding something precious, like the treasure he vowed he would treat her as, and brings their mouths together. It's gentle but firm, pressing her close and before he lets her go, he teases her with a swipe of his tongue across her sensitive upper lip. It causes her to shiver and he smiles against her lips.

They're married.

Derick is pleased, and the beast inside him roars in triumph that he has captured his prey. Alina will never get away from him again. If she tries to run, he will chase. If she tries to fight, he will conquer. She will belong to him in every way, and he will never tire of taking from her.

Alina is resigned, and hesitant. There's so much unknown and uncertainty before her. She wants to trust Derick but for now she can only trust herself. Alina makes a promise to do her best, but keep up her walls. A lifetime is a lot of opportunities to be hurt.

They all leave the gazebo and head into the house and the formal dining room for dinner.

11

Alina

As we walk to the house, Derick holds my hand.

When we sit down at the table, he takes it again. During dinner, he keeps his left hand on my thigh. Not pressing or inappropriately high, but there and claiming me even though no one here is going to challenge his ownership. I don't know why he won't stop touching me.

There's quiet chatter between everyone at the table, except from me and Derick. Jack is regaling my sisters and my father with stories. I can tell he's a charmer, and lures people in with an easy smile and a carefree laugh.

I wonder if Derick sees how much Jack is hurting, and that his brother is looking for something from him. As someone who has navigated all sorts of insanity from her sisters, its easy to recognize when the dynamic is off. Like a skip in a record that's not enough to ruin the song but obvious enough you notice when you pay attention. Derick isn't paying attention.

After the meal, our cook brings out a small round cake.

"It's the yellow with the raspberry frosting," she smiles at me, and leaves. That's my favorite cake, the one she's made for all my birthdays.

I wonder if I'll ever have it again.

Derick and I cut the cake, and I let him feed me a piece. His finger touches the tip of my tongue and drags across my bottom lip. It's sensual and dangerous, and I see his eyes dilate.

When I feed him a piece, he catches my wrist before I can pull away and sucks the frosting from my thumb. He might as well have sucked my clit for the way I feel it inside me, and my body is throbbing instantly with need. I hate that I react to him this way, but giving him my body will distract him from trying to take anything else.

I know what I'm getting into there, and I can't deny how good it will feel.

Derick stands abruptly. "Thank you, everyone for this lovely day, and for uniting our families to both our benefit." He raises his glass and we all follow suit. "To growing our family."

Everyone repeats after him in a murmur, even me, and I drain the rest of the champagne from my glass. I expect Derick to sit back down but instead he takes my hand and pulls me up.

"Now, I'd like to be alone with my wife."

Before I can say goodbye or goodnight, Derick is pulling me out the back door. We have a small guest house shielded from the main house by trees for privacy. I knew from Aro that they'd readied the house as a makeshift wedding suite for Derick and I because it wasn't worth going to stay anywhere in the city.

Apparently I'm not moving fast enough for him because he stops and picks me up. I squirm in his hold, aware of my weight, but also begrudgingly impressed by his strength. He takes long sure strides, never flagging. He doesn't even put me down to open the door.

Derick steps inside the guest house and kicks the door shut, then sets me down on the floor.

"We exchanged vows, I carried you over the threshold, and now you're mine, *lleidr bach*." He takes off his suit jacket, then his tie. I watch, entranced, as he continues to undress like it's my own personal striptease. Its only a few steps back to the bed, and I sit down on the edge, watching.

Derick catches on and slows his movements. His hand are gorgeous, strong and defined. He undoes the cuffs of his crisp white dress shirt, then he removes his belt. The slide of the leather against the wool makes me squirm, and my nipples get hard. Derick smirks. When he untucks his shirt from his pants I get a quick peak of the trail of dark hair that leads down to his groin. His cock is already tenting his pants and I'd be lying if I said my mouth wasn't watering.

This isn't going to be gentle. It's not going to be love making.

I know Derick is angry with me, and I know he's going to make me feel it tonight.

It's sick that I want it.

When he starts to unbutton his shirt, I stand up and reach behind me to undo the zipper of my dress but he stops me with a hand.

I sway slightly on my feet as he removes the shirt, baring his muscular chest and abs. He undoes the button and zipper on his pants and leaves them open, gaping obscenely. When he steps closer I have to remind myself to breathe.

Derick turns me around and slides down the zipper on my dress. He does it slowly, so slow that I fidget. I'm embarrassingly wet, ready for whatever he's going to do.

A rumble of approval comes from him when the dress drops easily from my body to pool on the floor. I'm not wearing a bra, and my panties are a tiny white thong. Derick pulls me back into his body, and taunts me by running his hands up and down my stomach, letting them brush the bottom of my breasts but never giving in to touching the places that would give both of us the most pleasure.

"Have you ever been spanked before, *lleidr bach?*"

I don't trust my voice so I shake my head no.

"Then I'll go easy on you. Bend over." I do as he says and he steps to the side of me, resting one hand on my back while the other starts caressing my ass cheeks. He trails a finger down the string of my thong, until he gets to my soaking wet center.

"I think you'll like this, Allie. I want to spank you once for each day since you left me, but I don't think I can wait that long to be inside you."

I don't say anything.

"I'm going to smack this delicious ass, and after each time, you're going to say that you're sorry. I'll stop when I think you mean it."

Before I can say anything, his hand cracks down. There's a sting, but the vibration also touches something inside me, and my clit pulses.

"I'm sorry," my voice is a weak gasp.

He smacks the other cheek a little harder. "I'm sorry, Derick."

Then he catches me off guard with a series of sharp, quick slaps, alternating cheeks, but so fast that I can't apologize and all that comes out is a moan of nonsense. He chuckles and I feel that inside me too. I am being undone and I don't know how to stop it.

My pussy is throbbing and wet, and I think if he did this enough I'd come from the stimulation alone. One solid thrust now and I'll explode.

His hand comes down again, firm and perfectly placed for maximum vibration.

"I'm sorry!" It's a strangled shout.

"Almost there Allie," he purrs at me and I want to beg him to fuck me and get it over with.

Derick smacks down again, and I flinch, overly sensitive now. "I'm sorry, Derick!" I scream it and then moan, "I'm sorry, I'm sorry."

"There it is."

He kneels behind me and gently kisses and licks at the flesh that he abused, soothing me. He runs his nose along the seam of my body, his breath tickling my pussy as he inhales.

"I missed you." It's so quiet I don't know if he intended for me to hear it.

There's a heavy pause before he stands up, rips the thong off my body, tearing it as it gets caught around my knees. Derick rolls me over until I'm on my back, naked and shaking, desperate for release.

He divests himself of his pants and boxers and I get a quick look at his gorgeous cock before he's leaning over me, pressing me into the bed with his heavy body.

"Cry for me, Alina."

Then he presses inside me and I scream, pleasure overwhelming me. I had forgotten how full he made me feel, and it's a different experience doing it raw like this. There are no barriers between us now and it makes everything more sensitive. I'd swear I can feel the ridge of the thick vein on the underside of his shaft rubbing against me.

Derick slides out, then slams into me, his pace slow and measured. He's holding back because he knows I'm about to come.

"Please. Please, Brody," I beg him.

That seems to set him off because he puts one hand around my neck, gripping me at the nape, and he pulls my head up so that our foreheads are touching.

Then he fucks me.

Derick pounds into me like a man possessed and after a few seconds, I detonate. My legs squeeze his body as every muscle in mine tenses, paralyzed by the pleasure. I'm screaming into his face, into his mouth, and he's eating it up - his eyes never leave my face as I lose my mind and my sense of self. Even as I come down, Derick's pace never slows.

"Again, Alina."

"No," I beg, but he holds me up harder and reaches down to toy with my clit.

"You don't get to tell me no Allie, not now." His thrusts slow, becoming harder and deeper, and I can hear the sounds of how wet I am as he slides easily in and out of me. I can feel my arousal dripping down my ass and spreading down my thighs. I've never been this turned on in my life.

Derick rolls his hips and I start to come again, my eyes rolling back in my head. I try and squirm away, get away from the over-sensitivity of his onslaught.

"Derick!" I scream, and then tears fall from my eyes, down my temples and back into my hair as it feels like lightning is shooting through my skin every time his hips slam into mine.

"There they are." Derick leans to the side and licks my tears, then kisses down my face until he's biting and licking my neck.

My arms wrap around him, holding on like he's a rock and this is a stormy sea. He's the only thing that's solid and steady and if I don't hold on I might fall under and never come back up.

"You're mine, Alina. I'm going to come inside this pretty little cunt right now. Do you want that?"

I think I say something resembling yes, but I'm terrified that I'm about to have another orgasm. It might kill me.

Derick moves harder and deeper inside me, his thrusts becoming erratic but electric. I start to come again, my pussy clenching down so hard it almost hurts. The room around me goes black and all I can feel is pleasure.

With a groan, Derick empties into me, pressing himself as deep as he can go as his cock throbs with his release.

We're holding onto each other, sharing sweat and air. I know my punishment is far from over, but a weight has lifted inside me. This was pure physical engagement - he didn't even kiss me. I survived this, and that seems like an auspicious start to my marriage.

12

Derick

I know what my wife is doing. She thinks that she can put up a barrier between us and wall herself off from me. Alina thinks I won't notice that we haven't kissed, but she forgets that our first night together was revealing. One night stands usually are. Knowing you won't have to face someone later means that your inhibitions are at their absolute lowest and you're more comfortable demanding what you want. I know she likes to be kissed when she comes.

I'm not going to kiss her.

I'm going to wind her up and make her desperate. Alina will break, and she will kiss me. I'm going to make my wife as obsessed with me as I am with her. Then she'll never even think of walking away from me ever again.

Jack doesn't understand why I'm so fixated on her, and I don't either. The two extra days we're in Chicago I do my best to give her space even though I don't want to - it makes me itch.

He and I go in to Designation's offices, tour some of their facilities, and establish connections between our two companies to start creating a plan to work together and expand our businesses. Most days I don't feel like much of a CEO but I do know my people and know what they do. A good business leader delegates and hires the best people to do the work well and creates a communication structure that encourages transparency.

A good criminal knows that he needs to do everything himself, and that loyalty is earned with blood and blackmail. All information is need to know, or go to the grave knowing it.

While I've been working, Alina has been packing up her life. I'm not insensitive to the difficulty of that, and force myself to stay away so that she can be with her family. It's also teaching me things about her that I didn't know, but aren't surprising.

She's unsentimental. Most of her packing was done in a day. There were very few things to be packed because she didn't like to acquire objects, but experiences. In the few boxes she packed were some memory boxes and albums from her trips, a few pictures and things from her mother, and a small jewelry box.

We had to arrange for special transport for a painting from her room.

Everything else was clothes and toiletries, and even that was small for a woman of her means. Alina had everything done in a day.

Then she grabbed her sisters and they holed up in Anora's room.

When it hit 10pm, I'd had enough. I'd carry her out of there if I had to, but she was surprisingly cooperative when I demanded that she come to bed in the guest house. I didn't miss the way they all blushed, and wondered how much she'd told them.

In the guest house, Alina lets me punish her.

She gets on her knees and sucks my cock, and then I eat her until she's crying again. Then I fuck her but don't kiss her, taunting her with touches of my lips on her jaw and neck, licking her skin but never touching my tongue to hers.

When I wake up on Sunday morning, she's still in bed with me. I watch her, touch her, and she responds to me. Her thick ass is pushed back into my waiting cock and I slide inside her, taking her slow and steady while she starts to wake. Her hand comes up to dive into my hair and she pulls me close because she's not quite aware of what she's doing when she's still half asleep. This could be a dream for all she knows.

We move together, slowly pleasuring one another. I cup her pussy and put broad pressure on her clit.

"Brody," she breathes out as she starts to come and it makes me happy. I bite down on the juncture of her neck and shoulders. She cries out and it tips me over the edge. I press deep and come inside her.

She sighs as I pull out and rolls over onto her back. We stare at each other for a long time.

Then she gets up and goes into the bathroom to take a shower.

It's just the beginning.

13

Alina

My entire family comes with us to the airport.

Derick, Jack, and Owen are all talking in a circle while we say goodbye. After an initially icy introduction and suspicion on both sides, the three of them seem to be getting along fine. I'm especially surprised by the connection developing between Derick and Owen. There are a few times when business has been discussed that I've seen them share a look, communicating without words. They understand one another.

I hug my dad for a long time. It's only April, so I don't know when I'll be back to see them before Thanksgiving. Derick already committed to coming back for it.

"I am proud of you, Lina. You are my warrior."

"Thanks, dad."

"But also give yourself a chance to be happy. To be more than one thing, okay?"

That's not what I expected him to say and I don't understand, but I nod. He steps away towards the other men to leave me with my sisters.

Aro and Anora are crying, Aster's usual frown is a little deeper than normal.

"If you need me to fuck anyone up, literally or digitally, I can be there in 4 hours." She steps forward and gives me a brief, short-armed hug before stepping back. Aster isn't big on expressing emotions but I know that she'll miss me. While she is oddly close with Aro despite the fact that they are opposites, I've always been the one that accepts her for the predator that she keeps on a tight leash. I am worried what she'll become without me here, but almost excited. She's only 22 - there's a whole world of hell she'll take on.

Aro hugs me and makes gasping nonsense noises. I'm not worried about her, she'll have Anora. I kiss her on the head and she steps back, tears sliding down her face.

Anora is the one that almost breaks me. We've been friends since the day I was born. I can try and promise that I'll call her every day, but that's a promise I can't keep. I'll have responsibilities, and so will she. She'll keep taking care of the house for our father, doing the social scene to keep us legitimate, and now that she's not getting married she'll have to figure out what comes next.

I take a deep breath, holding in my tears.

"Like I said, call me when you fall." Anora whispers in my ear and then pulls away, smiling. Like the well-mannered rich kid she is, she goes to say a gracious goodbye to Derick and Jack.

Then it's as if time is moving faster than usual because then we're in the plane, in the air, and I'm staring out the window as we fly over states I haven't been to yet. I'm sitting in the front of the plane and Derick is on the other side of the aisle, working on his laptop.

Jack got a shot of something from the flight attendant and then passed out. He's snoring lightly in the chair behind Derick.

The closer we get to landing, the more I retreat into work mode so that I'm not nervous. This is something and someplace unknown to me. Obviously I've read about the area, had Aster send me everything she could on Venture and the financial situation - not that I understood all of it. That wasn't my area. Still, I did my best to familiarize myself with everything on paper. I don't know how much Derick will tell me or let me be involved, but I won't be walking around blind if I can help it.

By the time we land, I couldn't make a facial expression if I tried I'm so far removed from myself.

Derick doesn't say anything, but he takes my hand when I walk down the stairs to deplane. He doesn't let me go and I'm a little bit grateful. This is his territory, and after his first inhale of Pacific Northwest air, he grins. There is something nice about the smell of the place. It's moist and heavy. The first time I was here, I loved it immediately. Anora would hate it. She loves the cold clarity of Chicago. This overcast softness would make her grumpy. It makes me feel relief.

We get in the back of an SUV, just the two of us.

"The staff will be at the house to meet you, but then you can rest or do whatever you want for the rest of the day."

"And then what?" I try to formulate the multiple questions that are stirring in my mind. "What's expected of me here? What's it mean for me to be your wife, Derick?"

He puts his hand on my thigh, heavy and possessive.

"You're the main point of contact for anything that has to do with the house. Elliot really runs things so you won't be needed for much, but when a decision needs to be made it'll be you. Venture also has a foundation and throws the usual fundraisers - you have to be involved. Then I'd also like you with me - you've valuable, Allie."

"What do you mean?" His last statement blasts through my hints of panic about having to throw galas and shit.

"You worked alongside your father for years - he never kept the business from you. You know things, and you'll have a perspective different from my men. I didn't marry you to stand next to me and look pretty, Alina. I married you to stand next to me and rule."

Well, fuck.

"Okay."

There's not much else to say to that, and I retreat back into my own thoughts as we drive. The house, as he tells me, is up in the foothills not in the city. It gives him the privacy of the woods and the isolation to take care of business. Derick tells me I'll always have a driver because it takes awhile to get used to going in and out of here, as well as for my protection.

"I know you can handle yourself," he holds his hands up before I can start a fight. "But you're more of a target now. Two against one is always better odds, right?"

Derick talks more about places we're going to go and where he wants to take me, as well as the things we'll need to establish and what my schedule will look like for the next week so I can start to settle in to life here. He's been thorough and the attention should feel flattering, but part of me is afraid he's going to bury me here now that's he's conquered me. I'm another trophy or acquisition. Derick might talk a good game about working together but I also know how charming he can be.

The car turns into a harshly curved driveway that leads to a clearing with a house made of wood and glass. I can't even say how many stories, since it goes up and down like a child put a bunch of different rectangles together and called it a house. It's beautiful, lit up and cozy looking. The wood is stained rather than painted, and the warm color blends with the woods that surround the house.

I stretch as we exit, following everyone else into the house slowly. There's an advantage to such an odd house, which is that there are a lot of vantage points to keep watch. The woods are tricky, offering places for enemies to hide, but I'm sure any approach would be noticed this far out.

Jack and his guard, Remo, walk straight into the house. Remo is very pale - his skin, his hair, his eyes, but he's strong and observant. I'm not sure he likes Jack, given the way he looks at him sometimes, but he seems dutiful.

Derick usually travels with his assistant, Jonah, a skinny ginger with a perpetual frown, but he went straight home from the airport. Derick's other shadow is Andrew. Andrew is a sad, serious man with dark hair and shark eyes. I like him. He and Derick are very in sync, and it makes me feel like Derick is protected.

I might not be completely sold on this marriage, but I've seen enough to know that I don't want anything bad to happen to Derick. He's trying to make this into something that works, and I'll find a way to adjust. I always do.

Derick waits for me at the door, and I go to him as we enter the house. It's interesting - the woodwork is all gold but the walls are dark, most of them black, and the glass carries through the house as well. The entrance is large, a staircase in front of us. To the left is a large dining room and I can see a doorway leading to what I assume is the kitchen. To the right is a living room, but I can see doorways to other areas. There's a hall in front of me, and underneath the staircase is an open stairway leading down. It's a bit like entering a maze.

I will definitely need a guide.

Derick draws my attention to the three men and a woman lined up and waiting to meet me.

An older man in his 50s with solid gray hair and serious green eyes is first, "Elliot, the...butler?" Derick laughs. "He runs the house and supervises everybody else. You'll work together on most things." We shake hands and he seems pleasant enough.

"This is Eifa, the chef. You can meal plan with her or leave it up to whatever she's in the mood to cook." The woman is probably 70 with a short cap of white hair and a steely glint in her pale blue eyes.

"My specialty is desserts, I got tricked into cooking for this *dynan*."

"Excellent," I grin at her. "I'm partial to anything with raspberries and never get sick of cinnamon rolls." Eifa nods in response, and then with a wave, turns and heads through the dining room.

Elliot takes over and introduces the last two men. They're young, in their 20s, and both have olive skin, brown hair, and dark brown eyes. The uniform of the staff is basic - dark pants, white shirts, and I appreciate they seem comfortable.

"This is David and Saul. They keep the house clean, run errands, do general maintenance. If you can't find me, they can do anything you need."

I nod at them and they nod back, both looking a little nervous.

"All of them, except Eifa, are trained for protection as well, and armed at all times."

"Eifa is probably armed," Jack jokes from over my shoulder and I shoot him a grin. "The woman has some very sharp knives in addition to a sharp tongue.

"You're just mad because she still calls you *bwlyn*." Derick puts his hand on my lower back and leads me away, dismissing the staff. "You're free to go, Jack. I've got this."

Jack looks at me, as if waiting for my okay, and I appreciate it.

"You'll be with me tomorrow going over some things, as well as Ethan, our accountant. Goodnight, *chwaer bach*."

Jack salutes us both and walks through the living room, then disappears through a doorway. This house is going to confuse me, I know it.

"His rooms are in the back of the house. The staff are on the floor below, as well as our home gym. We're on the third floor." Derick takes my hand and I don't fight him as we go upstairs. The second floor is long dark-painted hallways going in both directions. "This is guest bedrooms, an office, and a small library room. It's not used much, but it might be now."

Then we turn and go up the next set of stairs. The landing is smaller and there are only two doors. He opens the one on the right.

"This is ours," his voice gets husky as he pulls me inside. This must be an upper corner of the house, high enough that he feels like he has privacy because two of the four walls are glass, looking out over the trees and then distantly the lights of Seattle.

The floor is warm wood with a huge fuzzy rug in dark blue. The bed is a massive king with the same color blue in the sheets and pillows. There's a seating area with a love seat and two chairs, a plain desk, and short bookshelf with a record player on top. The bookshelf is full of albums.

He pulls me toward doors on the left side of the room. "Our closet," he gestures to one, "and the bathroom." He opens that door and leads me inside. The bath is done in all white and gray, with a huge shower, a separate free standing tub, and an area for the toilet that's hidden by a pocket door.

Derick smiles tentatively at me and takes me through to the next room. It's a smaller version of the bedroom, but empty.

"This is your room. I wanted space you could make your own. After Ethan gets you set up with the accounts tomorrow, get anything you want."

I turn to face him, defiant. "A bed?"

In an instant his face goes dark and he crowds me. "No, Allie. You're mine. Your place is in our bed."

I glower back at him, not backing down and getting up in his face. "Our bed? For how long?"

Derick inhales sharply and wraps a hand around my throat, pushing me back into the wall. He brings his face so close to mine we'd be touching if I moved a millimeter. I'm pissing him off on purpose and while my mind is angry, my body is enjoying the results. My panties are soaked.

"Until my last breath, or until we break it and have to get a new one. I've never had a woman in that bed. I've never had a woman at this house. You're the first, the only, and I will fuck you in every room on every surface until the air is saturated with our pleasure. We're going to start right here."

Derick lets go of my throat and rips open my shirt, buttons tinkling on the wooden floor. He massages my breasts roughly and I moan, throwing my head back and arching into his touch. While he teases the points of my nipples with his rough thumbs, I undo my pants and let them slide to the ground. An approving rumble comes out of Derick, and he pulls my shirt down my arms and then undoes my bra.

The air in the room is warm so I'm comfortable standing in nothing but a lacy, cheeky pair of panties.

Derick lays hot kisses down my neck, between my breasts, across my stomach until he's kneeling before me. I gasp when he presses a breathy kiss over my pussy, taunting me, before pulling my panties down my legs and exposing me to him.

"Should I remind you that you're mine, Allie? In this room, right now?"

I don't say anything.

He stands up and moves his hand to me, parting my folds and diving into the slick wetness pooling at my entrance. I clutch on to him as he pushes two fingers into me, causing me to shake with pleasure.

While I stand here naked, Derick is still in his suit. His soft brown hair is slicked back from his face, his scruff carefully maintained, and his gray jacket and trousers fit his body perfectly. The erection he's sporting isn't so bad either. I want him inside me, I want him to fuck me on the floor or against the wall, but I'm not going to ask. Asking is giving in to him. He has to take it if he wants it too.

I cry out when he removes his fingers from toying with me, but watch eagerly as he uses both hands to undo his belt and pants to free his cock.

"Will you take me, *lleidr bach*?" He whispers as he steps closer and rubs his cock down my abdomen to taunt my clit.

"Yes," I whimper as I lift a leg and wrap it around his hips.

"Good girl," he groans before grabbing my ass in a brutal grip and lifting me up. He presses me against the wall like it's nothing to lift and hold me, and keeps me there with one hand while he reaches down to guide himself inside me.

The intrusion of him feels so good, and my hips grind against him wantonly as we start to fuck against the wall. I hold onto to him and enjoy the view of him sliding into me, pressing into me harder and harder as we get worked up.

He bites into the skin around my collarbones, leaving marks but right now I don't care.

"Derick," I moan, "harder."

Shifting his grip, Derick pumps into me, slamming his hips against mine and hitting my clit with each thrust. I'm going to explode. I won't be able to be quiet and I don't even care.

I tense as it hits me, squeezing down hard on him and crying out as the pleasure rockets out from my core. For a few seconds I can't even breathe as I'm trapped in the sensation. Derick rides me through it and then presses in deep, groaning as he fills me.

We both breathe heavily and he lets me down gently, making sure I'm steady on my feet before he lets me go. Our foreheads are pressed together, and I can't stop myself from looking at his soft, perfect lips. They are nice, but off limits.

I jolt when Derick reaches out to touch my pussy again, gently teasing my clit with the mix of our come. He slides a finger inside me again. The audible wet sound of it is obscene and sexual, and I'm almost embarrassed that it turns me on again.

Derick removes his finger and brings it to my mouth. "Taste us."

Caught up in the moment, I do as he asks and open my mouth. He gently runs his finger over my tongue, and together we're a salty, musky flavor.

"Perfect," he rasps.

14

Alina

After getting thoroughly pleasured, I collapse naked into the bed next door. I'm surprised that it's dark out already when I wake up. The clock on the bedside table says it's 9:30, so I've missed dinner for sure. Surprisingly, I'm not hungry. Although lack of appetite is my usual response to stress I also don't feel as stressed as I expected. This house is comfortable and it sets me at ease.

"What's that smile for?" Derick's voice comes from the far end of the room and I see that he's in one of the armchairs in the sitting area, reading through documents. He caught me in an unguarded moment.

"I like the house. It's lovely."

"Thank you." He stands up and walks over to me, sitting on the end of the bed. When he tries to take my hand I move it away under the premise of tucking my hair behind my ears. I wrap the blankets around my naked body and take a deep breath.

"Ask." His voice is quiet and raspy again, the voice that resonates in all my sensitive parts.

"Ask what?"

"Whatever is on your mind right now."

I sigh, frustrated that he can read me. When I look into his face it's easy for me to read him too but I think it's because he's letting me.

"First, what language are you always using? I tried looking up some of but it all comes out German and I know it's not."

Derick laughs and it's real and loud.

"Welsh. It's Welsh - which is a Celtic language. Our grandparents immigrated here from Wales and they and our mother taught us Welsh. I think they felt the weather was similar. Washington isn't for the weak."

I give him a wan smile.

"What's the thing you call me mean?"

His smile turns heated. "I'll tell you when you're ready."

My response is to roll my eyes and I press on. "What about tonight? Dynan and bwlyn?" The words and pronunciation are uncomfortable on my tongue and I know I basically slaughtered them.

"*Dynan* is little man - Eifa has always called me that. *Bwlyn*," he stops and laughs, "means little ball. Jack was very round before he hit puberty. It's really meant to be sweet but Jack's sensitive."

I laugh as well, and file away that Eifa has been with the family a long time and knows them well. She's also the only woman on the staff. Not to embrace internalized gender norms but household staff are usually women. Even if they double as protection, I'm a clear example that women can get the job done too.

Which is why I approach the next question carefully.

"Why are there no women on the staff?"

Derick's face falls as if he knew that was the question I was going to ask and he was hoping that I wouldn't.

"I'm going to tell you this as an act of trust, and because it's important you know that I view you as one of us. You're a Clayton now. I expect you to protect our secrets as your own." Derick is deadly serious, and doesn't say anything else until I nod in agreement.

"We used to have a mix of staff. Women whose families had been with us or whose loyalty we earned. I felt they could be trusted."

He rubs his hands across his eyebrows in a stressed gesture and then continues.

"Jack started sleeping with one of them. He was 19, they were both wrapped up in this young forbidden love bullshit. Then she got pregnant, and it got real for him. He disconnected from her - doing what I made him but never really stepping up. So, I did. I made sure she was provided for and had the best care.

"And then she lost the baby. At 18 weeks. It was traumatic for everyone, but her most of all. Jack didn't react. He stepped away and acted like it never happened. He didn't go to the hospital, he wouldn't see or speak to her. It was as if he had nothing to do with it. She was heartbroken. There was no expectation that they be together, we would've taken care of them either way, but she was hurt by his lack of any sort of emotion for her.

"After, I made sure she had somewhere to live, a therapist, and the promise that I'd help her find a job when she was ready."

Derick shakes his head and looks away, still hurt by something that must've happened years ago. Jack is only a year older than me.

I reach out and take his hand. "What happened to her?"

"She stepped in front of a bus. Witnesses say she was waiting at the stop with them - for a therapy appointment - and when the bus pulled up she turned away and walked straight past it into traffic. I had her buried with her daughter."

"Jack is why there's no women? You think he can't control himself?" Jack hadn't struck me as the kind of guy who would chase the nearest available woman but maybe I was wrong. I'm usually good at reading people. This would also explain my feelings about the connection being off between Jack and Derick.

"No," he replies darkly. "When some of the women who worked for us, here and at Venture, saw how I'd taken care of - her." I notice that he hasn't said her name but let it go. "They saw dollar signs. It got out of hand - some of them getting Jack drunk to sleep with him, throwing themselves at me, making claims. It was easier to retreat. There are plenty of amazing women at Venture who would never behave that way in a million years, but when it comes to home we decided to be cautious."

"Not worried Eifa is going to throw herself at you?" I joke to lighten the mood. That was a heavy truth and I don't know what else to say.

"Since we're related, I really hope not." He sees my shocked face. "My mother's cousin. All the family we've got left, but she wouldn't take a handout."

"I understand that." We lapse into silence as I process everything he told me, and how it alters my perception of the dynamics of the house, and between him and Jack. It's not my place, not yet, to try and repair the damage between them but at least I have something to consider when trying to fix them.

"Thank you for telling me."

"I told you, you're one of us now."

A cold ball forms in my stomach so I break eye contact with him and shift away. Derick sighs but lets me.

15

Derick

After letting Alina know that dinner is wrapped in the fridge for her if she's hungry, I head down to the second floor and into my office. Talking about Jack's mistakes, and what happened to Nora, always takes a lot out of me. She was only 21.

We hired Nora because we saved her, and she was loyal to us. Her family had been murdered as part of a plot to kidnap her and her sister for trafficking. They were poor, immigrants, working under the table, and it all went down in a building that we owned under a shell corporation. We owned a lot of low income housing to keep the families of some of our more illegal employees safe and comfortable.

When my men found Nora, she was holding the dead body of her sister, a knife in her hand, and one of the men dead at her side. Little, but fierce, and only 16 years old. After getting her cared for, I brought her into the house. She was like a sister to me, a brave tiger cub I needed to protect until she grew into her own. I wasn't going to let her be staff forever, just until she felt confident enough to go out on her own.

Jack broke her. I raised my brother most of our lives and he should've known better. As much as it hurt to lose Nora, so soon after losing her daughter, my disappointment in Jack's failures runs deeper. I don't care that he was 19, still a kid in most ways - he knew better. It's why I've never been able to trust him with the bigger things in the businesses even though he's 27 years old and this fuck up is almost a decade behind him. Every time I test his judgment he fails me. I love my brother but I'll be cleaning up his messes for the rest of my life, and I think telling Alina that story planted the seed of that reality because as my wife, she will be too.

Jack is also the reason I'm heading to the office in the house. He sent me an urgent text to call him.

I push the speed dial button on my office phone and he picks up after one ring.

"Someone burned the shipment."

"What the hell do you mean?" I'm pulling out my phone at the same time, texting my main enforcer Kade. He needs to go see our men inside the docks and find out what the fuck is going on.

"I got a call from Leo that the cops confiscated one of the containers. They only knew about that one, but that's a third of the shipment." He sounds pissed. Jack is generally in charge of our off the books underworld stuff, mostly the clubs and 24/7 convenience stores, but he's also got the reputation as our contact for anything related to our business. Especially when people fuck up, they wouldn't dare call me. I step in when things need to be handled.

"We can still fulfill orders with the other two." I add another text to Kade telling him to speed up delivery of the other two containers. Normally we wait a bit to extract our product to alleviate scrutiny, but we can't afford to lose another shipment.

"Okay. Who's doing this? A rival would steal our shit, not get it taken away."

"I'll get some people on it, don't worry about it."

"Derick -" Jack starts but I cut him off.

"No, you did your job, now it's my problem. Check the clubs, I'll see you in the morning."

Jack doesn't say anything, but hangs up the phone. I know he's pissed but there's a reason he called me. It's my part to take care of shit like this.

I log in to my VPN and then into the encrypted drive where I store our data. The upside to being the owner of a company like Venture is that there are tech savvy people in the world who don't care about committing crimes, they care about pushing limits. To find the ultimate ways to keep digital secrets, and I have a lot of them working for me. They have no problem doing work for our criminal clientele, and they setup digital storage units for me that can be deleted with the send of a text. It's dangerous, but they know without a doubt that I will kill them if they snoop on my shit. It's happened before and I'm sure it'll happen again, but the ones who believe in discretion flourish.

My record of the orders we have to fulfill against the product coming in still lines up. We aren't in trouble, and we have another shipment coming in a few weeks from now. Then I shift over to our financials. I haven't been as vigilant here lately as I should've been, and I can see that we're thousands down from our usual profits at several of the clubs. It's Jack's job to report that stuff, and also notice when things like this are happening. It's his job to figure out why. Now I'll have to get on his ass about that too - and check on the men he's keeping around him, and in charge of the clubs.

Blood and blackmail, I think to myself. I'll have to make the time to figure it out.

My cell phone rings. Kade is calling.

"What did you find?" I don't bother with niceties. Kade would see it as wasting time.

"Ecklie wants a meeting."

That's the port supervisor we mainly work through, and if he wants to meet it's either to confess he fucked up, ask for more money, or both. If he knew something or suspected something that was easy, he'd tell Kade. Ecklie's been useful for years now but eventually everyone gets greedy.

"Make it happen. You and I will meet Thursday. Be at the house by 4."

"Done." Kade hangs up and I put my head in my hands.

There's too much going on. Allying with the Sorrelles and Designation Tech protects our legitimate interests, and it shores up the work we can do for our criminal clients, but what's happening now is outside of that bolstering. This is the side of our business that's always been strong, and now it feels as if it's crumbling. There are pieces I can't see yet because I don't even know the right places to dig. Someone is coming at me, trying to tear down my underworld.

Part of me is tempted to let them. It's easier to keep my hands clean doing illegal work through Venture. I don't give a shit about the clubs, except Cartref, and we can keep running the housing developments through our shell corporations. Those are acts of charity, not criminal enterprises and sometimes it's better if people don't know where the help is coming from.

I want to be done. If I could find a way to shut it down or get bought out in a way that truly disconnects us, I would. But I don't think it's in the cards, not right now.

There's nothing more I can do at the moment. Kade will tap into his network and use his men to gather information, and when we know everything we can we'll make decisions. I'm half tempted to have someone check on Jack, but I'd never go as far as distrusting him that deeply. If he ever found out, the injury would never be repaired.

Instead, I'll focus on conquering my wife. One orgasm at a time.

16

Alina

The week goes quickly, and my schedule for the first few days feels more like being on-boarded for a job than entering a marriage. Then again, marriages are historically business arrangements so maybe it isn't so different.

Ethan arrives promptly at 10am on Monday. He's an attractive Black man who can do terrifyingly complicated math in his head and tells me he has a nearly eidetic memory. He goes through the process of authorizing me as a user on various accounts, ordering cards, setting me up with my own usernames and passwords, as well as making sure I know which I can talk about and use in certain places and which I can't. He also informs me that I'm expected to purchase furnishings for my room, and can change anything in the house that I wish. I'm also expected to increase my wardrobe since I'll be attending formal events with Derick. He gives me a list of stores where we have accounts that can be billed directly.

I fucking hate clothes shopping, and now I wish Aro was here to do it with me. I need a woman friend in Seattle.

Ethan also gives me a laptop, a new phone with the same number but better encryption, keys to the house, and an access card to get into

Venture. It's overwhelming how much power and access I have and I haven't even been married for a week. This kind of generosity would not be reciprocated by someone coming in to the Sorrelle house.

I spend the rest of Monday purchasing furniture for the upstairs room. I'm getting real fancy and calling it my sitting room, like a proper socialite. When I can't make decisions, I video call my sisters and they help me pick everything out, so it feels like they're a part of it. I don't quite miss them yet, but I feel their absence. Despite our differences they've been included in my every day decisions and to be doing so much without them feels both uncomfortable and liberating.

I am on my own in a way I never have been before. No one else's opinion matters in this room and that's kind of insane. The furniture I end up buying is all big, deep, and cozy, in a variety of jewel tones that will look good with the bright wood. I even buy one of those cheesy vinyl wall decorations to make one entire wall look like the silhouette of a forest. I'll need help to put it up but I'm kind of excited. I've never gotten to focus on anything like this before.

Tuesday I get up early, despite being sore in all the right places, and find my way down to the gym. I go hard, and the men start heading in to work as I'm heading out. They give me weird looks, but that's something I'll deal with another day. Derick is relentless in attacking my body every night and I think he's trying to orgasm me into submission.

It isn't working but it's fun for him to try. Pleasure isn't the way to earn my trust. I'm not sure what is, or if that's even what he's trying to do.

After showering, I'm whisked into the city to meet with Jonah and get a tour of Venture.

Jonah's waiting at his desk and through the glass walls of his office, I get a peek at Corporate Derick. He's glowering while listening to two staff talk, and I have to squeeze my thighs together to relieve the tension. It's sexy as hell. He's in a dark suit, deep frown on his face, jaw tight, and all I can think about is sliding under his desk and sucking his cock to relieve that tension. To make him lose his cool when he's all tied up in business mode.

I file that away for a time when I might need it. It's pointless to deny my physical attraction and our explosive chemistry.

Jonah and I step into a small conference room.

"Here's a printout of your calendar for the next few weeks, but from here on out everything will be digital and accessible from your phone. Please keep any appointments or time that's set aside up to date."

"Not a problem." I flip through the calendar, seeing only a few things over the next two weeks, but one of those things is a charity dinner that I definitely don't have a dress for yet. Fuck.

"He goes to a lot of charity dinners and donates a lot. You don't have to stay long but you have to show up. Has he talked to you about the foundation yet?"

"A little."

"Great. Every other week there's a luncheon of the volunteer planning committee, you have to be there. We have two full time staff who run the foundation and therefore the fundraiser, Melinda and Casey."

"Where are their offices? Where is the foundation?"

Jonah looks at me for a long second. "There is no office for the foundation."

I don't say anything, and file that away again. I might have to change that, and we'll see what I learn at the first lunch next week.

"I've also chosen one of our administrative staff and assigned them to you part time. Lauren will be a point of contact for people who want to meet with you or invite you to events."

"Why her?" I cut Jonah off as he takes a breath to continue his prepared speech. I can tell how much he hates doing this and see his shoulders tighten with every ring of Derick's phone, even though someone else is working the desk and taking his calls.

"Excuse me?"

"Why did you choose Lauren?" Jonah doesn't know it, but this is a test. I'm assessing his skills. He might be an organized and committed assistant, but I need to know that he's also looking out for Derick and Venture's best interests.

"She's a married mom to four kids, and the boost in pay for taking on your schedule helps her." I stare at him longer and he sighs. "Lauren is a local and knows a lot of the players, so if you ask the right questions she can give you answers. She's also the only female staffer who has never made eyes at Derick. Not that the others would ever try anything," he holds up his hands to assure me, "but they look. Lauren doesn't look. She's stupidly in love with her husband and they've been together since high school. She takes no shit, is awesome at her job, and can take care of things so you don't have to."

"And if at some point I need her full time?"

"She knows it's a possibility."

"Thank you, Jonah."

"Right." He wraps up our conversation and then hands me off to his back up staffer, Keith, to give me a brief tour of Venture. I want to meet Lauren today but she'd already planned to have the day off. It'll happen another time, and I leave a note on her desk for her to call me the next day. I need to know more about this charity dinner before I commit to a dress.

Wednesday is when things get interesting.

I work out later than usual, and the men are in the gym, including Saul and David.

It's a wide open room, built under the ground and into the side of the hill because it's bigger than the footprint of the house above. The walls are lined with machines and weights, and the center is three mats for sparring matches.

I want to spar. It's what I'd be doing today with our men at home.

I stand on the edge of the mat after doing a quick run on the treadmill to get myself warm and loose. It's a clear invitation.

One of the men, one that's obviously a leader and the others look to, steps up to me.

"They aren't going to fight you." His voice is cautious.

"Why? Afraid their egos can't handle it?"

"You're out of your league with us, ma'am."

"You can call me Alina."

"I'm Roe." He points to the other three men in the room besides Saul and David. "That's Louis, Sean, and Riley. We're here to protect you."

"I can protect myself."

"I'm sure," he smirks. "But we're still not going to spar with you."

I don't want to play this card, but I will, because this is his territory. "I guess I'll have to call Derick..."

"Wait," Roe holds up his hands. "Don't interrupt the boss." He steps onto the mat and beckons me with his fingers. "I'll go easy on you."

"I can't say the same."

I step onto the mat and don't wait, I attack.

I'm not a small woman. I never have been. I'm 5'10" - I'm three inches taller or more than my sisters. I weigh 180 and most of it is muscle. My body is broad and built for brute strength; it's my own work that made me quick and sharp too. Despite the fact that my body is imposing, even for a woman, men still consistently underestimate me. It's not like my muscles aren't on full display right now - I'm in tight workout pants and a sports bra. I have abs that show without me flexing, and my biceps are bigger than my fist when I flex.

There's a powerhouse inside me and I love being underestimated.

Without hesitation, I dive for Roe's center and get him down on the mat, then roll him to grab his arm behind him and twist his wrist.

We struggle for a second before he taps the mat. I let him up, and we face each other. He still looks hesitant, but my smirk also pisses him off.

"Let's do this for real."

It takes two more matches for Roe to beat me, but we're fairly evenly matched. He's an inch shorter and about 30 pounds heavier, and he gave me a good workout.

Someone must have called Derick anyway because he's waiting for me upstairs when I'm done. Sweat is dripping down my body and I don't look at him as I enter the kitchen and get the water pitcher from the fridge. I pour myself a glass and drink it before turning to lean on the counter.

"Can I help you?"

Derick's eyes are on fire as he eats me up. It makes me shiver and my nipples are instantly and obviously hard. I take a deep drink and feel him watch a bead of sweat drip from behind my ear down my neck, and across my chest. He's hungry and I like teasing him.

"Good workout?"

"It got there eventually. Do you mind me sparring with your men?"

"No. I made sure they know that now."

"Thanks."

I turn around to put my glass in the dishwasher and he's behind me in a few quick steps. He pulls my sweaty body hard against his suited one, and I don't miss the press of his cock against my ass. Derick licks the sweat from my neck and my head falls back.

"I like you this way," he bites my shoulder. "But I know what I'd like better."

Derick pushes me into the counter, and I brace myself, waiting for what comes next. I don't expect him to grab a knife from the block, pull the waistband of my workout pants, and then cut along the seam. He drops the knife to the floor and then rips my pants open, baring my ass and pussy to him.

He slaps one cheek. "Up on your toes and bend over."

Derick, in his fine, expensive suit, gets on his knees behind me, spreads my cheeks open, and licks me from pussy to asshole. He groans, diving in to my soaked core, lapping up my arousal and my sweat.

"I like you dirty, Allie." I gasp as he presses his tongue against my asshole and clench automatically. "I like the taste of your sweat. I want to taste it with your come."

"Then work for it," I say through clenched teeth, trying to hold back.

Derick pulls back and starts to tease me with his thumb, grazing it across my clit, along my lips, and then to my ass. He does it over and over, and I'm shivering with the need for more. More pressure, more penetration, more something.

I cry out when he presses two fingers into my pussy while he slides his thumb into my ass. He works both hands slowly, and I have never felt so full in my life. After a moment he stops moving his thumb, just presses hard into my ass. Before I can ask what he's doing, he starts fucking me hard with his fingers. My juices are sliding down my thighs, all over his hand and I'm sure getting onto his suit.

Imagining how he looks right now, how we both look - me ripped open and bent over, penetrated in both holes, him looking all put together in his suit but doing something filthy - throws me over the edge. I come hard, clenching onto him and rolling my hips to get the friction I want. My legs are shaking when I come down and as he slides out of me I feel empty.

But then he licks me again. "Sweat and come. Delicious." His tongue presses on my sensitive clit and I squeak, making him laugh.

Derick backs away and I turn around. From the front you wouldn't know my pants were cut open.

"There's a meeting tomorrow I'd like you to be at. Lauren added it to your calendar."

"Okay," I agree. "This lunch next week for the foundation - anything I need to be aware of?"

He thinks for a second and then looks something like guilty. "Maybe. There's a woman - I saw her to...blow off steam."

"Did you end it?" I hate the fact that I feel jealous of this woman, and that talking about this puts a pit in my stomach.

"Not officially, but she knows we're done. The last times I saw her nothing happened -I wasn't interested."

"Why was that? Got bored?" I sneer at him.

Derick's face flashes with anger and he cages me against the counter, pressing his hips into mine, his mouth so close I can't help but look at it.

"No. I met a woman at a club and spent a night inside her. After that, no one compared. I couldn't even get hard without thinking about her." He grabs my ponytail and yanks my hair back, exposing my throat to him. "I knew that no one else would do, and I had to find her, take her, and keep her."

"I see," I manage to get out. Derick moves me around like a toy, adjusting so that our foreheads are pressing together and all I can see are his dark eyes.

"I'm yours, Alina. All you have to do is claim me."

I stare into his eyes for a long moment. "We'll see."

He lets me go slowly and gives me space, but he's still close and still touching me.

"You need to end it with this woman. Officially."

"Why?"

"Because I don't want a mistress thinking she still has any access to you. You vowed to be faithful - and you meant it, right?"

"Yes." Derick is vehement, and I'm sure he means it right now.

"Then make that clear to her. That you're married, thanks for the fucks, see you around."

"If that's what you want."

"It is." I do want it. I want it clear that for the moment, I own him. I want it known, even if he falls back on other habits in the future, that as his wife I have the power. I am the commitment and the priority. They were before, I am now.

"Will you come with me?"

I frown at him. "You want me to come with you to break up with your mistress?"

"Wait in the car. I'll need something to look forward to after dealing with her."

"Fine." It seems like a weird request but he's following through, so I'll do it.

"After the meeting tomorrow." Derick presses a kiss to my collar-bone and then leaves the kitchen. After a few deep breaths I make my way upstairs, and no staff are accidentally treated to a view of my ass.

17

Derick

The small table in my office at home is full, and the room is tense with anxiety. Jack is fidgeting, nervous and frustrated. Kade is still, patient and angry. His right hand, Niles, is tapping his fingers on the table, ready to be out of the house and into the field looking for answers. I'm tense, like usual. The only one who appears calm is Alina.

She's wearing a dark suit and a dark purple button up. I can see her holster across her back and shoulders, and I know she's carrying even though there's no reason to be. It demonstrates her competence and I like it.

The suit is straight, clean lines, trying to hide her curves. Somehow, knowing what's beneath the clothes makes seeing her all buttoned up like this incredibly sexy. I can't be distracted by that right now - I invited her for a reason. I need an outside perspective.

"What's the plan?"

"We'll meet Ecklie at the docks, on the east end where it's mostly shut down. Quiet, open, and good visibility in all directions. Two of the warehouses down that way are abandoned so any signs of life will be noticed." Kade explains this to me, and Niles nods.

"That's a bad idea," Alina steps in. "You should meet on more neutral territory, especially if you suspect he's already betrayed you."

Niles sneers at her. Kade stares, his face blank of expression. His silence allows her to continue, and I listen as well. I've never questioned how Kade wants to run things like this. He has good instincts and he's never let me down. We've worked together since my father died. He has been the most trustworthy person in my life.

"This is his turf. He knows it better than you do, and he knows where he can hide what. It won't matter that it's open with good sight lines because it also gives you nowhere to run if this is a trap. The docks are a bad idea."

"What would you know about it?" Niles scoffs at her.

I see red, but wait. Alina needs to be able to handle my men as well as I do.

"It's not my first meeting, sweetheart, or my first time feeling out a traitor," she talks down to him and he stiffens. "This is a trap."

"Kade?" He's the only other opinion in the room that I trust.

"She has a point."

"Are you fucking serious? Who is she?" Niles stands up and gestures at Alina. Now it's my turn.

"She's my wife." My voice is low and dangerous, and Niles pauses immediately. Jack and Kade both subtly move away from him, distancing themselves from the trouble he's about to get into. "She was the head of security for Don Sorrelle, and I know how many bodies she's buried."

Alina sits up straighter, surprised by that statement. I'm sure I'll be questioned about it later and I don't mind that I showed some of my hand when it comes to how thoroughly I've gathered information about her and what exactly she did for her father.

Niles scoffs again and sits down. "This isn't Chicago."

"Exactly," I snarl at him. "We've been getting our business sniped and our security compromised, and it's someone who knows our operation. An outside perspective is necessary. We will be blind to our own weaknesses until it's too late."

"Fine," he scowls. "If not the docks, then where?"

"Where would he feel secure? It has to be public, obviously, somewhere he thinks you wouldn't make a move on him." Alina stares off into the distance for a second.

"What?" I prompt her. Everyone is looking at her, and only Niles is still frowning.

"This is going to sound crazy, but what about on the ferry?"

"Why the ferry?" Kade asks.

"It's isolated for both sides, so there's vulnerability there that will make him overconfident. In his mind, you wouldn't dare make a move against him in such a public place. Except he doesn't realize that the best place to hide is in a crowd."

"What if he brings reinforcements?" Jack asks.

"I think we can handle that," Kade answers. "My sources indicate that he's on the outside, not running the show. He's alone and wants us to think he's more."

Jack pulls up the ferry schedules and we settle on Seattle to Bremerton. It gives us two hours to sort out our shit, there and back, and we can always throw him overboard if needed. I want to think we're kidding about that but when things go sideways, water destroys evidence and that's always useful.

They start plotting and Alina sits quietly and observes. She's staring at Jack, who isn't adding anything to the conversation. As usual. They make eye contact and he shrugs. I have no idea what that's about.

When we've got our plan outlined, Kade and Niles leave. I'm still not sure about Niles, but he didn't put up a fight once everyone else was in on the plan. Ecklie is up to something and I'll either make him spill his guts, or cut them out of him. He's dealing with me now, not my lieutenants.

Jack stands up. "I'm taking tomorrow night off. I need to decompress."

"It's been a long week, you deserve a break," I nod at him.

Alina stays in the room, and we're sitting across from each other.

"That guy was kind of an asshole."

"Yes," I agree.

"I like Kade though. Where'd you find him?"

I give her a small smile. "Prison." That's not the entire story, but the answer is fun.

She gapes at me, and my eyes are drawn to her thick, pink lower lip. When she notices the way I'm staring at her she swallows and looks away.

"Are you going to tell me more?"

"No," I stand up and stretch, pleased when she watches my body. "We have an errand to run. Do you want to change before we go? I'd like to take you to dinner afterward."

Alina looks at me, and I wish I could read her mind because the conflict is clear on her face. I don't understand what's holding her back. I have literally given her the keys to my kingdom, given her free rein to do what she wants with our home, and made it clear I will be her personal jungle gym if she wants it. Her mistrust in me is rational, I guess, but it still chafes.

"Okay." She gets up and walks out. I reach out to stop her, but she doesn't see. I don't know what I would've done anyway. Hugged her? That's awkward as fuck. That's not what I want but I have to let her come to me. This is a marathon, not a sprint.

Half an hour later, Alina looks fucking delectable in a simple gray dress. It's fitted to her waist and then flares out softly, landing at her knees. The shade of gray she's wearing matches my tie, and I like to think that she did it on purpose.

I'm taking her to Canlis. It's one of the most gorgeous places to eat in Seattle, and I can't help but want to impress her. Cat lives in Queen Anne so it's not that far to go after I end something that was never anything at all.

Cat Mason is the sole heiress to old money, and never thought to do anything else with her life except spend it. It made her the perfect person to have an arrangement with, not that we ever spoke about it formally. She wasn't going to want money from me, or even that much attention. Cat wanted to get fucked, and she wanted the cache of people knowing that I had chosen to fuck her. We didn't do dates, families, or events. Even at my foundation's annual fundraiser gala we barely spoke to one another.

But Cat didn't keep it to herself that we hooked up, and I didn't care. I knew she had other toys she played with occasionally, and she knew that I had mine. Still, when it got out that I was getting married, something changed with her. I didn't want to acknowledge it because I didn't want to deal with extricating myself from it. Then I didn't have the motivation for it.

Alina is more than enough motivation. If it makes her believe my vows to her and makes her feel more comfortable, then I will face down what I'm sure is going to be an Oscar-worthy performance.

People don't walk away from Cat Mason.

We pull up in front of the house, and Alina raises an eyebrow, but says nothing.

I take her chin in my hand and make her look at me. "I'll be right back."

"I'll be here."

I want to kiss her so fucking bad but I won't.

Instead, I step out of the car and ring the bell. Cat answers after only a moment, dressed in a pair of short black shorts and a sports bra. Cat likes to talk about how much yoga she does and I'm sure I interrupted a session. The smile on her face makes me feel sick. It's knowing, as if she's not surprised to see me.

I look back at the SUV before I step inside, but I can't see Alina through the tinted windows.

"You haven't even been married for a week, Derick," Cat purrs at me. She pulls me into the living room by my tie and I am filled with the urge to rip it off and burn it. Then she puts her hands on my chest and starts to rub on me.

Gently, I remove her hands and push her back from me.

"I'm here to end things, formally."

"Oh? Formally?" she grins at me and starts playing with the waistband of her shorts. Cat is beautiful, objectively. A soft, symmetrical face that hides a cruel, clever mind, a fit body with a tight ass, and long brown hair that came in very handy when fucking. It was purely physical, but it's not what I want. Not ever again, from anyone.

"You know I'm done, Cat. I've been done."

A flicker of anger crosses her face but she quickly hides it. "I don't care that you're married."

"I care that I'm married. She's all I want."

Now Cat looks pissed. I brace myself for the onslaught and wonder how long I have to stick around before getting the fuck out of here. Cat knows better. This isn't who we are, but I'm hurting her ego and I get that. I don't want an enemy but there's only so much I'll put up with.

"So you no longer have a use for me and you're letting me know. I was just a warm fucking hole to you, huh?"

"And I was just a hard dick to you, Cat. Don't make this something it wasn't. But I'm not actually an asshole, and this is me not ghosting you."

"Fuck you, Derick!" she lets out a sob but there are no tears on her face or building up in her eyes. "Fuck you."

"Not anymore, Cat. I'll see you around." I take a few steps back. Cat puts her hands on her hips, her mouth open and closing as she really works up a head of steam.

"Fuck you!" she yells again and grabs the nearest thing off the end table in her living room. It happens to be a paperback book, which I'm grateful for. It thumps off the wall next to my head and I turn and hustle my way to the front door. It closes behind me and when I glance back as I walk down the steps, she's standing in the living room still, ranting at no one. I have no doubt she'll move on easily.

18

Alina

The woman, Cat, is beautiful. She's small and lithe, obviously fit and overtly sexual. I am nothing like her. Even if he's breaking things off, it still hits at insecurities any woman like me might feel. I'm not small. I'm actively resisting him. It's clear from the look on her face that she thinks he's there to hook up.

I feel sick, and then I feel stupid for feeling sick.

From the front of the car, Andrew speaks. "Don't worry, Mrs. Clayton."

I jolt. It's the first time anyone's called me that. The paperwork tells me it's true but it's different hearing it said out loud.

"I'm not worried."

"You are, it's okay. I've been with him for 6 years, and Mr. Clayton is a man of his word. He's very...dedicated."

There's something Andrew is trying to tell me, and I feel like I understand a small piece of it but I don't want to grasp the whole. I just nod, and then let out a breath when Derick walks out of the house.

When he gets back in the car, he's radiating tension, and sits close to me.

"Drive up a block and park," he directs Andrew, who does as

instructed immediately. When the car stops, he nearly growls. "Take a walk."

Andrew doesn't say anything, but exits the car, locks it behind him, and starts walking down the street. For a second I worry, but this is a pretty swanky neighborhood and I'm sure that Andrew can hold his own.

"Are you okay?" I ask.

"Fine, *lleidr bach*." He moves to kneel in front of me in the large backseat, and maneuvers himself between my legs, gently pushing them open with his body. "Regretting ever touching a woman who wasn't you."

"Don't be ridiculous," I say immediately. In response, Derick reaches up and rips my panties down my legs, then pushes up my dress. I'm bare to him, and he spreads my thighs open to look at me.

"This," he leans forward and licks me, "is the only pussy for me." He slides his hands under me, gripping my ass hard and tilting my hips up so he can dive at me from a better angle. His tongue parts my lips and he sucks hard at my clit before swirling his tongue around it, making my hips work on their own as I fuck his face.

I grip the seat and roll my hips, taking what he's giving me both physically as well as mentally. Whether it's on purpose or not, he's making his want for me clear. Derick is destroying me one swirl of his tongue at a time and I can't stop it.

"Derick!" I scream out as I start to come, my hips lifting off the seat as he holds me to his face and lets me ride him. Even as I come down, he still licks gently at my pussy, lapping up my come and teasing me.

When he lifts his head he licks his lips and closes his eyes like he's savoring a meal and fuck if that doesn't get to me. He wipes his mouth with the back of his hand. I lean back when he presses into me, our chests meeting.

"It's not only your pussy, Allie. It's you. You are the only one for me."

I don't say anything.

Derick moves to sit beside me, arranging my dress so it's down around my knees again. He puts a proprietary arm around me and keeps me close as he pulls out his phone to text Andrew that it's safe for him to return. It smells like sex in here but I'm sure that won't come as a surprise to Andrew.

"Can I have my panties back?"

"No." Derick pockets them. "I want to be sitting across from you at dinner knowing that I'll have easy access to dessert."

This time I don't say anything because I don't know what to say. I've had plenty of pleasure with men, but no one has ever been as obsessed with my pussy as Derick. He eats me out every day, sometimes more than once. It's like he's conditioning me to get wet the second he pulls off my panties.

And it's working.

Andrew comes back and doesn't look at us as he starts the car and heads back into traffic toward the restaurant.

Derick leans over and whispers in my ear. "My beard is going to smell like your pussy all night. I fucking love it."

I gasp, and he continues. "Who needs dinner when I can just eat you? Spread you out on the table until I have you screaming. Begging me to fuck you."

Even though I just had a fantastic orgasm, I'm wetter than I was before. His voice when he whispers like this is raspy and when I can feel his breath on my skin it makes me break out in goosebumps and feel like I can't breathe. I want him to stop, and I want him to keep talking.

"You will beg me by the time I'm done tonight, Alina. Beg for my cock to fucking pound into your tight pussy, and I can already hear the way you'll scream when I fill you up with come."

I'm lightheaded, and swallow hard. He notices, and runs his fingers down my throat. Derick tightens the arm he has around me pressing our bodies together. Can you come from someone talking to you? One touch on my clit and I'd probably explode right now.

"I love seeing your dripping pussy after I fuck you. Seeing the evidence that you're mine." His fingers trace my jaw, and then my lips. They part slightly and he slides one finger inside. I tentatively move my tongue forward to touch it. He groans and buries his face in my neck. Without thinking, I reach over and palm his cock through his pants, squeezing it.

"Dirty girl," Derick's voice is harsh with arousal. "Would you let me fuck your ass, Allie? You liked when I played with you there the other day. When my cock is covered in your cum and mine, would you let me spread you open and take you there?" He groans again. "I want to feel your ass tighten on me when you come, because I'd make you come from fucking that sweet, tight ass."

I bite my lip hard, because all I want to do is cry out. I want to beg him. I want to beg him for everything he just promised me, every filthy fucking thing. Right now I'd let him have absolutely anything he wanted.

"Andrew?" my voice is high and thready.

"Yes, ma'am?"

"Forget dinner, take us home."

Andrew nods and Derick laughs in my ear. "That's my dirty fucking girl."

19

Derick

This is the longest car ride that has ever been. Alina and I are rubbing on each other like cats in heat, she's moaning softly, I can't stop running my mouth with all the things I want to do to her and ways that I want her. As we turn into the driveway, she deep throats my finger and I nearly come in my pants.

When Andrew stops the car, we don't say anything.

We don't say anything as we go inside and straight up the stairs. Our movements are restrained, like both of us are trying not to run. When we get to the second floor, Alina grabs me and drags me down the hall to the office.

"You said every room in the house, right?"

Fuck. I might be falling in love with my wife.

She pulls me in to the office and pushes me into my desk chair, then kneels on the ground. I watch her intently as she undoes my pants and frees my cock. Her tongue feels incredible, hot and soft, as she licks my shaft.

"I thought about this the other day when I came to Venture. I saw you through the window and thought about sucking you off under your desk."

"Fucking hell," I groan, and that's the moment she takes the head in her mouth and sucks. I watch with adoration as she works my cock into her mouth, and love the feeling when I hit the back of her throat. I don't touch her but grip the arms of the chair as she finds her rhythm, sucking my cock with dangerous enthusiasm.

Alina works me, warm and firm, and I know that I'm going to come. Nothing will stop it.

"Swallow me, Allie."

She nods and hums around me, and it gets me even closer to the edge. Her head moves up and down faster, and my hips start to pump into her mouth as I get closer.

She takes me all the way to the back of her throat and I groan, watching as she closes her eyes and sucks, swallowing my come. It's so fucking sexy. I've had her suck me off before but not to the end like this. Alina moves to rest on her heels and looks up at me, her eyes hooded and her gaze hot.

I stand up, cock still out and still hard, and she follows me from the room. Before she can turn and head to the stairs, and I grab her and open the door across from the office. It's an unused bedroom, fine but plain, with a large queen size bed, a chair, and side tables.

I throw Alina on the bed and reach behind her to undo the zipper of her dress. In one tug I pull down her dress and bra straps until they're tight at her elbows, binding her together. I tug at the cups of her bra and her breasts spill out, nipples hard and waiting for my mouth.

I alternately lick and suck them as I push up her dress again, grateful I've already stolen her panties. She's wet as hell and there's a moisture spot on the inside of the dress from how dripping fucking wet she is. I fuck her with my fingers as I suck her tits, loving the inviting softness of her pussy and the way she flutters around my fingers.

When she's on the edge of coming I pull out, and climb over her. My dick slides in all on it's own, knowing exactly where it wants to go. I'm pressed to the hilt inside her and she comes immediately, screaming and clawing at the bed because she can't get hands on me, tangled like they are. The clench of her on my cock almost sends me over again, even though it's only been minutes since my own orgasm.

It feels incredible inside her, and I slide in and out of her heat at a ruthless pace. The sound of our skin slapping together echoes in the emptiness of the room and her screams bounce off the walls. It's all music to my ears.

I grab her hair and yank her head back, licking and biting at her throat.

She's breathing hard and heavy, her breasts heaving beautifully.

"Brody," she gasps, and every time she calls me that it sets me off. It calls to something new inside me that I don't know how to explain. I know that night lives in her mind too, and when she's weak she goes there.

"Allie," I groan against her throat and come inside her.

My arms come around her, pressing her to me and pressing myself into her. She feels perfect up against me, my cock still inside her, and the way she fits with me. This woman is strong and I get to have her when she's weak. I know that she can kick the ass of most of my men, that she could probably kick mine, and yet I have her now. This woman is mine.

After a few minutes of this, she taps my back.

"We should go to bed."

I get off her and go to help her up, but she doesn't let me. Without another word to me, she leaves the room and heads toward the stairs, holding her dress up to cover her breasts. It should make me hot that she's walking through our house like this, but all I can think of now is the distance she's putting between us.

20

Derick

Allie is pulling away from me.

The other night got too real for her, and I'm trying not to be pissed as fuck and force her to let down her walls. She has to do it on her own. If she needs to retreat again, I'll be patient. I have the rest of our lives.

Kade and I are on the ferry, waiting for Ecklie to approach. We saw him get on, and per the terms of our meeting agreement we aren't talking until we're 30 minutes into the trip. Solidly out on the water.

Ecklie looks nervous and twitchy, and as far as we can tell he didn't bring anyone with him. He's on the upper deck of the ferry, staring toward Seattle like he's considering jumping off and swimming back. It would probably be better for him if he did.

"I like your wife."

"Excuse me?" I snap my head to Kade.

"This is smart. She's an asset." For a moment it was funny because Kade didn't even realize he'd said something that gave me pause. He is a bluntly honest man - he likes someone or he doesn't, and there was nothing romantic or sexual about his statement. Kade saw everything in terms of usefulness. He had come to the conclusion that Alina was useful.

"Hopefully this goes down without us having to kill anyone."

Now Kade smirks. "Where's the fun in that?"

My watch beeps letting me know 30 minutes has elapsed, and we turn and put our backs to the railing. Ecklie makes his way down toward us, trying to look casual but failing. He comes to stand beside me, facing out toward our destination.

"I was the one who told the cops."

His quick confession makes me instantly suspicious, especially when all his tics and tells are going off as well. He's sweating, his voice is shaking, and he's twisting his wedding ring around in a circle.

"Why?"

"Someone paid me to. You don't have as many friends as you might think. There are people who want to see you fall."

"Who was it?" Kade asks, palming his gun under his jacket.

"I don't know, but they offered me a lot of money to do it. It was a guy, he knew a lot about your operation, knew pretty much everything. He's not the first rumblings I've heard though."

"What are you talking about?" If he's going to be candid, I'm going to get everything I can out of him.

"You aren't the only people I have deals with, and a lot of them are not happy you've consolidated power by marrying that Sorrelle girl. Venture got bigger and people don't like it."

That's the first I've heard of it. Expanding our capabilities only allows more opportunities for people with less than legal dealings to hide their money and their information. We definitely charge them for it, but make it worth their while. It never occurred to me that it would look like a power grab. The deal had been in the works for months, and no one had said a fucking word.

Venture was strong, nothing would touch it. This was more reason to just say fuck it and get rid of all of this shit. Sell this all out to someone who wanted it. There were gangs and outfits that would have no problem taking over from me.

Now that I was seriously considering it, the path laid itself out before me in my mind. What moves to make and who to make them with, and even how to leverage this situation with Ecklie to my benefit. We'd keep the businesses that were legitimate on the surface but I was done with this kind of underworld drama. I didn't need it. The money wasn't even worth it. I'd stayed in it because my father had been in it and it hadn't truly occurred to me that I didn't have to be.

My hands would never be clean. I'd always have holds in the dark side of things, but I had the power to choose what was worth it and what wasn't. This wasn't worth it anymore.

"I'm going to increase your cut by 5% and you're going to agree not to fuck with business again. I have a use for you," I get in Ecklie's face, dropping all pretense of trying to keep our conversation low key. "If someone calls you, your next call is to me. Otherwise, I will make you disappear, but first I'll make it hurt. Got it?"

Ecklie gulped, glanced between me and Kade, and then nodded.

"Get out of my fucking sight before I dump you in the bay."

He runs away, back to the top deck. I turn around and face the water, kind of annoyed now that I'll have to spend another hour on this ferry going back to Seattle. Still, it gives me uninterrupted time to plan and that's a rare thing.

"What the hell was that?" Kade asks.

I consider him for a moment. He's been with me since just after my father died. He was a troubled kid that I caught trying to steal my car. Rather than turn him in, I asked him to show me how. We bonded over a similar outlook on life. Kade was as loyal as they come, and may as well have been my blood brother for the loyalty I gave him in return.

Then he got in a fight, a justified one, but he still ended up in prison.

I made sure he was taken care of in there, and by the time he got out, Jack had fucked up, and I was in charge of everything. There's no one I knew who was less greedy or less ambitious than Kade. There was nothing more he aspired to be than exactly what he was: a clear-eyed thug who didn't run from a fight. He was loyal and relentless.

"I'm getting out of this. Selling it off to whoever is willing to pay."

"Really? Explain it to me."

"We make more money with other enterprises, both above and below board. I kept doing this because there was a need but it's more trouble than it's fucking worth. It's too much organization, too many payoffs, and we don't even fucking use our own product because I don't need unregistered phones or sim cards because I'm a fucking tech billionaire. Someone else wants it more than me, they can have it."

"You're not afraid you'll seem weak? Losing a shipment and then backing out?"

Kade has a point there.

"I'll figure something out to cover that angle, but think how much time we wasted on this fucking meeting. We have better things to do."

"Like you're wife?" he smirks, and doesn't even hit me back when I punch him in the shoulder.

Pulling out my phone, I put in my passwords to get to the protected area where I take notes. I still put things in code as much as possible, something that is known only to me and will make sense when I read it again later. It's a to do list - who I need in my own organizations to get things moving, who I need to reach out to in the underworld to make the offer, what I'll be asking for in return for the trade, and how to approach my contact overseas that I'm stepping away. Whoever takes over has to be worth vouching for. Then again, if I step away cleanly, it's theirs to fuck up and has nothing to do with me.

I'd rather focus on Venture. Jack can handle the clubs and our other investments, make his own mark there. We've got promising things in the works with encrypted storage and data transfers, programs backtracking data monitoring and theft, and one of our more unhinged programmers is trying to create programs to track identity thieves and more efficient ways to heal the damage done. It's personal for him, and it's beneficial for us, so I let him run with it. These are the things that interest me. It's what I want to be doing every day.

I think my father could never quite let go of the criminal side of things because of the air of power more than the actual benefits. He liked the idea of people owing him favors but the world didn't quite run that way anymore. We were evolving beyond that.

Instead, all he got was kids late in life, a young wife who drank herself to death, and he was beaten by fucking cholesterol because he didn't believe heart disease was a thing. What a fucking champion of industry.

Looking down at the water churning and splitting in the wake of the ferry, I vow again to myself to never be that stupid. To never waste the power that's in my hands. I can't say that I'm a good man, but there are times when I try and do good work. This might be one of them.

21

Alina

I've been here a week, and every day has been busy. It feels like I've stepped through into another dimension, one where I've taken over the life of a different Alina.

Sunday I spend actual hours on a video call with my sisters. Even Owen steps in to say hi at one point. They miss me, and it was fun hearing them talk about their lives like usual. Aster is working at Designation and staying busy - she's been put in charge of her own special project team and is distinctly happy. Aro is about to finish her degree and has no idea what she wants to do with her life. Anora and I have talked about it, but don't know how to help her.

Anora is deep into the social scene at the moment, having volunteered to serve on the boards of two different foundations. Now that she's there, she's digging in deep roots in the things that always interested her before. I hope that when the panic hits me over the charity work I'm now expected to do she'll be able to talk me down.

Derick and I haven't been physical in days, and I'm grateful. I need a break from the relentless assault that is his body, his voice, his scent. We sleep next to each other every night, and it's nice to feel his warm body next to mine, but I need some distance.

Now it's Monday and we're eating breakfast together. It's a first. I'll be driving in to the city with him today because I'm going dress shopping. Jonah agreed to give me Lauren for a full day and I hope we get a lot done so I don't need to do it again. I talk to or text her frequently, trying to get a read on what I need to do. Last she told me on Friday, this is all planned and handled.

Derick is staring into his eggs like they're going to tell him something. When he came back from the meeting on Sunday he didn't say much except that it went according to plan, and he had things to work on. At first I felt like he was keeping me out, but based on what I'm seeing now, he's thinking things through. Derick appears to be one of those people who processes internally, and doesn't share where he's at until he's done. I make note of that.

"You need to pick a driver," he says out of nowhere.

"What?" I look away from my yogurt.

"On days when we're separated, I'd like your driver to be consistent. You've met the men, you know their capabilities."

I think for a moment. "Roe, probably."

"Why?" There's a hint of jealousy in his voice, and I like it.

"I trust him." I pause and consider my words, knowing that's not going to be enough of an explanation. "If we got into a situation where we needed to defend ourselves, I think he knows my capabilities the best, and we complement each other. I'd feel safe with him."

"Is there a reason you don't feel safe with the others?"

"No," I assure him, understanding what he's getting at. "It's that I don't think they trust my skills in the same way he does. Roe doesn't care that I'm a woman because I've proven myself, if that makes sense?"

"It does," he nods. "We should go."

We both clean up our breakfast dishes, handing them off to Eifa who is working on meal prep for the week and planning dinners. Other than sharing with her what I don't like, I let her have free rein to make whatever she wants. It's been delicious every single day.

Andrew gives me a nod when I slide into the SUV, and I'm surprised when Derick sits close to me, wrapping his hand around my thigh. Part of me wonders if he even realizes he's doing it because he's distracted and staring out the window. It's as if holding on to me like that offers him reassurance or comfort. It doesn't feel possessive in this moment, but like a man would hold his partner when he had a lot on his mind. My stomach flutters.

The drive is quiet, but not uncomfortable, and I find myself drifting to sleep. When I wake up, my head is resting on Derick's shoulder. He kisses the top of my head before giving me a little shake.

"I've got to go, *lleidr bach*."

I sit up. "Sorry."

He smiles softly at me, and his gaze drops to my mouth. After a second of hesitation, he cups my face and kisses my forehead. "I didn't mind."

"Have a nice day," I offer as he slides out of the car.

Andrew and I wait for a few minutes before a woman exits the building and starts making her way toward us. Lauren is a short blonde woman in her 40s with a pep in her step and practical flats. I've learned from our calls that she has three daughters and a son, who is the oldest. He's about to go to college and is concerned about who's going to look after his sisters when he's gone. Trust me kid, I know the feeling.

I open the door and step out to meet her. She smiles, big and happy, and we shake hands.

"We're going to get so much done today." Lauren slides into the backseat after me.

"I hope so. I really mean it when I say I hate shopping."

"It's not a problem. We're going to the Ellis Boutique," she rattles off the general location to Andrew and he starts driving. "They have everything you're going to need. I pulled up the next 6 months in the calendar and you have 4 events that require formal dress, not including the fundraiser gala for our own foundation. We might want to shop for that more specifically once the theme has been confirmed."

This all sounds horrible.

"We've been assigned a consultant, Kayla, and I shared with her all your preferences and had her pull dresses you might like. I was very clear with her on freedom of movement for your legs, and colors to stay away from. I did my best to make things as pain free as possible."

"Without you, I'd probably be showing up to these events in a pantsuit."

"With the right kind of pantsuit, maybe you can."

"Lauren, I think this is the beginning of a beautiful friendship."

I am not wrong. Lauren's efficiency made this as straightforward as finding my wedding dress. She makes me feel so comfortable I almost tell her about that, but I think the details of Derick and I are best kept within the family. Lauren seems great, but I don't know how much I can trust her with yet.

Much to my surprise, I end up buying 8 dresses from various designers in different shapes and colors. My favorite is an ice blue satin with a high slit - so high I definitely can't wear underwear with it. Derick will lose his mind for that dress, and I'm surprised to find that's what I'm thinking about. Not just how the clothes make me feel or if I'm comfortable in them, but how he'll react.

Lauren and Kayla also conspire to surprise me by finding me an amazing, and shockingly sexy, tuxedo. It's black with white detailing and makes my boobs look like my best asset.

They also talk me into several dresses that are more suitable for business occasions, and those foundation lunches I'm expected to be a part of. This is where I feel some doubt. I'm a suit woman. That's what I've worn my whole career because I've been the person who had to stand back on the side and observe and protect. Now I'm the person in charge in some of these situations. I'm the person people will be looking to for decisions and I have no idea how to handle that kind of scrutiny.

I guess it starts with dressing the part. Fake it until you make it.

The trip takes several hours and before leaving I arrange for anything that needed alterations to be delivered, and the rest we get into the back of the SUV.

"This was exactly what I needed today," I tell Lauren when we drop her off. "Thank you so much."

"You are so welcome, Alina. We'll talk Thursday for sure before the luncheon."

When she leaves, it's still a few hours until the end of the day so I assume Andrew will drive me back to the house before returning to get Derick.

It only takes a few moments to be proven wrong because before I can even ask, Derick is walking out of the building. He gets into the car and I move over automatically.

"What are you doing?"

"Taking some time off. How was your excursion?" he asks, and then glances behind us into the trunk area. I'm surprised when he laughs, and the look of delighted amusement on his face is so pure that it makes me smile back at him without reservation.

"I'm good for awhile. The rest will be delivered."

"The rest? Did you bankrupt me?"

"Not even close and you know it."

"Seriously, tell me about your day." Derick is so sincere that I find myself talking about the clothes and the time with Lauren, and before I know it we're back at the house.

It's not quite home to me yet, but it's getting there. No matter what happens, I do feel I have a place here. This space suits me. The way it functions, with the staff, with our lives, feels very comfortable to me. I didn't expect that.

Derick and Andrew are both needed to carry everything into the house, and we also grab David to help us get everything up to our bedroom. Garment bags of various lengths cover the bed.

"It's so much."

"Don't worry about it. It'll go faster than you think." Derick steps into the closet and changes quickly while I try and sort through the piles and bags. When he steps back out, he's casual in gray sweatpants and a black t-shirt.

I unzip a random garment bag and take out the dress. It's black and slinky, the material swished around my legs when I walked and it made my butt look amazing. As I stare at it, remembering how it made me feel, Derick walks over to his record player and puts on an album.

There's a long silence as I start working, and then eventually "Prey" by the Neighbourhood starts playing. I'm surprised, but don't say anything. It's from one of my favorite albums, and I wonder if he knows that or if it's a weird coincidence.

"Mind if I stay here and work while you do?" Derick asks.

"Not at all. It's your room."

He frowns at that but goes over to the love seat and stretches out, reading on his phone and typing notes. I think he could do his entire job from that phone and it's a little bit impressive.

I hang up one dress at a time after smoothing them out, and then move on to the next. There's a whole section of the closet that's built to house dresses that reach the floor. When I think he's distracted I put away the blue dress, followed by one in a soft lavender that I didn't think I liked but made my skin glow. The feelings I had when I tried on each dress return as I look at them, and I remind myself that Kayla deserved every penny of her commission from this sale.

It takes longer than I thought, and my arms are sore by the time I'm done. An unexpected work out. I collapse back on the bed and starfish out, loving the way there's still so much more bed because it's that damn big.

Maybe that's what I like about this house so much - it feels like there's enough room for me. Growing up with petite sisters, I think I always tried to make myself smaller. My height was always the first thing people noticed and the instinct became to retreat, to be invisible. Then it shifted to if I can't be invisible, then I'm going to be intimidating. That was fun, but it was just another shield against being a big woman.

Like shouting at someone to try and out crazy them. People notice my size so I make them notice so hard they can't talk about it.

Derick makes me feel normal. This giant bed that's long enough and wide enough to drown me makes me feel normal. The high ceilings and wide open spaces of this house make me feel like I belong.

It reminds me of the night we met. That we talked about loving wide open spaces and found comfort in emptiness. The windows in this room make the space feel so huge, and being up high makes me feel like I could walk off into the clouds. Despite my uncertainty, I can breathe here.

When I come back to myself and open my eyes, Derick is standing over me.

"Hi." He smiles. "What are you doing?"

"Thinking."

"About?"

"Do you remember talking about liking places that felt open and empty?"

Derick's face softens and my heart twinges in my chest. We're both back in the night we met. It's the first time I've mentioned anything from that night or brought it up at all.

"I do."

"This house feels open."

"I know. I feel the same."

When he lays down next to me, I don't move away. When he twines his hand through mine, linking our fingers, I don't move away. We stare up at the ceiling, listening to the music and not moving. It's oddly nice to relax with him this way, and I realize that most of the time we spend together is filled with tension of one kind or another. This is something new. It's nice.

22

Alina

Tuesday night I'm Derick-less. He's out doing some spot checks and I think he knows I'm still keeping some distance between us.

I make popcorn in the microwave, dump it into a bowl, and then try and find my way through the first floor to the back living room. It's got a huge TV and I am ready to stream something mindless on Netflix until I feel like crawling upstairs to bed.

On my way there, I bump into Jack leaving the hallway that leads to his room. Tuesdays are his official night off, and I assumed he would be elsewhere. He grins at me.

"Whatcha doin' Lina?" I think it's sweet that he started calling me Lina like my sisters do. I want us to have a sibling relationship.

"Thinking about some Netflix. Want to join me?"

"Absolutely."

Subtly, I let him lead the way and follow him down a hallway, around a corner, and down a short flight of stairs into the big room. It would've taken me a bit longer to find it, and I would've turned the wrong way at least once.

I settle in with my popcorn on the huge comfy couch as he works the remotes to get everything on. After some debate, we settle on watching the reboot of *Unsolved Mysteries* to freak ourselves out. It's fun to find that Jack enjoys documentaries of the strange and unexplained as much as I do.

Jack sits next to me and steals my popcorn as we talk about the cases and debate theories. When it's all gone, I put the bowl on the coffee table and shift so I can lay down, and I'm surprised when he takes my feet and puts them on his lap.

"Heard you had quite the shopping trip."

"I did. It was not as awful as usual."

"This is why being a man is great - a few suits, a tux or two, and we're ready for any event. At least we'll all be there together."

"That's true. I hope you'll tell me all the shit I need to know and who to stay away from."

"Everyone. The causes are good but the events eat your soul. Let me donate my money in peace."

We get pulled back into the show for awhile, and I'm starting to get sleepy.

"Are you doing okay?" Jack asks.

"Yeah. I like it here. I mean, I did choose to vacation here."

Jack smiles but it's small. "What drew you to Derick that night?"

I tense. "How much do you know?"

"That day, when he came home, he was rabid. Trying to figure out who you were, how to find you. It's not like you were his first one night stand, but he was obsessed. When he called me telling me that he'd found you, I wondered if he'd lost his mind."

My mind flies back to the club and seeing Derick for the first time. "He looked at me like there was no one else in the room." I stuff down the thought that he still looks at me like that now. When Derick's attention is focused on me, no one else exists for him.

"We talked too. We clicked, I guess, as much as two people who aren't being entirely honest about who they are can."

"It reminds me of our dad."

Inside I freeze but on the outside I play dumb. "What do you mean?" I don't know much about their parents, but what I've picked up isn't anything good.

"He was obsessed with our mom. Pursued her with single-minded intent. It lasted long enough for them to have us, but short enough that she became an alcoholic to cope with his rejection." Jack is watching the TV, unaware that every word he's saying is like a stab in the stomach. "When the obsession was over they stayed married but our family was broken all the same."

"I'm sorry." There's nothing else to say to this. Part of me wants to scream that Derick and I aren't like that, but isn't that situation my exact fear? That I'll be beguiled by Derick's fixation with me and then when it fades and he steps away from me, I'll be broken?

"It's okay. Derick has raised me my whole life because they were never meant to be parents. Our grandparents did their best, but every day it's been me and Derick. The kind of man I am, or try to be, is because of his example. I never thought he'd have anything in common with our dad but there's a first time for everything right?"

"Yeah," I laugh and it's brittle enough to make Jack look at me. I don't know what he sees in my expression but it makes him panic and backtrack.

"You two aren't like them. That's not what I meant."

"Were they in love?" I ask.

"Yeah, for awhile. From what I've been told."

"That's where Derick and I are different. We're not in love, Jack. Love doesn't last, and obsession fades. Derick and I are building a partnership, and that will be stronger than anything built on feelings." That's the truth. We might be enjoying each other now, and Derick might think this is more, but I know the reality. The fun ends, the connection doesn't.

Jack nods, but there's something like pity in his gaze. "Sometimes we can't help our feelings though."

We sit in silence for a minute, contemplating that.

"If you ever need to get out - you need a break - you tell me. I'll make it happen." His eyes are intense and he squeezes my feet. "Seriously."

"Thanks, Jack."

We settle back in to the show, both trying hard to return to the light banter we had earlier while dissecting episodes but it's obvious we're both wrapped up in our thoughts right now. Without betraying his brother, Jack was trying to warn me. Not necessarily away from Derick, but reminding me to keep myself in check because intensity doesn't breed endurance. We can feel a lot now, but it could be a burst of fire that dies, instead of a conflagration that endures as coals. Either way, as the song says, smoke gets in your eyes.

I know this, but the reminder was necessary.

When the next episode is over, it's time for me to go to bed. My thoughts will keep me up but I need to be by myself.

"I'm out. Goodnight, Jack."

Jack stands up and heads toward his room. "Goodnight, Lina."

"I always wanted a brother," I tell him before he leaves. "I'm glad I have you."

Something close to anger flashes across his face but then he gives me a tight smile, that sadness like pity in his expression again. "Glad I can help."

When I get upstairs, I crash faster than I expected. The next thing I remember is the movement of the bed when Derick gets home, and feeling surprised when he wraps his arm around my waist and pulls to him. I pretend to be asleep until I actually am.

23

Derick

Even though it's not Venture business, I set up a meeting for me, Kade, Ethan, and Jack at my office there. I'm not ready to talk to Alina about this yet, and I don't want her to think I'm doing things behind her back. This is a big change, and I need to sort out my plans before I go to her.

Kade is sold on this now that he's had a few days to sit with it. I gave Ethan a heads up so he could run the financial data, and because some of the irregularities were bothering me and I wanted him to take a closer look. There's definitely things coming at us from multiple sides, and I want to know what limbs to cut off and which to repair.

We sit around the small conference table in my office, and I feel like an ass because the only person who doesn't know the purpose of this meeting is Jack. I should've talked to him privately. At the end of the day, I'm going to be handing more power over to him but it's a big change.

"We're getting out of our business at the docks." I rip off the band-aid.

"What? Why?" Jack is stunned, leaning back hard in his seat. "Is Ecklie more connected than we thought?"

"No, but I realized it's trouble and work that we don't need. Ethan, talk about the numbers."

"At the end of the day, it's maybe 10% of your entire income, but when you consider the money we pay out for bribes and protection, as well as greasing the wheels overseas - you're paying in 2% more. Below board, way more money is made from the clubs even with the issues that we've identified."

"Okay, so we drop the phones and cards," Jack prompts.

"No, we're going to sell. Kade is feeling out some of our regular customers about cutting out the middle man."

"Right." Jack stares at the table, and the whole conversation feels awkward. "What about the clubs?"

"Revenue and collection is down compared to the last three years," Ethan recites. "Business could be down, but the amount is consistent. It looks like skimming."

Jack turns red and speaks through gritted teeth. "Who? From where?"

"I'm going to find that out," Kade answers.

Jack nods.

I take a deep breath as I head into the next part. "Aside from that, I want to pull back on everything else to focus on Venture. I'm happiest here and I think a lot more could come from our connections with Designation if I had the time to focus on it."

"What does that mean? We're shutting everything down? Where does that leave me?" Jack's voice is steady but I can tell he's pissed as hell.

"Will you excuse us?" I look at Kade and Ethan, and they both exit the office quickly.

"I want you to have all of it. It'll be yours, entirely."

Jack looks flabbergasted, but not mollified. "So I'm just going to be your underworld kingpin little brother? Some sleazeball who runs a bunch of clubs and obvious money laundering schemes while you're my suit wearing superhero brother?"

"You wear suits too," I try to joke but it falls flat.

"I didn't want to be a gangster."

"You're not. You are a successful entrepreneur." Jack scoffs but I continue. "We own 8 clubs and only 2 of them were my idea, the rest was all you evaluating trends and locations and they're all successful. The stores do good work, and you oversee the shell corporation that runs our residential properties. You're brilliant, Jack."

"That's my legacy?"

"I gave you opportunities and you ran with them. We have the success in those areas because of you."

"Whatever." Jack stands and fixes his jacket. He looks at me and I can't read his expression. This conversation didn't go at all how I expected. Even if I had pulled him aside privately before this meeting, I think he'd still be where he is right now. Jack has never said he's unhappy with what he does. His time is flexible, he's personable and charming, and even when he's off he ends up going out.

A few times years ago he asked about getting involved with Venture, but he still had a lot of growing to do and there wasn't a place where his skills would fit. I told him no, and that we'd revisit the idea in the future or if the right opportunity arose.

The time never really came, and he never asked again.

It eats at me all day. Yesterday was exhausting and after doing all the spot-checking at the clubs and making my presence known, all I wanted was Allie. She was sleeping when I got home but I needed to hold her. When I woke up this morning she was still in my arms, our bodies perfectly aligned. It had been hard to get out of bed.

Now all I want is to go back to this morning with the knowledge I have now and figure out another way for the day to play out.

I leave the office early. Andrew doesn't ask and I know that he goes over the speed limit once we're out of the city because my mood is radiating off of me in waves. When I get in the house I head straight upstairs.

As I get to the the third floor landing, I hear music from Allie's room. The door is closed but not latched, and I walk up and peek in the gap. The furniture got delivered today, and she's dancing and singing to a song from her laptop as she builds a bookshelf.

I look around at the things she's chosen to occupy her space.

There's a large area rug in a pattern of gray and blue, with little hints of pink here and there. She's got an L-shaped sectional against the glass walls in a dark purple color, an army green love sac, and a glass and chrome coffee table. The painting we had moved here is leaning against the wall and she probably needs help getting it hung up properly. There are two short bookshelves that will go next to the desk that she stuck in the other corner. It's simple and lovely.

"Need help?" I ask her. Alina jumps, and turns to look at me. Her hair is up in a messy bun and she's wearing black joggers and an old t-shirt from her high school. It's faded and the letters are nearly gone, but it looks soft. I want to feel what it feels like against her skin, but I'm trying to give her space.

"Not with this," she waves her hand at the shelves, "but are you any good at hanging things?"

"I can give it a try. Let me change."

I step over into our bedroom and quickly divest myself of my suit. Mirroring her, I pull on black joggers and a t-shirt. I cut through the bathroom and find her moving one of the bookshelves into place.

"I'll have your boxes moved up here tomorrow."

"It's taken care of - Elliot will have the boys bring everything up."

"Sounds like you're settling in."

"I am," she gives me a tentative smile.

I grab the tape measure that's sitting on the floor and examine the fixtures on the painting for hanging it up. I start making marks on the wall, estimating where it should be. I get lost in the work, the way that I can focus on this straightforward task and not have to think about anything. Before I know it, I'm hammering in the nails and then lifting the painting to rest on them.

When I step back, I snap out of the zone. I turn to look at Allie and she's standing with her arms crossed, watching me.

"Want to talk about it?" she offers.

"Not yet. But thank you."

She nods. "Aro painted this." We both turn to look at the painting and she steps up next to me as we look at it. It's a swirl of colors, compelling in the way that some modern art is. It communicates something through color and texture, and the variation of the sizes of the brush strokes. "She did one big canvas like this for each of us, even Owen and dad. This is supposed to represent me."

"I can see it," I nod.

She laughs, then stops. "Really?"

"The colors are all bold, but not necessarily bright or flashy. The strokes are strong and sure, the texture is smooth. Don't you think this is how your sister sees you?"

Alina doesn't say anything, and I feel like maybe I should talk about it. She's no stranger to sibling conflict and gets along with Jack well. She might know how I can even begin to fix something I didn't even know I was breaking.

"I'd hate to see how my brother sees me."

I breathe in sharply when she slides her hand into mine and squeezes.

"Did you and Jack fight?"

"Not exactly. I thought I was doing something good for him and he didn't feel that way. He said a lot of things that make me think I haven't been hearing him at all."

"He's 27 years old, Brody, at some point you have to offer him choices rather than issuing edicts. Jack admires you, and he knows he's disappointed you in the past. But you can't wall him in so that he goes the direction that you want."

"It never occurred to me he wouldn't want this. There's some decisions I've made about our businesses." She stiffens but doesn't move. "I wanted to talk to you about it as well but talking to Jack felt more important."

"I understand. Jack will come around too, but if he doesn't want what you do, figure out how to talk about what he does want. Okay?"

"Yeah."

We've had this whole conversation standing side by side, holding hands. It's simple and comforting, and I'm astounded by how much I trust this woman. The way she's crawled inside my mind and heart and is able to be so honest with me. I value her, truly.

The thought occurs to me again: I think I'm really falling in love with my wife.

I've never been in love so I don't know if that's what this is, and prior to this second I'm not sure I even believed in falling in love. I don't know what it means for anything, I just know that I would rather stand here holding her hand for an entire day than be with anyone else.

"Derick?"

"Yeah?"

"I'm going to hug you."

"Okay."

We turn toward each other and she puts her arms around my neck and pulls me close. I press my face into her hair and hold on tight to her body. All of the tension in mine leaves and I don't hesitate to lean on her. Alina holds me close and holds me up, letting me have a moment of weakness.

24

Alina

Lauren and I meet in a small conference room at Venture. She has a stack of folders for me, and when she hands them over I see that each one is labeled with the organization the fundraisers are supporting. Inside, there's a rundown of the cause of the charity or foundation, the people who run it, the major donors (and whether or not Venture or Derick are one of them) as well as the themes for each event if they are known.

She also has a fat folder for me about the Clayton Foundation. The work it does is specific, and frankly, incredible. They support single parents by providing sliding scale or no cost daycare if they qualify. They also provide doctors outside normal business hours at the centers twice a week so that parents can be present for their children's check ups and vaccinations without having to take time off work. It's a huge chunk of money because the centers don't generate revenue, but according to Lauren, Derick never blinks at the cost and it's small potatoes to Venture.

"The childcare the company provides is like that too. When my youngest two needed it, they had an awesome time. The center is on the first floor."

Lauren gives me more details about some of the other things Venture and Derick donate to, and a bit of a profile of the causes he backs away from.

"This is a weird question, but what's your actual role other than working with me?" I ask Lauren.

"Oh, I administrate all of our donations and charitable contributions. People call all the time wanting to get on Mr. Clayton's radar for causes and I sort through legitimate requests or find gentle ways to say no. He's a ridiculously generous man."

"Oh yeah?" It's fun to hear one of Derick's employees talk about him, especially in such a positive way. Although there's an intensity to the employees every time I come to Venture, they don't seem unhappy. They're motivated.

"One time, he told me to go through GoFundMe and pick 10 people who were close to their goals. He looked them over and approved for me to donate to all of them. He likes to support single parents or guardians who need to provide for their family. I think it's because -" she cuts herself off and pretends to be very busy organizing the files in front of her. I can tell Lauren had a moment where she was too comfortable with me and forgot she was talking to her boss's wife.

"Because why? You won't get in trouble, Lauren. You're indispensable to me already."

Lauren blushes, and continues quietly. "I think it's because that was him. This lone guardian raising a kid. If he struggled doing it with all his money and privilege, imagine people in that situation who don't have that. Plus, it's more money than he could ever spend in a lifetime."

"That's a very good point. I'm glad he has you to help him with that."

"I do what I can." She opens the folder for the Clayton Foundation. "Now, let's talk about the lunch tomorrow."

Two hours later, my mind is packed full of information about the Clayton Foundation and I think I'm going to have a very interesting lunch. While Derick has been generous with his money for the Foundation, he hasn't been as generous with making sure it's organized and well-supported. I plan on changing that. The board is small and needs to be expanded, they need permanent office space, and we need to be more selective about the volunteers for organizing the fundraising events. If it's the same people on every committee for every organization, you never get anything new or creative that might draw new donors. I'm excited.

Before leaving, I go over to Derick's office.

I've been thinking about everything Lauren told me. I had her print me a list of all his regular donations, not just the ones where there's fundraising galas to attend. It was 12 pages long and they weren't small potatoes. The only thing he seems to stay away from is political donations, and I can respect that. She was not wrong that he's generous, and there's a definite theme to the work he tries to support.

While a lot of it is about people raising kids on their own, he makes sure as much money as possible goes to the kids themselves. Most of the schools in the city have computer labs that exist only because of him, and that get updated every three years. He also has an intensive speaking schedule to 8th graders, encouraging them to go into computing and recruiting them early for internship opportunities or interest when they go to college.

It's adorable.

It's out there for anyone to see that he has this soft spot, and yet I don't think it was in any of the information I read about him.

Derick cares.

Derick cares and it's affecting me so much more than I want it to because it speaks to his ability to commit and follow through. I'm terrified. Despite what Jack said last night, my mind touches on the possibility that Derick's obsession won't fade. That what we are building toward is something other than a business partnership. Derick doesn't take commitment lightly - and he's said in so many ways that he's committed to me.

When I get to his office, Jonah isn't there so it's unguarded.

His door is closed but no one is with him. He's sitting at his desk, frowning down at documents. Except his eyes aren't moving, so he's not reading anything, he's staring. There's been a lot on his mind lately.

I don't knock, and he looks up when I open the door.

The frown melts off his face. "Hi."

"Hi." I can't stop the tears that spring to my eyes. I'm dealing with a lot of emotions and not sure how to process them.

Derick jumps up from his desk immediately and comes over to me. "Are you okay? Your sisters?" It's so sweet that I let out a watery laugh and shake my head, indicating that everything is fine.

I look up at him, letting myself really take in and enjoy his face. It's not something I do often because I like his face. He's gorgeous. Every line, every scar, every shape, appeals to me so it's dangerous to focus too much besides reading his expressions. Now I look. I appreciate the scar on his chin that's only visible up close because his scruff hides it. The way the hair on his left eyebrow is a little more unruly than the right. The small beauty mark under his right eye. The amazing green of his eyes themselves.

Because I can, I take his face in my hands. Derick stills. I trace his cheekbones with my thumbs before I pull his face down to mine and kiss him.

It's a deep, romantic connecting of our mouths. Even though he could, he doesn't make it sexual. Instead he wraps his arms around me and pulls me close, pressing us together as I enjoy this moment. My body fits perfectly against his, and his warmth soaks into me.

I know that Derick has darkness inside him and blood on his hands - so do I. No one who really knows him would ever describe him as a good man, but underneath it all there's someone who wants to do good even when he can't be good. There's gold inside his darkness and I feel privileged to get to see it.

When I break the kiss, his eyes are dazed and warm. I kiss him one more time, soft and brief, before stepping back.

"I'll see you at the house."

He nods, and I smile before leaving the office.

25

Derick

For the few hours left in the day, I pretend to work.

I don't know Alina as well as I think. Her capacity to surprise me only makes me fall harder.

I was sure that in a moment of sexual insanity, she would break down and kiss me. That I would taste her again in the heat of our bodies communicating, and get to devour her while she came apart on my cock.

But no.

Instead, for reasons I don't yet know, she comes into my office with tears in her eyes and takes the last piece of my heart. I didn't know kissing could be so emotional. Never in my life have I been so undone by something so simple. She looked at me like I was everything, and touched me like she was making sure that I was real.

That kiss will replay in my head every day for the rest of my life.

Fucking hell. I'm in love with Alina.

It doesn't surprise me, or scare me, when mere months ago I would've hated the thought. I don't know how this is happening because on so many levels, I barely know her. What I do know is that she constantly impresses me, and that she doesn't need me. The best I can do is make her want me, because I think that I do need her. In her presence, I become a better version of myself. I think I fell for her the second our eyes met, something in me recognizing that she was it.

It's been 10 days and already she's changed the way that I see things. I'm not thinking and waiting, I'm planning and doing. I'm seeing my own weaknesses and failures, and accepting that it's not too late to fix them. I wanted perspective and I got it.

I want to go home to her every night, or go out with her, or fight alongside her. It doesn't matter as long as she's there.

How did this happen to me?

Jonah informs me that Alina was at Venture today because she was meeting with Lauren about the Foundation and some of our other charitable work. I take a minute to track Lauren down.

She's sitting in her cubicle talking on the phone when I approach. She doesn't notice me.

"I'm sorry Mr. Forrester, but it's company policy that we do not participate in political donations. Venture does not invest in individual candidates."

Roger Forrester is a bastard who I'd never support personally either. I'm shocked he's calling himself but he must've thought his name had enough clout that he'd be put through to me rather than following the route all these requests make. Once again I send gratitude for Jonah out into the universe because I'd bet good money that he was the one that got the call and routed it to Lauren.

I can hear the asshole shouting at her through the phone and silently laugh when Lauren rolls her eyes and makes a few notes.

"Mr. Clayton does not personally assess donation requests."

More silence, more yelling that is unintelligible from my side of the conversation.

"Mr. Clayton is not available."

More yelling.

"Mr. Clayton is not available."

Lauren grips her pen and grits her teeth, taking a deep, slow breath through her nose.

"I understand Mr. Forrester, but it's policy. You have a good day now."

She hangs up the phone and sighs. "Jerk."

"You can swear at work, Lauren."

I feel bad when she jumps and slaps a hand to her chest. "Mr. Clayton! What can I do for you?" Lauren immediately slips back into work mode, and I see why her and Alina are a good fit to work together. I also need to look into how many of the calls she takes go that way, and if that's the case, give her a raise.

"Did anything happen when you met with Mrs. Clayton today?" I feel weirdly proud saying that. Mrs. Clayton. God I'm pathetic.

"No, not that I noticed. We went over a lot of information it could've been quite overwhelming." Lauren looks concerned, and grabs her notepad to look at the notes she took. "We went over the charities for all the upcoming fundraisers and then spent quite a bit of time on the Clayton Foundation so she's prepared for tomorrow's lunch. Mrs. Clayton was quite interested in the extent of your generosity. She seemed very impressed."

Hm. That still doesn't explain how emotional she was.

"Thanks Lauren. I appreciate all the good work you've been doing."

"Of course, sir."

I walk back to my office and pretend to work until the day is over.

Alina is upstairs when I get home. She's standing in our closet, staring at her clothes and biting her lip.

"Hey." I undo my tie and start putting my suit away on my side of the closet. When I look over at her, Alina is watching me. The night of our wedding she did the same. I turn to face her as I unbutton my

141

shirt, and then undo my cuff links. The shirt drops to the floor but her eyes remain on my chest.

"Care to help me out?"

"If you insist." She walks over to me and slowly undoes my belt, pulling at the strap as if she was tugging on my dick. I'm hard in seconds, and don't mind the smirk on her face. Aline teases a finger along the top of my pants, the light graze on the skin above my boxers is like an electric shock to my body.

Then she surprises me further when she kneels down as she undoes my pants. Alina frees my cock and without teasing puts the head in her mouth, sucking hard and eager. I can't control my hips as they thrust me further into her mouth. Instead of pulling away, she braces herself with her hands on my thighs and looks up at me, eyes heated as her mouth continues to slide up and down on my cock.

"You want me to fuck your mouth, *lleidr bach*?" My voice is raspy and I dig my hands into her hair, pulling it back into a ponytail that I can grasp in my fist.

Alina moans and nods, her eyes fluttering shut.

"Eyes on me, baby."

When her eyes meet mine, I grip her hair tightly and begin to pump, moving both myself and her head up and down. She's drooling, spit dripping down to my balls and down her chin. The sound of her slurping me makes me harder, and I pump faster as she relaxes her throat more.

"You're a slut for me, aren't you?" I stare intensely at her as I slow my pace and push myself all the way into her mouth. She struggles for a second and then swallows. The flex of her throat against my head has me groaning.

I start pumping again, loving the way my cock parts her pretty pink lips.

"Fuck you're sexy like this."

But that's not how I want this to end. I pull out of her mouth and she gasps. Ropes of drool drip off my dick and onto the floor, and she wipes her face with the back of her hand. There's wet spots on her white shirt and her jeans, and it makes me feel good to have gotten her a little dirty.

"Crawl to the bed."

Alina's eyes flash with defiance for a second, but then she turns around and starts to crawl. The sway of her ass is hypnotizing, and it takes a lot of self-control not to pounce on her right then, rip down those jeans, and fuck her right into the floor.

I follow her, watching her move like the strong fucking panther she is. She stops at the end of the bed and looks over her shoulder.

"Take off your clothes, then get on all fours. Put that ass in the air for me."

She puts on a show as she strips for me, taking her time, running her hands over her body and drawing attention to the hard points of her nipples, and the wet spot on her panties from her arousal.

Then she stands before me, every line and curve visible. I clench my jaw against the desire to bite into her flesh and mark her.

"All fours," I remind her as I step closer, getting out of the rest of my clothes as she moves to obey. When she's in position, it's my turn to kneel. I grab her ass hard, spread her cheeks apart and dive in. She is already so fucking wet, her arousal is thick and slick against my tongue as I fuck her with it, but not so she can come.

I want her insane.

I want her so worked up that she forgets the English language, both our names, how to breathe, because all she wants is for me to fill her.

So I swirl my tongue around her clit, feeling when she starts to move her hips faster, and then I pull away. I press my hand against her, rubbing gently as I lick her asshole. Alina is panting and moaning but she's not there yet.

It's time to overstimulate her. I do everything at once. My tongue in her ass, two fingers curving inside her tight pussy, and my other hand pinches her clit. Alina starts to writhe and then I pull back, stopping everything.

In anger, she stands up and turns around, coming at me. This is the moment I've been waiting for.

Before she can hit me, not that I wouldn't deserve it, I pick her up and fall down onto the bed with her. My cock nudges at her soaked entrance and she makes a high keening cry, lifting her hips to try and get me where she wants me.

"I'm going to kiss you now," I whisper against her mouth. Her eyes are wild and unfocused, but they meet mine and she nods.

As I take her mouth, I push myself inside her, gliding easily in until I'm snug to the hilt. I don't move as my lips part hers, aggressively stroking her tongue with my own. Alina's hips pump over and over and it's fucking ecstasy. She's topping me from the bottom, desperate to come on my cock right now.

She tastes so good - I've missed it. The last time I kissed her was after I married her, and now I'm going to kiss her every goddamn day until she feels the way that I do. The intensity of the thought gets me moving, and I start to drive hard into her, never breaking the kiss. We're sealed together, breathing the same air, as our flesh pounds together.

Even as she comes, I don't stop, swallowing her screams that only get me closer to my own end. Her cunt is squeezing me tight, practically wrenching it out of me. It's my turn to groan into her mouth, and when I do her arms come around my neck, keeping me close.

We aren't fucking anymore but she's still kissing me and clinging to me.

I keep kissing her until I'm hard again, and I won't stop fucking her tonight until she begs me to. I love this woman and I'm going to show her that with my body until she's ready to hear it and believe it.

26

Alina

Despite my extensive preparation, I am dreading this lunch. Roe is driving me to the restaurant where there's a standing reservation in a private room for this group. It's the two foundation staff, and the six lead volunteers that form the committee that plans the fundraiser gala.

I'm on the phone with Anora, trying to get advice.

"They're just women."

"I've grown up with sweaty dudes who speak with their fists. I don't know women."

"Pretend like they're me."

"There's no way they're as nice as you. One of them is Derick's ex-mistress."

"You think she'll still show?"

I scoff. "Anora. Of course she will."

She laughs, and I miss the sound. It's not the same over the phone, and she's too well-mannered to really laugh around most people. "I can't wait to hear about how this goes. What did you decide to wear?"

Before Derick came home and made me come for hours on end, I'd been trying on clothes and sending pictures to her, trying to figure out what to wear. When Derick got home and we got all dirty and depraved, I still hadn't figured out what I was going to wear. Lauren had convinced me to get all those dresses and while they were gorgeous, they didn't feel like me.

So I was wearing a suit. It was pretty sexy for a suit. It was navy blue and tailored perfectly, with flared pants, as well as flared sleeves on the jacket with obnoxious gold buttons. I was wearing a white button down with a few too many buttons open. I felt like I had to flash the girls and remind all these women that while I had masculine energy, I was as womanly as the rest of them. It felt like the most honest version of myself I could be in front of a group of total strangers who were going to judge the hell out of me.

Derick liked it. He kept grabbing my ass all morning and telling me how good I looked. It was so bad that at one point Jack rolled his eyes and left to eat his breakfast elsewhere. I'd had a couple errands to run so left shortly after Derick did.

I'd checked out the venue where the gala was usually held, and made a drive-by visit to the daycare center. The hotel where we would have the gala was lovely, and the event manager assured me that they could accommodate any theme ideas. The daycare center had melted my heart because it was such a clean, happy place. Derick did good.

Snapping to the present I hit the video button and put my arm out.

"Ooo the sexy power suit. I love that one."

"Me too." I take a deep breath as Roe pulls up to the restaurant. "I'll call you after."

"You are a bad ass woman, never forget that."

I end the call and make my way to the hostess, who shows me to the room. It's in view of the rest of the place, but it's got one big table where we can spread out and get comfortable. There are only three women there, and I'm glad that I'm not the last to arrive.

Two of them jump up and beeline for me. "Mrs. Clayton?"

THE SIGHT OF YOU

"You can call me Alina," I smile at them and offer my hand. "Would you be Melinda and Casey?"

"We are," the tall redhead answers. "I'm Melinda, and this is my wife Casey." Casey is a willowy blonde with clever eyes and a carefully neutral face.

"I'm so happy to meet you both. I'd like to set up time for the three of us to talk, separately, about how I can support you more."

Casey looks suspicious but Melinda nods as we move back to the table. I find that I'm supposed to sit at the head, and it's kind of intimidating. Melinda sits to my left and Casey sits next to her.

The other woman is in the middle of the table. She's a well-maintained woman in her 60s and tells me her name is Anita Cartwright. The first formal event I'm going to with Derick is for an arts organization that she supports. I ask her questions about it and she seems surprised but happy that I know so much. One down, five to go.

The next two arrive together - they're younger, barely in their 20s, and all giggles and smiles and only tell me their first names - Joanna and Leah. They look similar but I can't tell if they're sisters. They immediately order drinks and start whispering to each other.

The next is another older woman, apparently Anita's bestie, because she stands up to make my introduction to Carla Rodriguez. She's got dark hair and amazing fuchsia lipstick. She smiles blandly, and I feel like judgment is being reserved.

Last, Cat fucking Mason and her obvious crony, Gloria Oldman. They don't greet anyone, and go to the far end of the table. Cat sits at the opposite head, and it's absolutely a challenge aimed at me. Gloria is tiny, and clings on every word out of Cat's mouth. It's like watching a bobble head the way she nods continuously, agreeing with everything that Cat says.

The waiter comes over and we all order our food, and I clear my throat to get business started.

"It's about to be May and the event is in July - where are we with things?"

Melinda jumps in. "The venue and catering are secure, we use the same every year to keep our reservations. The last meeting we still couldn't settle on a theme."

"What were the ideas?"

I'm surprised when Joanna jumps in, and see her shoot an odd look at Cat as she rushes to speak. "I wanted to do the Sky's the Limit and have like, a cloud theme? Because this charity is aspirational. It's providing support for people to reach up, you know?"

Cat snorts but I don't acknowledge her.

"Tell me more."

"I have this artist friend who could create these cloud structures to use around the tables, and the stage area could kind of look like the sun - it'd be like spending a night in the clouds. This crowd loves when you do fantastical shit and it wouldn't cost much; he'd do it for the cost of materials and exposure."

"Can you send me some of his work, or an image of the cloud idea?"

"Definitely," Joanna nods and pulls out her phone.

"The other ideas?" I prompt.

There's a tense silence and then Cat speaks up. "In the Spotlight," her voice is falsely high and girlish. "I thought we could get some of the people we help to come to the event and share their stories, do their own work to get the donations that help them."

Gloria nods and bites her lip. Out of the corner of my eye I see Anita and Carla exchange a look, and Carla barely controls a sneer.

"Their stories are pretty private though," I start, thinking through my words. "Derick barely wants to take credit for setting up the foundation, I can't imagine he wants to put these vulnerable people at the mercy of this crowd to be exploited for their stories."

Cat simpers at me, and then throws down the gauntlet. "You aren't the only one at this table who knows what Derick likes."

The other women at the table stiffen, and Leah gasps. Even Gloria pales and looks at Cat like she's crossed a line. Cat stares me down, that smug smile on her face, and I know she expects me to get upset.

Instead, I laugh.

The smile falls from her face for a moment, and then she forces it back.

"Cat, you aren't the only person at this table who's fucked my husband." I see Melinda and Gloria both stiffen slightly, and find those to be fascinating pieces of information to mull over later.

"I think it's inappropriate to let that interfere with the good work this fundraiser does. He's my husband, present and future. Everything else is the past."

Cat smirks again and looks around at the other women before responding. "That's not what Derick told me on Thursday night." All the heads turn back to me, like watching a slow-motion table tennis match.

I grin at her. "Oh, Cat. Do you know why Derick came to see you on Thursday night? Because I said after two years you deserved more than having him ghost you. He was in your house for less than 5 minutes and I know because I was waiting in the car for him and saw you throw a book at his head." Joanna snorts and covers her face. "He's done with you, and you can't lie your way into making anyone believe otherwise."

She gulps, and leans back in her chair as I stand and lean over the table, dropping my voice low even though I know they can all hear me.

"Want to know what happened after Derick left your house, Cat?" She can't look away from me and I know I'm threatening as hell right now. "He got on his knees in the backseat and ate me out until I came all over his face." Anita and Carla both gasp but it sounds impressed rather than scandalized. "Then we canceled our dinner reservation so we could go home and fuck. We're trying to hit every room in the house. But you've never been there, have you?"

It occurs to me that this conversation is significant for two reasons no one but me is aware of: I called Derick my husband, and I called the house my home.

Cat's face is twisted in a sour scowl and I don't break eye contact as I sit back in my chair. Then I take a deep breath and smile, shifting my eyes to the other women, even Gloria. She's the only one that looks scared, the rest look amused.

"Cat, you've been very generous with your time serving on this committee but as a member of the board, I think it's best we part ways."

"You can't-" she starts.

"Actually, she can," Melinda interrupts firmly. "You are, of course, still welcome to donate and attend the gala."

"Thank you so much," I know it's sarcastic but I can't stop myself from saying it. Cat growls and stands up, grabbing her purse. She starts to stomp off but then realizes that Gloria isn't following her.

They have a stare down.

"My mother said I had to be here," Gloria's voice comes out weak and terrified. "I have to stay."

Cat throws up her hands and screeches, and then stomps out of our sight.

"I never liked her," Carla breaks the silence. "It took twice as long to decide anything if we disagreed with her, and then she never did anything. Just gave orders."

"Then let's get back to business - are we comfortable moving forward with the Sky's the Limit?"

There are nods all around, and we start discussing details and dividing up tasks. The invite list is assigned to Carla and Anita because apparently they know everyone, and they know just whose buttons to push to get more donations. Joanna and Leah kindly invite Gloria to work with them on the theme and the decor. I get assigned to work with the venue about scheduling, security, and other miscellaneous things that come with running an event, and weirdly it's the things that scare me the least. Melinda and Casey will oversee the budget and marketing.

I like this group of women. Once the awkwardness of Cat being there was gone, they all opened about why they supported this particular foundation.

Carla was a single parent herself, and worked hard for the money she had. She'd risen up in the world, socioeconomically, as a widow with three children. I knew her bad ass vibes were legit. Anita was raised by a single mom and married well very young; she was never able to have children of her own and she and her husband both agreed they didn't want to leave money behind, they wanted to share their wealth now. She was on boards and committees for enough charities to keep her busy every single day, and she loved it.

Gloria explained in a very quiet voice, that the Clayton Foundation was important to her mother, but she was busy working, and sent Gloria instead. The entire idea of it seemed to terrify her and if she was more scared of her mother than someone as vindictive and likely to hold a grudge as Cat, her mother must be a terrifying woman.

Joanna and Leah, who I found out were sisters, had decided to dedicate their time and money after Joanna got her degree in Sociology. She felt this was one of the most impactful ways to help people, and Leah, who was only 19 and had not decided on a major, was along for the ride to learn. Joanna, while giggly, was smart and I was excited to see what she came up with to turn it into a night that had the money flowing into the foundation and made people remember it.

As soon as I got in the back of the car, all the stress left my body. I'd scheduled a meeting with Melinda and Casey, we had all agreed on what needed to be done by the next meeting, and I was worn out from all the talking and communication and eye contact. People were a lot. This is why I was such a physical person. I didn't like talking.

Roe left me alone as he drove back to the house, and I texted Anora that it went well but I was tired. The drive was uneventful and soothing, and even though it was nice to have a driver at times like this, I needed to start driving myself sometimes too. I needed to know where I was going, just in case there was a reason I needed to go quick and didn't have my phone. At the very least I should know how to get from the house to Venture and back.

My first thought was to bring it up with Derick tonight, but I didn't need his permission, and I wasn't going to seek it. If he challenged me when he found out about it, I'd push back that it was for my own protection.

At the house I went upstairs, stripped off my clothes, and collapsed onto the bed. I fell asleep before I could even get under the covers.

I wake up to the feeling of Derick's warm body settling over mine, his scent wrapping around me, and his tongue sliding along my lips and demanding entrance. I give it to him, kissing him in slow, lazy strokes as I slowly come back to the waking world.

When I'm fully present, I push him off of me and roll off the bed until I'm standing.

He sits up, sexily rumpled. He's already taken off his tie and unbuttoned his dress shirt, his hair is sticking up a little like it gets when he's thinking hard and needs to do something with his hands. I can see his cock straining against his pants, and when I look up to meet his eyes he's smirking at me.

"I need to punish you."

Now his expression turns into a full on grin. "For what?"

"Cat Mason."

His expression drops, genuine concern taking over. "What did she do?"

"Well, I kicked her off the planning committee, but it's not that." I bite my lip, trying to find a way to articulate my thoughts. It's not jealousy exactly, more like disappointment that he would be with someone so self-centered. It was clear that it was purely physical - they never went on dates or dinners, they barely acknowledged each other in public - but she is so different from Derick. There's a river of gold inside him and she's got a pit of coal.

"I don't understand how you could be with someone like her." My distaste is clear in my expression.

I expect him to laugh but instead he pulls me closer. "I forgot every other woman the first time I touched you."

My heart clenches and then panic flutters in my chest.

"Don't say things like that," I push at his shoulder, trying to blow it off.

"Why not?" Derick's hands trace up and down the backs of my thighs and I can't answer for a moment as my eyes flutter shut, my entire body lighting up in reaction to him touching me.

"This..." I swallow, and then steel myself. I lean over and massage his cock through his pants, trying to find some form of control in this conversation.

"This is a business arrangement with benefits, Brody. Not a love match."

Pain flashes across his face and then his expression hardens, the angry, dominant man I've seen before taking over.

"Right," he stands and gets into my space. Then catches me off guard when he grabs me and throws me down on the bed, then turns me over and pulls my ass up until I'm on my knees. Roughly, he yanks

154

down my panties and runs his hand along my already soaked slit. He gives my clit a quick pinch and I cry out.

"Not a love match," he mutters under his breath.

Before I can say anything else, he lines his freed cock up with my entrance and slams inside me. There is no possibility of anything other than a scream coming out of my mouth. I grab the comforter with both hands, fisting it tightly as he starts to pound into me at a rapid, unyielding pace.

I can feel every inch of him sliding in and out of me, and his hips slam into my ass cheeks hard enough that I know it's going to hurt later. Derick holds me tightly around my waist and fucks me like he's mad at me, and it feels so damn good I can't think.

When I come, I scream his name, and that seems to make him even angrier. He gets impossibly faster, then leans over me, one arm wrapping around my torso and his other hand grabs my throat.

"Fucking scream, Allie," he growls. Then squeezes my neck just enough to make me see stars, and I come hard but can't quite breathe. When he lets me go, heat and pleasure race through my body as the over-sensitivity of his body hitting mine makes me cry out, and he groans as he comes inside me.

We stay like that for a moment before he slides out of me, and goes into the bathroom without another word. I feel like I did something wrong but I have no idea what.

27

Them

Alina and Derick find a rhythm to their life together. Before they know it, it's July. They've been married for three months.

It's more pleasant than either expected, but Derick wants more. He chases, and Alina runs and blocks. She gives him her body, often, but runs every time it seems like he's getting close to her heart. Sometimes she still hesitates to kiss him, but won't retreat when he comes for her.

They've made their way through most of the house now, sharing memories of them fucking in different places and on different surfaces that get them both worked up to engage in a repeat performance. Their bodies are marked from their lust for each other and the damage they've done to themselves while breaking the furniture.

Things at the house have settled into a routine - a bubble away from the danger outside.

Derick dismantles the criminal side of their empire, but things are only getting worse rather than better as he puts distance between the Clayton name and the underworld.

Their convenience stores get hit by a string of robberies, one of them resulting in the cashier being shot to death. The money is a drop in the bucket to the Claytons, but the loss, the chaos, and uncertainty make things worse.

The money keeps being skimmed from the clubs as well, and despite everything, despite turning to violence, neither Derick or Jack have figured out what's happening or how. One of their longtime bouncers turns up dead, stabbed in the chest, and no one has any answers. Jack spends longer hours at the clubs when he's working and most days he's surviving on coffee and sarcasm.

Then the threats start coming, and the tension builds in the house.

First, it was a photo in the mail of Alina and Derick leaving Venture, and a note telling them to tread carefully. Derick thought it might be a threat from the group he rejected to buy out their shipments, but they claimed to have no idea.

Derick sold their pipeline of phones and supplies to a digital anarchist group called the Handle. They believe that no one should be tracked by their digital footprints and that the landscape of the future is already too regulated. They were one of their biggest customers, paying most of the cost of the work anyway. Plus, they were less likely to feel like they needed to take out the Claytons to keep control of what they'd just gained. It was done, and Derick could wash his hands of it. It was easier than he expected.

Alina started getting anonymous text messages from burner phones telling her to leave Derick, to hide because they'd come for her to get to him, and would send stalker photos of Derick to let her know that they were watching him. Sometimes the messages would threaten Alina, but the majority of the time they were trying to divide her and Derick.

Then someone slashed the tires on Derick's car while he was at work.

A picture of Alina was under the windshield wiper, a big black X across her face.

Derick didn't tell Alina about it, but Jack did.

As Jack and Alina got closer, things got more tumultuous between Jack and Derick. Derick was trying to keep everyone safe and he could only do that if he was exercising complete control. Jack often disagreed or ignored him, seeing his brother rather than his boss, and it put them increasingly at odds with one another over every little thing.

Every Tuesday night, Alina and Jack made popcorn and watched a true crime documentary. They'd spend hours talking about serial killers and conspiracies, about famous and infamous crimes, and who they'd be the most afraid of, and who they thought they could take out. Spending the time with Jack made her miss her sisters a little less, because now she had a brother.

Sometimes Jack would say things that made her confused or uncomfortable, telling half the story or half truths because he wasn't always sure how to talk about what was on his mind. Those nights they turned in early, Jack going off in a melancholy mood to his side of the house.

Alina wanted to ask him what was upsetting him, she already had some idea, but she also knew that if Jack confirmed it, she'd go straight to Derick. It wasn't Alina's place to speak for Jack and explain to his big brother how he was pissing him off and hurting him. Jack could barely stand to be in the same room as Derick anymore. He didn't eat any meals with them, avoided them at the gatherings they were all required to go to and always drove in a separate car, and in most meetings he wouldn't even speak. As far as Alina knew, they were only communicating via text message and it was never anything pleasant.

So when Jack told her about the threat on the car, it meant they'd had a face to face conversation. It meant that Derick was worried enough that he made a point of telling Jack.

But he didn't tell her.

The next day, Alina drove herself to Venture for her meeting with

Lauren.

Derick waited until they were both home at the end of the day to fight about it.

It got ugly. There was screaming, a thrown shoe, and slamming doors. It was their first true fight and a sign of the way the outside was starting to eat into their home life.

In the end, Derick said he was sorry because Alina was right - if she didn't know there was a threat, she couldn't protect herself. She apologized for leaving the house without protection, and he agreed not to fire Roe because it wasn't his fault that Alina booked it before anyone could notice that she was leaving.

They made up with their bodies, harsh and angry the first time, and then slower and more languid the second.

While pressed deep inside her, Derick took Alina's face in his hands, making her look at him as he whispered to her. "I can't lose you."

She frowned at him. "You won't."

Derick silences her with his mouth, and swallows all her moans and cries as she comes around him. Then he buries his face in her throat as he comes, thinking things that he can't say out loud because she'll run. He might never be able to say them out loud because she might never be ready. This might be one sided for the rest of their lives, and he'll have to find a way to live with that.

Because he will be faithful to her, he sees no one but her, he thinks about her when she's away from him, and has come to trust her more than almost anyone else in his life. Alina never says what he wants to hear, she tells him the truth. She tells him things that he needs to hear to be better, safer, stronger. When he chose her, he wanted a partner. He got a queen.

28

Alina

To my surprise, I have a life here. I still talk to at least one of my sisters every day, and my dad once a week, but I've slowly found a circle in Seattle too.

Lauren has officially crossed over to being my friend as well as my assistant. I met her family - and even Derick came along. That embarrassed the hell out of Lauren but she managed to hold it together, and he acted like a person rather than her boss for the night.

The women on the foundation committee are indispensable to me. Carla and Anita took me under their wing, and I'm more confident in my role now. Not just with the foundation and the fundraisers, but that I can be myself and also be the things that Derick needs from his wife in these circles. I barely wear dresses except for formal events, although I have definitely upgraded my suit game. Even Gloria has warmed up to us.

I did eventually ask Derick if he'd slept with Gloria because that one surprised me.

I was even more surprised when he actually turned red with embarrassment.

"Have you met Gloria's mother yet?"

"I've only seen her at events, we haven't met."

Derick puts a hand over his eyes. "Regina Oldman is possibly the most difficult woman in the world. Gloria is a constant disappointment to her - and also does anything that her mother says. No matter what it is."

That made sense given the fact that she managed to stand up to Cat to stay on the committee because it was something her mother expected of her.

"At a dinner, Regina made a comment that Gloria needed to find a man, and then very pointedly said she needed to find someone like me. Gloria took that as a command and tried to seduce me in the coat closet later that night." He's practically glowing red to the point where I already feel bad for Gloria for whatever it was that happened.

"She...she unzipped her dress and just stood their naked, offering herself to me. I basically swallowed my tongue in horror and looked up at the ceiling. Then I threw a coat at her and left. We never spoke of it again but I also don't think we've made eye contact since then either."

"Oh poor Gloria." I cover my mouth to stop the laughter at how genuinely uncomfortable he is over the experience.

"Poor Gloria? Poor me!"

"Oh yes, poor you, women literally throwing themselves at you. How terrible."

The taunting led to Derick pulling down my yoga pants to thoroughly spank my bare ass, then gripping my ponytail tight as I sucked his cock. He slid in and out of my mouth, taunting the back of my throat with unexpected deep thrusts, before he pulled out and came on my face.

There was so much heat in his gaze when he looked down at me and ran his finger through the mess before sliding it into my mouth. "Poor you," he said gruffly at me. "My dirty fucking girl."

I'd squirmed under his gaze and at his words, my feminism angry at me because I loved it when he talked to me like that.

Derick confuses me, and I lock that confusion and questioning in a box that I throw down into the deepest ocean of my heart and mind. We've been together for three months and his attention has never wavered. If anything, he gives me more attention. Part of me never truly believed him when he said he wanted a partner, but here I am, part of the decisions about divesting the Claytons from some of their criminal businesses, how to protect what they're keeping, and so many other decisions in between both important and arbitrary. Half the time, Derick makes me pick his tie before he leaves the house.

It's all very domestic and I don't trust it for a second.

Tonight is another meeting at the house - I've started calling his office the War Room because more often than not, that's how it feels. Sometimes we're at war with each other, disagreeing and circling until we come to some sort of agreement on the next step. Sometimes it's being strategically at war with the outside, with the unknown entity that wants to see Derick Clayton fall.

Tonight, we're arguing about selling the clubs. Derick finally listened to Jack when he said he wanted to tighten his circle and focus on the three most profitable, and get rid of the rest. Outside of Derick's club where we met, that leaves four very profitable nightclubs to offload. As usual, it's Derick, me, Jack, Kade, and Ethan. Tonight Kade also brought Niles along.

Our relationship has not improved.

"Forrester Entertainment has already agreed to keep all staff for a year - it's an excellent deal." Niles shoves the file with the offer across the table toward Derick.

"Except Roger Forrester is a cunt," I shake my head. "While our money laundering operation is an unwritten part of the deal, on paper we do not want the Clayton name or Venture associated with him."

162

"His money is good."

"His reputation is bad, and he's running for office. We can't tie ourselves to him."

"What's this we?" Niles sneers at me. "You're barely a Clayton. I'm still not sure why there's a pussy in the room."

Jack and Derick both stand, but I put up my hand to stop them. Because they're not complete jackasses who have a problem with a woman being in the room, they respect my silent request and resume their seats.

"First, is your dick that small Niles, that you're threatened by a vagina being in the room?" I laugh but it's flat and humorless. "Second, can you honestly point to a decision I've made or advice that's been taken in the last three months that didn't work out?"

The answer is no. The longer Niles sits there trying to think of a time, the redder he gets. I share a glance with Derick, communicating silently. He nods.

"We're done. The offer from Forrester Entertainment is being rejected. Thank you for your perspective, Niles."

I get up and leave the room, heading straight to our bedroom. Derick will take care of wrapping things up but I couldn't be in the room with that fuckwad for another minute or I'd kill him. I'm sure Derick was verbally eviscerating him right now, and it would make a bigger impact than anything else I would've said. It fucking sucked to have men overlook my abilities, but at least I knew every other man in that room believed in me.

By the time Derick comes upstairs, I've already changed into pajamas and gotten ready for bed. I'm putting Cigarettes After Sex on the record player because they always calm me down, and a broody sort of zen is appealing right now.

"Kade is letting him go."

"Is that code for killing him?" I sigh.

"No," Derick laughs. "I can't trust him if I can't trust him with you."

"Thank you." My tone sounds anything but grateful.

"There's nothing to thank me for. You have more than earned your seat at the table, Allie. That seat was waiting for you to fill it, and make us better."

"Okay." While I believe him, Niles did shake my confidence today. As much as I can keep my cool and the veneer of being impenetrable, every once and awhile the reminder that a lot of men in the world reduce my entire sex to our genitals hits me right in the face. All I've ever wanted was to be in a place where my value was recognized. Working with Derick creates a false sense of security sometimes because the inner circle of our lives clearly do value me, and that softening of my walls leaves me vulnerable to hits some days.

Derick comes up behind me and rests his warm hands on my hips. I'm wearing a pair of cotton shorts and a t-shirt, nothing under either one. He buries his nose in my hair, sending tingles down my neck and back. I want to lean on him right now, physically and mentally. I know he won't judge me for what I'm feeling, and I know that if I let my body fall into his, I'll relax.

With steady persistence, Derick is winning over parts of me I've been trying very hard to keep closed. I trust him with everything except my heart and even that might be only a matter of time. I'm on a precipice right now. Maybe I can fall in love with him and he'll love me back and everything works out. More likely than not, I'll fall and get hurt - but I'm getting to the point where being hurt may be worth it. Letting Derick love me, and letting myself love him, might be the making and the breaking of me.

Tonight, I give in a little. I lean back on him, let my head drift back to rest on his shoulder, and turn so our cheeks touch. He has carefully maintained stubble and it's just long enough to be soft. I nuzzle him with no shame, letting his clean scent into my lungs. I pull his hands from my hips so that his arms wrap around my body. We sway to the music for a long time. Until my heart stops racing and my stomach stops swirling and the adrenaline of my anger fades.

Derick lets me go and strips off his clothes. He leaves everything in a pile on the floor like he's afraid if he gets too far away from me I'll run. Maybe I would, I don't know. The restless awful feeling inside me wants to run and scream. Wants to find Niles and claw up his face.

Instead of running, Derick pulls me into bed and wraps his arms around me, holding me until I fall asleep.

29

Alina

Roe pulls to a stop outside the large warehouse on the far side of the city. When Joanna showed me what her artist friend, who went by Michael - no last name - was capable of, I knew we had to do more than what the hotel we reserved could provide.

The warehouse was the perfect blank canvas for him to create a world in the clouds. Plus, it was easy to put security on the warehouse and control the movement of the guests and media that were attending. The hotel had too many vulnerabilities - this was a site that was only our event that we could fully control.

The event was in a week, and this was the final check on the general decor before we had to set up the stage and the tables. I was actually excited. Not just about seeing the setup, but about the entire event. No one was more shocked than me. Okay, maybe Anora, but I was a close second.

When I walk into the warehouse, Joanna and Michael break apart quickly, but their lips are both swollen and it confirms my suspicion that something was going on between them. He's in his mid-30s so I was worried that he was taking advantage of the surprisingly innocent Joanna, but he looks at her like she hung the moon. He even called her his muse, and as I look around the warehouse I think that if she is, he'll be famous in no time.

There are huge mounds of clouds in each corner, shaped like the most decadent cumulonimbus puffs of fluff, made from starch and cotton. They're also covered in glitter and sparkle even in the dim light of the warehouse windows. When we have the overhead lights on for dinner, they will look spectacular. I look up and see the stretches of clouds across the structures on the ceiling, as well as long dark stretches of cloth painted to look like the sky and stars. You can't even see most of the walls inside the warehouse - it truly is like being up in the clouds and looking out into the darkness of space. There are smaller cloud mounds all around the warehouse that mark where we will put the different tables.

"This is incredible, Michael."

"It was fun. I never thought I could create something on this scale."

"Everyone is going to freak," Joanna chimes in, squeezing his arm and they smile at each other. "No one has ever seen anything like this at a fundraiser. They're usually stuffy things in hotel ballrooms. This - this is an *event*."

Joanna is absolutely right. This is spectacular.

"Credit where it's due Joanna - this was all you and Leah, and Michael, of course."

"Surprisingly, Gloria too. She was the one who thought of doing the ceiling."

"Excellent," I grin at them both.

Michael takes me through and shows me the different pieces, as well as hidden spaces inside them that curious party guests might find if they are willing to look. The large clouds aren't just art, they're actual structures. My mind is completely blown standing inside one of them. It's lit up soft and pink inside and I feel like I'm standing inside cotton candy.

After discussing a few more details, I leave them alone in the warehouse and go back to where Roe waits for me. I can't stop smiling and he smiles back. We've bonded, not just because he's my driver, but we've really learned one another's fighting styles now and push one another.

"Looks good?"

"Looks amazing. Derick is going to love it, and I think it'll set a record for donations."

"Really?" Roe pulls away and drives back toward the city. "Are we headed to the office?"

"Yes. I should only need a half hour there, I need to sign some checks and then we can head home for the day."

Unable to keep my joy to myself, I text Derick and tell him that if he's good I'll take him to the warehouse for a sneak peak at the decorations. He responds almost immediately.

What do I have to do to be good?

It's suggestive and I figure he deserves a little torture today. We've both been too exhausted to get physical the last few days and now that I'm worked up from excitement, I'm horny as hell. I look up to make sure that Roe is distracted by the road and shift slightly so that my cleavage is showing when I take a selfie.

I send it to him with the message: *Worship me.*

Derick sends back a picture of his crotch, his cock obviously hard in his blue dress pants.

Always. What does my goddess want tonight?

Make me cry.

Embarrassed and excited that I said that, I switch over to my group text with my sisters and send them some of the photos I took of the inside of the warehouse. Anora and Aro respond immediately. Anora says it's lovely, and Aro sends a series of heart-eyes emojis. It's a challenge to get her to respond with words most of the time - she likes to communicate in images and for some reason I always know what she means when she sends them to us. We all do.

I'm surprised when my phone buzzes with a response from Derick, and it's a long block of text. I blush at the first sentence.

> *Should I finally fuck your ass tonight, lleidr bach? Do you want to know how good it feels to come on my cock when it's deep in your ass? I'm going to eat that sweet pussy until you're begging me to stop and crying for me to do anything to you but toy with that sensitive little clit. You'll be begging me to fuck that sweet ass, my wife. You'll cry for me.*

Holy shit.

I almost orgasmed from his words and the flood of moisture that fills my panties is intense. He doesn't usually talk that filthy unless he's really riled up, it's why it always catches me off guard when he does it. I have no idea how to reply to that. It's what I asked for, and the anticipation is going to keep me aroused and heated for the rest of the day.

I'm still worked up when Roe pulls up to the short, squat office building where I arranged for space to be rented for the foundation. It was ridiculous that they didn't have a permanent space and had to keep files at Venture or their home, and that they had no formal meeting space or place to work from. The office space is a small suite with a lobby, a break room, and two offices.

Casey's office is empty and the light is turned off. Melinda sits at the

169

table next to her desk, rearranging the seating chart for the gala. Even though Carla and Anita had rounded up an incredible and generous list of donors, they wanted nothing to do with the drama that always ensued from choosing the seating arrangements.

"Hi," I greet her with a smile.

She jumps, looking a little frazzled. "Sorry, I didn't hear you come in."

"Seating chart not going well?"

"I have to call Carla every 20 minutes to make sure there's no drama between people that I might have forgotten about. They're adults! It's a dinner!"

I laugh and walk into her office. "Treat them like they're toddlers, maybe that will solve the issues."

Melinda shakes her head and steps away, flipping through the files on her neatly arranged desk until she gets the one she wants. She grabs a pen and hands both it and the file to me.

"Final checks for catering, rentals, Michael, and the extra security. It should be the last of all the payments as everything else was covered up front."

"Great. You're amazing at this."

I perch at the edge of her desk and note who each check is made out to, that it's consistent with the previous checks, and what the amounts are. It's not that I don't trust Melinda, it's that too much weird shit has happened recently for me to take anything at face value right now. She's given me no reason to mistrust her, or to think she's doing anything less than the same stellar job she's been doing for years, but my paranoia is up.

I got another text last night, and it was Andrew driving Derick through the city. It made me anxious, and I haven't told Derick about it although I did text Kade. He's been trying to look into all of this, but he's got a lot on his plate.

I sign the checks.

It occurs to me that all of these messages are warnings directed at me, not necessarily threats directed at Derick. I pause in front of the table that Melinda is staring at like it's a pile of unexpected dog poop.

"When did you sleep with Derick?"

She flinches hard and the little place notes shift on the layout. As a redhead, she knows that her skin immediately betrays her as she turns bright pink rising from her cleavage to her hairline.

"Right when I started. It was one time."

"Okay." I wait, seeing what she'll say now.

"I, uh, think Derick knew something about me that I didn't know about myself. He introduced me to Casey shortly after and I never - I looked at her and then never looked at anyone else." She takes a few deep breaths and the color recedes. "I'm sorry."

"Nothing to be sorry for."

"Did he tell you?"

"No," I smirk a little, "I figured it out."

"You're scary when you do that you know, it's like you read minds."

"Just attuned to body language. I like you Melinda, I think you and Casey do great work, and I want to make sure that I don't have to worry about you. Does Casey know?"

Melinda nods, opens her mouth, closes it, and then finally says, "Is something going on? Are you alright? I know - I know not everything the Claytons do is entirely above board and," she starts to flounder and gives me a pitiful look.

"We're figuring it out. Thanks Melinda."

I leave the office, focusing on the night that I'm going to have with my husband, and hoping that he can follow through on his dirty promises.

30

Derick

My slutty little wife wants me to worship her…and she didn't say no to me taking her ass tonight. We've been teasing around it and preparing her for awhile, and I think she's ready. My cock is going to be hard the rest of the day just thinking about all the things she's going to let me do to her tonight.

Except I immediately deflate when Kade walks into my office, a thunderous look on his face. He almost never comes to see me at the office because his work has nothing to do with Venture.

"Niles is dead."

"What?" I lean forward. That was not the plan and I want to know what the hell he's talking about.

"His body was found this morning in the parking garage of his apartment. He'd been shot 12 times."

"What the fuck."

"I don't know. And that's not actually the worst news I have for you."

Today can already go fuck itself. I wave my hand for him to continue.

"You've been hacked."

"Venture is fine, and we're monitoring our phones."

"I know, this is the crazy part - they hacked the cars. Your car for sure, maybe Alina's and Jack's. We've been monitoring computers and phones, thinking that's where they'd believe we were vulnerable, but one of the new programmers looked at the car GPS and that's where we found it."

"New programmer?" We hadn't hired any new programmers.

"From Designation. I got an email - I assumed that you'd put them on it since things lately might be compromising Alina's safety."

"Let me see."

Kade slides his phone across the desk and I read the email and look at the unintelligible attachments showing the code that's been added to the GPS. It's signed Aster Sorrelle, and the signature notes that she's a lead programmer at Designation.

"That's Alina's sister."

"Really?" Kade seems intrigued and I glower at him.

"She must know something is going on - and put herself on it. From what I hear she has an interesting variety of skills." Part of me is frustrated that Alina shared so much with her sisters, but the other part is glad that they are looking out for the both of us. The threats and weird incidents are getting beyond my control. This city has never hid so much from me that I couldn't track down with either money or a threat.

"That's what I hear as well," Kade says as he reads the name. "She's a killer."

I brush that off because it's not relevant right now. "What do we do?"

"The cars are being wiped and reprogrammed right now. I'm coming over tonight and the four of us need to have a conversation about security at the house."

"Why?"

"We've worked hard to keep the location of the house as low key as possible. It's not public, you don't have visitors there, we're careful. If the person who did this didn't know where you lived, they do now. We need to make sure it's secure because that's where you're most vulnerable. It's not like you're going to put a security staffer outside your bedroom door."

"Damn right I'm not." I'd have to have a new one every day, killing them for hearing Alina. If my bedroom hadn't already been on the third floor I would've moved it there to keep all her cries to myself. I know she'd been with other men but it was not relevant to our current reality. Now she belongs to me and I would never let anyone see or hear what it was like when I made her come undone.

For fuck's sake she asked me to make her cry.

There had never been a more perfect woman for me, and every day she gave me a new reason to be completely obsessed with her. For all the power she held out in the world and her physical strength and skill, Alina's secret was that she liked to be owned in the bedroom.

Last weekend she'd let me tie her hands behind her back and I put her on her knees and fucked her face. Then she'd ridden me reverse cowgirl and I'd held on to that tie, pounding up into her and watching that perfect ass move as I imprinted my cock inside her body.

Afterward, I'd massaged her in the shower and soothed the marks I'd left on her, washed her hair, and then held her all night. We'd fallen asleep talking about plans for the end of the summer, and she hadn't pulled away when I suggested we take an actual honeymoon.

I was fucking gone over her.

The tension in my body never quite went away anymore. I'd made Jack take more security with him, and I made him turn on the tracking on his phone so that I knew where he was at all times. Jack and Alina were the two most important people in my life - the two people I would die for without hesitation. The world that had been handed to he and I was now putting all of us in danger.

Someone wanted the Claytons - or maybe just me - to fall and

174

they were doing a good job of it. The unknown was driving me mad. Long after Alina would fall asleep, I'd be up staring at the ceiling, the reassurance of her breathing my soundtrack as I tried to figure out new ways to approach the situation.

Even Alina had no idea what else we could do. Everyone had been questioned, everything that could be tracked was, and we had people we could trust combing through the details of our lives trying to figure out who was trying to burn down my empire.

An empire I didn't even want.

Maybe that was the motivation - to get me to give up everything that wasn't Venture. So far they'd left the company alone. No hacks, no attacks, and no threats made inside the building. It was all the ways that we made the kind of money we didn't pay taxes on.

The only other relief was the ventures that I hid behind shell companies - the low income housing units, and no one had messed with the daycares run by the foundation. So whatever was going on, there were certain places even they wouldn't mess with.

What would happen if I sold every last piece of the underworld my grandfather and even my father built? My father was a bastard and I would have no problem wiping any piece of his legacy off the map. It was bad enough his blood ran through my veins. The pompous, selfish piece of shit was barely a father and I didn't miss him.

It would certainly be a financial blow, but it would also give me time to focus on the things I cared about - Venture and the charity work I'd started.

The only sticking point was Jack. Although we'd been fighting more than ever recently, he was the man in charge of the illicit side of our lives. He ran the clubs and the stores, he controlled the money, made changes and controlled staffing. That was his slice of the empire because he'd never been all that interested in Venture. Even when I'd talked to him about it, his answers had been so noncommittal. When he graduated college and asked about working at Venture, I knew he felt obligated but his heart wasn't in it, so I gave him control over the party scene instead.

I could find something for him at Venture. People loved him - he was the more charming of the two of us. Jack could find a way to talk to anybody. I also loved that he'd bonded with Alina. They both needed someone right now and I was glad they had each other. I know she missed her sisters and heard her telling them how much she loved having Jack as her brother now.

One of these days I'd hear her saying how much she loved me.

31

Alina

We'd spent two hours going over new security protocols and deciding what the best measures were to increase safety at the house. It was the longest meeting of my life because from the second Derick got home and shared a heated look with me, I was turned on. I was squirming in my chair the whole time from how uncomfortably wet I was.

The moment Derick confirmed with everyone that we felt everything had been addressed, the two of us made a completely obvious beeline for the stairs to our bedroom. Kade had called out a laughing "goodnight!" but we didn't answer. Today had been full of nasty surprises and now we both needed something good.

"Take off your clothes and get on your knees," Derick demands the second he closes the door. I do what he says, and his gaze is so intense I can feel it on my skin. He strips down to his boxers, and I can already see how hard he is. Our bodies are screaming for each other and ready for release.

Derick comes over to me and leans down to tease my nipples with a fingertip. I arch my back, leaning into his touch and he rewards me with a light pinch.

"What do you want, *lleidr bach*?" His voice is just above a whisper, husky and aroused.

I look up into his eyes, so dilated I can barely see the color. "Make me cry. Make me scream."

Derick grins but it's tinged with darkness and my body shivers with excitement. He pulls off his boxers and his cock springs free, right in my face - right where I want it. Without prompting I reach up and wrap my hand around the based before putting it in my mouth. I love the velvety softness of his skin, the salty, musky taste and scent of him. When I take him deep in my throat he groans, and the motion plus the sound of him causes my mouth to flood with saliva.

He pulls out of my mouth and I pout, which makes him laugh.

"My turn." He wraps his hands around my waist and throws me on the bed, then kneels beside it and yanks me forward by my ankles. I spread wide open for him, and he taps my clit, causing my hips to lift. "Good girl."

Then he attacks - alternatively sucking my clit and then swirling his tongue around it, he slides two fingers into my pussy and moves them in and out at a rapid, almost painful pace. The sound of my wetness echoes in the room, and with one shift of his fingers and suck from his mouth I come hard, rolling my hips as I ride the wave of pleasure that hits me.

I sit up and pull Derick to me, tasting myself on his mouth and seeking to feel all of him with my tongue. He pushes back on me until I'm spread on the bed again, and he's moving his head to my entrance and sliding inside.

We've had sex hundreds of times by now but that first thrust never feels anything less than ecstatic. I moan and immediately clench around his pleasurable invasion, my nails digging in to the skin of his back as he presses deep.

Derick rolls his hips in a steady rhythm, torturing me. "You're going to come again like a good girl," he tells me. "Get this cock nice and wet before I slide it into your ass."

"Fuck," I barely manage to gasp as my body grips him tighter, so insanely aroused that I'm already on the brink of coming again. "Please," I beg him. There's never any shame in begging for pleasure in my book.

"You're my dirty fucking girl, Allie. You'll let me fuck you any way I want. Won't you?"

"Yes!" I scream. "Fuck me, Brody. Fuck me however you want."

He picks up the pace, and I am so close that my body starts clenching and shaking as I chase the edge. With one hard thrust I'm launched out of reality as I move on his body and feel the insanity of this orgasm from the tips of my fingers to the tips of my toes. It's almost hard to breathe when I come down.

Derick kisses me, then licks and nips at my neck and tongue. When he gets to my nipples he taunts me further with wet laps of his tongue, exposing the skin to the cold air after making them wet. His finger brushes my clit softly.

"Are you ready, Alina?"

"Yes," I nod. I wipe the tears that have fallen down my cheeks and take a deep breath.

"I'm going to own all of you after this."

You already do, I think to myself.

Derick gets up and stands over me. "Say it."

"You own me," I manage to rasp out and get treated to his sexual deviant smile.

"Good girl."

Then he climbs onto the bed and lays down, beckoning me with a crooked finger.

"Suck my cock," he commands, and I listen. I taste myself on him, and love the mix of our flavors on his skin. "Nice and sloppy, baby," he groans as I take him deeper, coating him with my saliva.

"You're going to get on top of me and ride my dick with your sweet little ass, Alina. That way you're in control, and I get to watch you come apart as you fuck yourself."

I moan around his cock in my mouth and my pussy clenches.

"Whenever you're ready, dirty girl."

When he's nice and wet, I do exactly as he says. I straddle him, sitting a little farther up his body than I normally would to ride him. Derick holds his cock steady as I line it up with the tight hole - it burns at first, but I move up and down a little at a time, in and out. He's played with me there enough that the sensation is familiar, and I relax quickly. When I finally sink down on him, my ass resting on his thighs, I think I'm the fullest I've ever been.

He reaches down and massages my clit, relaxing me as my ass adjusts to the invasion and the new sensation. It isn't unpleasant, but it's different.

"Rock your hips," he tells me, and I follow the motion of his hand on my clit, rocking my body back and forth. The friction is incredible. I lean forward, bracing myself on his chest, and start grinding faster. Come from my pussy slides back, pooling around the base of his cock. As I rock, he starts sliding in and out of my ass.

The feeling is like nothing I've ever known - it's deep and right on the edge of being painful. As my confidence builds, I lift my hips more, chasing the feeling.

"That's right, fuck my cock with your ass," Derick groans, never stopping his movements on my clit. I'm getting closer and closer to orgasming, moving fast and erratic as I pound my ass down onto his hips and thighs, grinding myself against his body.

"I knew you'd love this. I'll worship every hole you have, every fucking day. I'm going to come in that ass tonight - you want that?"

"Yes," I moan hard, almost there.

"You want to feel my come deep in that pretty ass?"

"Please," I'm moving fast and feeling the burn in my thighs, but I'm almost there. I slam down, taking him all the way in to the hilt and everything clenches all at once. As I start to orgasm, Derick slides his fingers into my pussy and I think I levitate for a second. I am full in the best way, coming apart on his hands and cock, and it lasts for nearly 2 minutes as I shake and grind, never letting up.

Derick wraps his hands around my hips, holding on in a brutal grip, and starts to push his cock up into my body. I'm beyond pleasured and can do nothing but hold onto his wrists to keep my balance and moan with the aftershocks of my orgasm.

"Tell me you want it, Alina."

I look down into his eyes. "Come in my ass, please."

"Fuck," Derick groans and releases, pressing himself inside me and coming, his hips thrusting shallowly as he stays deep.

I collapse on top of him, and he gently pulls my body toward him as his cock slips out of me. My asshole definitely hurts, but I think the experience was worth it.

"Want to take a shower?" he asks softly, running his hands through my hair and down my back, soothing me after such an intense experience. I can only nod because words have escaped me.

This man is wearing down my resistance, and I'm starting to run out of reasons to hold back.

32

Alina

It's Tuesday, and it's Jack's turn to pick our viewing for the night. Derick is out doing the usual spot checks on the club and decided that rather than make sure my car wasn't hacked, he was going to get a new car altogether.

I've been rich all my life but never spent money like that - just deciding to get a new car out of nowhere. But it also made me feel safer because who knew what else had been tampered with.

Tonight was the last day of quiet we'd have for a bit. Tomorrow the woods around the house would get all sorts of bells and whistles installed to alert us if anyone tried to get near the house. They were also going to build some new fencing closer to the house and get a gate by the driveway so it would slow down any cars that tried to come up this way. As much as I loved the views and the isolation up here, it did have it's downsides.

In the middle of the woods, no one can hear you scream. I guess that answers the question about a tree falling in the woods too.

It also meant that I didn't go anywhere, even inside the house, without being armed. Right now I had a knife strapped to my calf beneath my baggy sweatpants.

I was drowning in clothes at the moment - besides the pants I had also stolen a hoodie of Derick's and had my little rice pack tucked in the pocket. In addition to all the drama of the week, I'd gotten my period this morning. The first few days were always the worst, but I was happy the timing worked out that it would be over by Saturday night for the gala, otherwise I'd have to wear an entirely different dress. Even I wasn't brave enough to go pantyless with a tampon in.

I sprawl out on the couch as Jack flips through options before settling on the documentary series about the murder at the Cecil Hotel. I'd watched it before but it was interesting every time. I was pretty sure he'd seen it before too, which meant Jack was feeling chatty tonight. I hope that I have the energy for whatever he has to say tonight and it's not another weird conversation where he's trying to get in mine and Derick's business.

After I get sucked in to the show, I look over to find him watching me. He looks worried.

"What's up bro?"

Annoyance flashes across his face. "Are you feeling okay? You don't look great."

"A little under the weather but it's fine."

His frown deepens and he looks me over. "Have you been sleeping? Is everything that's going on stressing you out?"

I shift and sit up. "Not as much as I thought it would. I feel pretty confident that I can protect myself," I give him a weak smile. "I just don't feel well."

There's a long pause and then he says so quietly I have to focus hard to hear him. "Do you want to leave? I can get you on a plane in a few hours. Get you home and away from all this shit."

"No, Jack," my voice is harsher than I mean it to be, and he flinches. "This is my home now. I made a commitment, so I'm here."

He stares at me, and I can't read his expression. There's something removed in his gaze and it's more than him being mad at Derick or worried for me. Whatever is going on is really bothering Jack.

His eyes drop to where my hands rest over the rice pack. "Shit, are you pregnant?" There's a hint of disgust in his voice and I ignore that for now.

"Uh, the way I'm feeling today would indicate otherwise."

We stare at each other for a second and I lift my eyebrows before he blushes and turns away because he finally understands what I'm saying. I'm the literal opposite of pregnant right now. And now would be the worst time to get pregnant - if I thought that Derick was in a feral protective mode now, I can't imagine if he knew that the next generation was growing inside my vulnerable human body. Nope, definitely no kids until this shit was sorted out.

It surprised me that I wanted them. That I could picture the babies that Derick and I would make together. I had kind of figured that I'd start having kids with him when he started getting bored with me. It would give me something to focus on and help us transition to being friends who parented while he got his more carnal satisfaction elsewhere. Someone like me didn't keep someone like him interested forever.

I never imagined I'd even get the chance to be a mom, and now I found that I was looking forward to it.

"Are you sure you don't want to go?" Jack asks again, reaching over and squeezing my foot. "Is this the life you planned on?" He prompts.

"Not at all," I answer honestly, but not unhappily. "I'm a fighter Jack. I'm not going to leave you all in the middle of a war with an anonymous enemy. Derick needs me."

"He really doesn't."

That stings but I press on. "I brought in an outside perspective. A threat to him is a threat to me, to all of us. Do you really think leaving him, even when our business alliance still stands, would be enough for them to leave me alone?"

"Maybe. At least you'd be far away and safe."

"If there's anything I've learned in my life Jack, it's that nowhere is safe. Did you know I lost my spleen?"

He seems caught off guard by the change in topic, but it's really the same. "What?"

"When I was 21, early days on my dad's protection detail, this disgruntled employee who got fired attacked my dad. I did my job and took the hit - I got stabbed in the stomach and they had to take out my spleen. But you know where we were?"

Jack shakes his head.

"Broad daylight, going into the post office. I don't know how he knew we'd be there, or if it was a random sighting, but that man tried to kill my dad and I made sure that didn't happen. I've been hurt, I've worked my body to it's absolute limits so that I could fight anything that came at me, or at someone I was supposed to protect. I'm strong, Jack."

"Sometimes strong and smart aren't the same thing." At my glare, he continues. "Just because you can fight doesn't mean you should or that you have to - sometimes it's being smart enough to know that you should walk away."

"I'm not walking away from Derick."

Silence falls for a long time, and I turn my eyes back to the show even though I'm not really watching.

"Do you love him? Are you in love with Derick?"

My heart beats faster and says of course I am, but that's not possible. I keep him at a metaphorical arms length. I listen but don't always share. I don't let him in. I don't talk to him about the mundane things that happen during the day, or text him with random thoughts. I listen when he needs to talk and offer advise when he asks for it, but I haven't let him in. I've been careful.

But I also get to see a side of him that no one else does. That side of him gets under my skin and crawls into all of the places I am trying to hide from him. I'd be lying if I said I didn't have feelings for Derick. They're strong and complicated and I wish they weren't there. I wish I could keep things casual between us. Our relationship could fade into a nice, friendly partnership.

Instead I know that I'll end up shattered on the inside while keeping my game face on on the outside. The fall has already started - I'm waiting to see what kind of landing I'll have.

It's taken me too long to answer because Jack squeezes my foot and shakes it a little, drawing my attention back to him.

"Please tell me you didn't fall, Lina. I don't think I can pick up the pieces of your broken heart and not deck him in the face."

I huff out a laugh. "Not in love, Jack. It's all good."

33

Alina

The Clayton Foundation fundraiser gala is finally here. I'm less nervous than I expected to be. If you'd told the Alina of months ago that I'd be not only confident, but excited, about this event…it's like I'm a different woman. I've become someone else since I married Derick.

I spent the morning at the venue going over the last minute details and making sure that everything was set. When Casey and Melinda arrived to take over, that was my cue to head to my hair appointment and then back to the house to get dressed. I banished Derick to a downstairs bedroom to get himself ready so that I could surprise him with my dress and the finished look.

I've been saving the blue dress. Lauren agreed that it was perfect for the theme and looked great on me. I was even happier because I'd convinced her to come tonight and enjoy a fancy date with her husband. There are plenty of seats left at the Clayton table.

Melinda had informed me that they kept a few seats empty at our table regardless so that it was easier for people to come up and speak to Derick.

Despite my teasing and my urging, Jack had declined to bring a date tonight. Maybe I'd conspire to hook him up with Gloria. Life without Cat had been good to her - I almost liked her now, and she'd been an excellent member of the committee.

The stylist had done a great job with my hair - it was whimsical but practical. The front half was an intricate braid crown with light blue crystals stuck in the plaits, and then the rest of my hair was soft, large curls that flowed down to the middle of my back.

I did my makeup myself because I still liked to keep things minimal. My sisters are on video chat with me as I stand in front of the bathroom mirror and try to do wings with glittery blue eyeliner.

"It's like this," Aro has her face close to the screen and is demonstrating for me how she does it.

"That's the hard way!" Aster says and shoves her away. "Do it like this," and she draws three quick lines along her eyes, and then fills in the gap. It looks much easier than the careful line that Aro was drawing. I do what Aster said, and it looks pretty good. Now to do it evenly on the other eye. I take a deep breath and it comes off pretty good.

"Now use the mascara, but don't start at the root," Anora chimes in, "Build up the end of your lashes so they look longer." I take her advise and it's the last thing I need to do.

"You look like a fairy. Put on the dress!" Aro demands. I'd described it to them but they hadn't seen it yet. I toss the phone on the bed so they're staring at the ceiling as I step out of my robe and take the dress of its hanger.

I'm wearing pasties over my nipples because the dress is also backless, and that was a new and awkward experience. I step into the satiny blue material and pull the straps up over my shoulders. It sits perfectly on me, and I adjust the floor length skirt so that the slit is all the way to the side as it should be. It goes all the way up past my hip, but the layers in the skirt swirl more perfectly because of it, and every step shows a tantalizing flash of leg.

I pick up the phone and aim it at the full length mirror so they can see me. I'm not wearing my shoes yet but it still looks amazing.

"Holy shit."

I'm surprised it's Anora, since she never swears.

"That dress is amazing," Aro adds. When I look at the screen, Aster is nodding as well.

"I've never seen you wear anything like this. You're glowing," Anora smiles softly. "Fall yet?"

I snort, ruining the moment. "Absolutely not."

"Lies," Aro adds, handing the phone off to Anora. Her face fills up the screen.

"Why not? Why are you holding back?"

I look away from her and look at myself in the mirror. In the past, I'd thought of myself as a confident woman who took pleasure in her body. I've never been small - I'm tall, I'm broad, and I'm obviously muscled now in a way that gets me noticed. In this dress, I can see how defined my arms are and my flat stomach. I know that I don't look like the social ideal, especially not to be on the arm of someone like Derick. It's stupid, but I did compare myself to Cat - someone who had a tiny body and feminine style. Even though it's very clear Derick is physically attracted to me, and has no problem throwing me around like I weigh nothing, I still get self-conscious.

I wasn't as confident in myself as I thought I was. I also thought dressing more feminine was giving up a part of who I am. What I've learned is that I can be more than one thing. So what if on the weekdays and when I'm working I wear suits and hide my body? That doesn't mean I can't celebrate my body at fancy events like this. I can wear whatever I want and it doesn't change who I am - it's expressing a different part of myself. Before Derick, I would never have worn a dress like this because I would've believed that I couldn't pull it off.

That I would look like an awkward box trying to play curvy vixen.

That's not what I see when I look in the mirror. I see myself as powerful, curvy, strong, and even beautiful. I know that this dress is going to drive Derick insane. I know exactly how to push his buttons and he knows how to play all of mine. We have gotten closer on a lot of levels, and I can admit that I am content with the status of my marriage at the moment - but agreements like this aren't for love, they're for stability.

"Things are good as they are. I don't want to get hurt and become bitter - I don't want my pain to make what we could have irreparable."

Anora looks sad for me, and I don't want pity. There's nothing to pity.

"If all he wanted was the business, he would've married me, Lina. He wanted you."

"For now."

"Why are you so cynical about relationships? Where did this come from?"

I ignore her question and glance at the clock. "I have to go, I'll text you later."

She tries to stop me but I end the call, and grab my shoes. I walk quietly down the stairs, wanting to catch Derick off guard when I come down to see his reaction. As I turn to head down, I can see that he and Jack are waiting together in the foyer. Tension radiates from both of them and they are facing in opposite directions rather than interacting with each other.

They turn at the same time when they hear my soft barefoot steps, and both their jaws drop in matching expressions. Jack's cheeks turn pink as he closes his mouth, but my focus is all on Derick. After he gets a grip on his reaction, I can see his jaw flex as he walks to the bottom of the stairs to wait for me. I stop on the bottom step so that I'm a head above him and look down into his handsome face.

Out of habit, I run my finger over his disheveled left eyebrow. It's becoming a thing now. His eyes flutter shut for a second and then focus back on me, dark and intense.

"You look incredible."

"Thank you."

He takes my hand and tucks it into the crook of his arm as I step down. I'll put my shoes on in the car, already dreading wearing heels for the night. I smile at Jack as I walk by him, and he gives a half-hearted smile back.

Andrew is waiting with the door open as we step to the car, and I slide inside.

Derick moves close as soon as the door closes and slides his hand into the slit of my dress and wraps it around my thigh.

I press a finger to his lips and stop him when he leans in to kiss me. "This is your punishment, Mr. Clayton."

"For what, Mrs. Clayton?"

I get a shiver when he says that, his tone and the sentence rushing through my body and making my nipples hard.

"For making me such a dirty girl," I whisper against his mouth, leaning close. "We have this gorgeous party to go to and all I want is to stay at home and ride your cock. I'm already wet for you."

"Fuck, Allie," he groans, his eyes dilating and darkening even more.

"So tonight you get to watch me in this dress, knowing that you can't have me until we get home."

"Well I hope you get the most out of wearing it because I'm going to rip it off you."

We gaze into each other's eyes and I love how riled up he is. "Good."

Then I look away from him and out the window, trying to hide the ridiculous grin on my face. Derick shifts so that his arm is around my shoulder and pulls me close to him. I don't mind because it's a little chilly in the car and he keeps me warm. We don't say anything as we drive into the city, sitting in the comfortable silence of people who don't need to fill it.

I think about what Anora said about falling - and what made me cynical. It wasn't anything in particular. Our parents were obviously in love with each other but maybe that's what did it. I know the devastation my father experienced after mom died and maybe I'm afraid to ever let myself be put in the same position. Love only hurts you in the end, even if it's not on purpose. Letting myself fall for Derick means that my feelings for him are bigger than my fear that he will hurt me.

I'm not there yet, but when I think about ever turning away from him, it makes me think that someday I will be. Sooner than I'm ready for.

34

Derick

The little minx I'm married to is driving me the best kind of wild tonight. As the car slides to a stop in front of the warehouse, I adjust my half hard cock so it doesn't get it's own story in the society pages. I step out of the SUV and hold out my hand for her. The cameras start flashing immediately, and she smiles softly and tentatively, uncomfortable with the attention.

The dress makes her skin glow, and even in the bright lights of the camera flashes, she's still the brightest thing that I see. We make our way into the warehouse and I stop, stunned.

Alina had described to me what they were doing for the decorations and the size and scale of what the artist did, but I had grossly underestimated what she was talking about. It was like we'd walked in from the humid night and into the sky. Giant cloud structures all around us and smaller clouds around the tables, as well as a star-painted sky above us.

People are already mingling with drinks from the bar set up along one wall. The crowd is younger than I'm used to, and that's impressive. It's harder to get the younger wealth to donate money and not just spend it.

We're immediately pulled into conversations and I make sure that every time someone mentions the decor of the event that Alina gets credit for taking things in a different direction. Ever humble, she credits the rest of the committee and the artist, but I can see the faint blush on her cheeks every time I compliment her. This is all new to Alina - my beautiful warrior - and she's fucking crushed it. No matter what, this event is successful, but she's helped elevate it to something else and I hope she's proud of herself. I'm proud of her.

Carla and Anita descend on us, wearing the same dress in opposite colors - Carla's dress is pink with black details and Anita's dress is black with pink details. They do this every year, and I have to admit it's kind of cute.

They each kiss both my cheeks before surrounding Alina.

"This dress is gorgeous, my dear," Anita runs her hand over Alina's hair, reassuring her in a motherly way.

"It's not too much?"

"Definitely not," Carla answers. "You fit right in. This was good work - I can't wait to see what you and the young ones come up with next year."

Anita sneaks over to me as Carla and Alina discuss the artist and if they think he'll show up with Joanna as his date tonight. It would be a bit of a scandal, but what's a gala without a little drama?

"You landed yourself a good one, Derick. Don't fuck it up."

"No, ma'am," I agree with her. "I don't plan on it."

Anita smiles at me and then pulls Carla away.

We get swept up in conversation after conversation, people complimenting the party, congratulating us on our marriage without questioning how quickly and randomly it occurred because this kind of thing happens in the world of wealth. Many of them make a point of promising hefty donations that will keep the work of the foundation going without any funds needing to be stretched or finessed.

Melinda comes rushing to us both, Casey on her heels, big grins on both their faces. "We just smashed our record for donations. We'd already made most of the budget for the year for the cost of a plate, but the extra money has been rolling in non-stop."

"Congratulations," Alina says to them both. "Maybe now you'll take a vacation after this is over."

"That's what I said," Casey adds, smiling at Alina. I'm surprised again because Casey doesn't like most people outside of Melinda, and isn't one to smile because it's the polite thing to do. She has active bitch face the majority of the time, but appears to genuinely like Alina. I shouldn't be surprised. Her mix of strength and vulnerability appeals to people. They want to protect her - and she doesn't even realize it.

Before dinner starts, Alina pulls me toward one of the giant cloud installations. It's got a blue and gray tint, and lights inside flicker through it as if it's a thunderhead full of lightning.

"I have to show you something," she gives me a coy look and I follow her. Alina takes my hand in hers and I jolt. It's a simple gesture but one that she never does. It's something couples do, and she's always careful to draw lines around things like that. Looking over her shoulder, she checks that no one is watching and leads me to the back of the cloud.

There's an opening.

You wouldn't see it if you didn't know to look for it, or weren't curious enough to go around the entire cloud itself. Alina pulls me into the little cave with a bench set up inside. It's truly like being inside a storm cloud - there are blue string lights set up across the space, and the lightning flickers can be seen from the inside as well.

"Isn't this incredible?" she smiles and turns in a circle.

I can't not touch her right now. I pull her close, my arms wrapped possessively around her waist, one hand resting on her ass.

"You're incredible."

Her eyes soften, and close as I lean in to kiss her. She tastes so good, fresh and sweet at the same time. I slide my tongue into her compliant mouth, taunting and teasing until she's moaning and going soft in my arms.

"I can't wait until this is over," I say against her mouth, then kiss along her jaw and down her neck. "I need you right now." We maneuver until the backs of her legs bump the bench, and she sits down.

"Take me," she whispers in the quiet.

I get on my knees and peel her dress open at the slit, and she lets her legs fall open, exposing herself to me.

She's bare.

"Fuck," I grunt. "You've been like this all night and didn't tell me?"

She smirks. "The slit is so high, I couldn't wear anything."

"*Lleidr bach*, you are going to kill me one day."

Alina laughs but it stutters into a gasp when I dart forward and lick her soft, smooth pussy. She leans back and puts one hand on the bench to brace herself as the other dives into my hair to hold me to her. I tease her clit with a few firm swirls of my tongue and she whimpers.

"Please, Brody. Please." She uses my nickname, and as always it makes me feral for her.

"Please what?" I tease her by sliding a finger along her slit, but not with enough pressure to provide any satisfaction. "Please fuck you with my tongue? Please let you ride my face?"

"Yes," she moans and her hips roll.

"I want to taste your come every time I lick my lips during dinner tonight." Then I dive in and eat her in earnest, licking and sucking at her clit as I slide two fingers inside her tight, wet heat. Alina grips my hair so hard it hurts but I like it, and she thrusts her hips against my face, chasing her orgasm as I devour her.

"Brody," she gasps, and I love hearing her say it again. I love hearing her say the name I only gave her, that belongs to her, just like I do. "I'm coming." Her whole body tightens and her calves wrap around my shoulders to hold herself up because she needs her hand to cover her mouth as she orgasms. I can still hear her moans and cries, muffled as they are, and it nearly makes me come in my pants. I've never been so turned on from eating pussy the way I am with Alina's.

As she comes down and puts her feet on the ground, she pulls me up by the lapels of my jacket and kisses me, the taste of her mouth and her pussy mingling as our tongues clash.

"I want to suck your cock."

"Right now?" I look down at her as I stand, and she's mussed and eager. Her hands make quick work of my belt, buttons, and zipper, freeing me easily. I'm already hard, and it won't take much for her to make me explode.

"Come in my mouth, Derick." Then she sucks on the head before sliding down until I'm nearly in the back of her throat. She slides back and forth along my length, hollowing her cheeks. It's not fast, but it's hard, and I can already feel my balls pulling up to let go.

"It's coming, baby." My voice is gruff and I look down to watch as her pretty pink lips wrapped around me. On their own, my hips pump into her mouth and I swear quietly as I start to come. When her eyes close when I press deep into her, I can't hold it back anymore.

"Allie, fuck," I grunt as she holds me deep and I shoot down her throat. For a few moments, everything goes bright white and all I feel is the way she swallows me down, over and over. When I'm done, she keeps sucking, moving her mouth softly up and down, cleaning off my cock with her tongue.

I barely have myself put away when a throat clears behind us. Alina looks around my body and frowns, and I turn to see Cat standing at the entrance with her arms crossed.

"If you're finished," she talks in that high breathy voice that always annoyed me. It's not her real voice and everyone knows it but pretends like they don't.

Turning my back on her, I help Alina up and make sure she's covered, and hold her close to me as we head to leave.

"It's all yours," Alina says to her with a soft but fake smile. Cat doesn't smile back, just glowers, and then looks at me.

She puts her hand on my arm to stop us, and Alina stiffens in my arms.

Cat looks at me as if we have something shared between us besides bodily fluids, her eyes big and wet.

"Can we talk?" She's really laying it on thick, her voice heavy as if she's about to cry.

"We have nothing to talk about, Cat. Enjoy your evening, thank you for coming." I slide my arm out from under her grip, and walk off with the only woman I need in my arms. We step back out into the party and the air is much cooler than inside the cloud. I lead her toward our table near the stage without looking back.

"You can talk to her, I'm okay," Alina barely moves her lips as she talks, not wanting anyone to hear.

"I don't need to talk to her. There's nothing she needs to say to me, or that I need to hear."

"I'm just saying, you have the freedom to talk to who you want to." There's the words that she's saying, but then there's what she really means underneath them. It makes me angry, but now isn't the time and I can't blame her for feeling the way that she does. I haven't exactly declared how I feel about her with words, hoping that my actions will speak for themselves until she's ready to trust me when we talk about our feelings.

It would be easy for me to tell Alina that I love her, that I want to be married to her, and that I want to work the rest of our lives for there to be only her and us and what we make together. I feel those things freely, easily, and without fear.

If I said that to Alina, she'd freeze. She'd panic, and would try to argue with me to downplay my feelings, doubting their verity. Alina isn't ready to be loved by me, and that's okay. However, I still need to make sure she knows I want no one else.

I pull her aside and turn her to face me. I catch her chin with my hand so she can't look away.

"I don't need freedom," I press a chaste, publicly acceptable kiss to her soft mouth. "Chain me, baby, you have my consent."

She laughs. "Maybe another night," and surprises me by leaning in and kissing me. Even though she was the one who had to choose when we could start kissing again, she rarely, if ever, initiates them. It's always me giving and taking from her, and she lets me. She never asks for anything from me and that's got to change.

We resume our walk to our table.

Lauren and her husband, Arthur, are already sitting at the table and talking to Jack. Jack looks more relaxed than he did before we left, and at least I know he won't be hostile while there are other people at the table.

He's so angry with me he's past arguing. Jack is firmly in the camp that we should dump everything as fast as possible. No more clubs, no more stores, no more money laundering. It's not that simple though. Not just the actual sales and control, but I want to make sure that our people are going to be taken care of when we step away. Or at least give them enough warning to go elsewhere if they don't want to work for someone else. I'm not cutting ties like it doesn't mean anything and the people who work for us and keep our secrets don't matter.

I've told him that he doesn't have to do any work if he doesn't want to - lord knows we have the money for him to be an insouciant playboy if he wants that, but that only made him more pissed off. There are other people who can do his work - I'd need multiple people to cover all the things that he does - so if he's unhappy, he can step away. I'll sell off what we have until we're clean, but the timing matters so we don't look suspicious as hell either. His impulses and impatience stop him from seeing the whole picture.

As we sit down, Lauren turns to Alina and they start whispering to each other, smiling and laughing. The only person Alina texts more than Lauren is her sisters. They're close enough that when the danger passes, I might even break my cardinal rule and have Lauren and her family out to the house for dinner.

Jack ignores me, and I don't push it. Now isn't the time.

35

Alina

The night is going off without a hitch. The food is delicious, the tension between Jack and Derick is only noticed by me, and we're getting as many donations as we are compliments. Melinda starts off the speeches, sharing information about the foundation's work supporting single parents and the goals they have to increase services and access. She gets polite applause.

After her, it's Derick's turn to speak, and then the night will turn into more socializing and dancing. He walks up on stage, face relaxed but unsmiling. It surprises me that he doesn't like public speaking.

"Thank you all again for coming tonight - my lovely wife kept me away so I was as surprised as all of you when I walked into this amazing setup." He smiles slightly and looks over at me before continuing. "I started this foundation to help people who didn't have anyone to lean on or help them shoulder the weight. I'm lucky that I have my brother, and now my wife, to stand by me. We are doing incredible work with your gifts, and I hope that it continues for years to come. Before I step away, please give a round of applause for our amazing committee." Derick holds out his hand and I see all of us stand to be acknowledged. I see Gloria on the other side of the room and her usually scowling mother has a small smile on her face. We sit back down, and I adjust my dress.

When I look up, Jack is watching me, a frown on his face.

Derick steps off the stage and sits back down beside me, pressing a brief kiss to my temple before whispering in my ear, "How much longer until we can get out of here?"

"At least an hour." I reach over and squeeze high on his thigh and enjoy watching him squirm.

"Then we might as well dance."

We do.

Derick is possessive and even though it would be polite, he doesn't let me dance with anyone else. We sway side by side and talk to people, making the small talk that we're supposed to and expressing endless amounts of gratitude, but the whole time his arm is banded around my waist and he holds my right hand gently in his as we move around.

I see Joanna dancing with Michael, and they both look happy and dreamy. I hope it works out for her - she thinks he's brilliant but life with an artist will always be a challenge. If they're still together next year maybe we'll give him another shot at creating an interactive dinner like this.

My heart soars as I look around the room. People dressed in gorgeous clothes are dancing in the clouds, and we made a shitton of money for people who really need it.

There's something off, though.

I keep looking around, keeping my face pleasant and neutral as I try and figure out what's bothering me. No one looks out of place, everything is where it should be...

When I look toward the entrance, that's when I realize what's off. Security isn't where they should be. They were there when we arrived, but right now there's no one at the door. Even though it's unlikely we'll get late arrivals who need to be checked in, that door and the two exits were supposed to be manned at all times.

We've stopped moving. Derick must have felt me change with awareness.

"What's wrong?"

"Security isn't at the front door." Before Derick can ask for a further explanation, I walk off the dance floor to check the other exits. No one is there. We had arranged for a 10 man team to protect this event and the six of them that should be inside the building are nowhere to be seen.

I feel Derick come up behind me. "All of the security staff are gone. Something is going on."

"Let's go find out." He puts his hand on the small of my back, not pushing but quietly reassuring. We walk to the front of the building, looking relaxed to the untrained eye as we head toward the door.

When we walk outside, one of the security staff is there and puts his hand up to stop us. His eyes widen when he recognizes who we are.

"It's best if you go back inside right now Mr. and Mrs. Clayton."

"I think it's best you tell us what's going on," I step in front of Derick and take charge of the conversation. They were hired by me, and they answer to me.

"Ma'am, it's - we - " he stutters. At that moment, Roe and Andrew come over from where our cars are, noticing that there's an issue. I almost laugh when Roe slides a small knife into my hand. As soon as I feel the grip settle into my palm I feel safer.

"What's going on?" Andrew asks. I'm annoyed when the guard answers him while he tried not to answer me.

"Someone approached the back of the building - they set off a smoke bomb. Staff confronted them but we haven't been able to find them. They've likely left the area."

"Why didn't anyone alert us?" I snap. This is ridiculous.

"They didn't get into the building, we thought discretion would be best."

"Well discretion is about to get your ass chewed out," I snarl, and Derick puts a hand on my hip to pull me back to him and calm me down. "We hired you to help, not make decisions for us. I should've been alerted."

"Keep everyone inside for now, and get your supervisor," Derick advises. We step to the side as another guard comes over to take the first one's place, and the first one steps away talking into a walkie.

"What the hell is going on?" I look around, unconsciously putting Derick between myself and the building, moving to protect him. My eyes are watching the dark shadows around the warehouse, and I'm suddenly regretting this location.

A taller, older man in a dark suit approaches us. When he comes into the light I recognize him as the team leader, George, and he gives an update on the situation.

"Whoever they were, they left. We searched the perimeter, no one got inside, and there's no sign of anyone. I think you can return to your party."

"Figure out what happened here and I expect a call," I direct him. "We were just leaving."

George walks away and I tamp down my annoyance, focusing instead on the feeling that something is still wrong. All of my senses are keyed up and my skin is crawling. The smoke bomb was a distraction. A good assassin is a lot like a magician - they use misdirection to pull all your focus on something irrelevant so they can hit you before you notice the actual trick.

Roe and I share a look, and he dips around the side of the building to take a look for himself. Derick and Andrew are talking in low voices, and Andrew is typing on his phone. Probably arranging for our own staff to come and back us up. We gave them the night off because there was going to be security at the party - security who were extremely well recommended. They won't be getting that same recommendation from me.

Then again, maybe this is my fault. I thought that controlling the flow of people at a hotel in the city would be more difficult, but the isolation of this location might be more dangerous than I thought. At least the event inside isn't being interrupted.

"Let's go." Derick holds out his hand and I take it, and we start moving toward the SUV, with Andrew behind us keeping a lookout.

As we get closer, a dark shape moves out from between the two vehicles. It's a shapeless person in black with a hood pulled low over their face and black gloves on their hands.

Everything then happens in slow motion, and my body reacts so quickly that my brain doesn't catch up until it's already over.

They raise their arm, aimed straight at Derick. I move to push him down and away, and throw the knife that's in my hand at what I can approximate is the shooter's chest. I don't hit center mass but I think I hurt him, still focusing on making sure nothing happens to Derick.

Derick hits the ground as the gun fires. Something, or someone, rams into me and I'm heading toward the pavement. But they're too late. The bullet rips through my shoulder and the burn of it goes across my chest and down my arm. I can't stop myself from screaming out, unable to contain my instant reaction to the pain.

36

Alina

More shots fire but I can't see anything. Roe is holding me down to the ground, shielding me from the chaos over my head. I'm feeling around with my uninjured arm trying to find Derick, calling his name, terrified that he's hurt and I failed him.

"Alina!" he shouts and moves over to me, shoving Roe away and pulling me close. "Fuck, you're bleeding." He puts his body around mine and I immediately feel anxiety because I should be protecting him. I might be hurt but he's the one they're after. I push at him and hook my leg around his, turning us over. Blood soaks my dress and his suit, and grit from the damp pavement sticks to my skin.

Roe pulls at us both. "We need to get in the car, now."

We move quickly - Derick stands and helps me up, but it doesn't stop another burst of pain radiating up and down my arm. I can feel the blood dripping across the back of my hand, and a warm wet spot over my rib cage where it's stained my dress. Well, it did get ruined, just not in the way that I wanted.

Derick and I get into the back and Roe drives, getting us away from the warehouse. He's on the phone, taking care of the situation because that's what we've trained them to do. Derick is in danger, so they handle it.

"What about Jack?" Derick's voice is furious but controlled.

"Andrew is getting him." Roe says over his shoulder. "We're going back to the house. Elliott is awake to take care of Mrs. Clayton's arm."

Instead of focusing on the pain, I'm focusing on my breathing. Big deep breaths through my nose, and slow and measured out through my mouth. It doesn't help, but it keeps my head clear. Being stabbed really fucking hurt, but I'd passed out from the pain pretty quickly. This is keeping me wide awake. I take that moment to look at where the bullet hit me. It's a wound in my deltoid, a bloody, meaty circle that goes all the way through. I know they say a through and through is better, but the idea that there's a hole in my arm makes me want to vomit. It's oozing thick blood, and I look away.

Keep breathing. Do not puke, do not show weakness.

Derick is moving, taking off his jacket and unbuttoning his dress shirt. He has a plain white shirt on underneath, and then he takes that off too. I'm about to ask him what he's doing when he rips it, and starts wrapping strips around my arm. We're quite the pair right now - me in a shiny bloody dress, and Derick shirtless in his dress pants.

His hands are shaking as he covers the wound, and I reach over to put my hand on his.

The party ended for us in chaos, and I hope that the guests have no idea what just went down outside of it. I hope they are ignorantly having their drinks and dancing, and assume that Derick and I snuck off. There's no reason to upset anyone because at the end of the day this was specifically about Derick. They were aiming for Derick.

"Are you okay? Are you hurt?"

"I'm fine," he says through clenched teeth.

"That's all that matters." I squeeze his hand.

"No, it's not." The fury in his voice burns me.

"What are you talking about?"

He grabs my chin and turns my face, fire in his eyes. "You took a bullet for me, *lleidr bach.*"

I'm still confused. "Of course. I did what I'm supposed to do."

"No," he snarls, and I flinch because I've never had his anger directed at me - not this kind of anger, and not like this. "You are not my bodyguard. You are my wife. When the bullets fly you don't worry about anyone but you."

"Derick." My voice is uncertain and shaky and I hate it. "No. You could've been hurt."

"Then I'm hurt. If anything had happened to you..." His eyes drop and the breath he takes is tight and stuttering. "If anything had happened to you because you were protecting me, I could never forgive myself."

"It's instinct for me," I argue, but keep my voice soft. "I didn't think about it, I did it, because that's who I trained to be. I'm the person who steps in front of the gun."

"Not for me." He takes my face in both his hands, holding me like I'm the most precious thing in the world and it does something to me. My stomach drops, my breathing becomes shallow, and I am utterly lost in his gaze. There's so much emotion in his eyes as he looks at me, and I'm afraid of what those emotions are. Afraid of what they mean for both of us.

"We vowed to protect each other," I remind him, but it's hollow. Hard as it might be, and even if it goes against my instincts, I will do anything this man asks of me.

"Not like this, Alina."

Derick drops his forehead to mine, and after a few moments our breathing syncs and slows, relaxing us both.

"I would rather die than you be hurt," Derick whispers, and a shudder that's nearly a sob leaves me. "That's how you protect me - by protecting yourself."

"Okay." It's all I can think to say because anything else that comes out of my mouth right now will only come back to hurt me later. I can't tell him that losing him would rip my heart out of my chest. I can't promise him that I'd never step in front of a bullet for him again, or do whatever I could to keep him safe. I can't make a promise that I won't keep because I'm at a point now where I can't imagine a world without Derick in it.

I'm still holding myself back from falling, but all it would take is the tiniest push.

I press forward and kiss him, scared and desperate, and wanting him to stop talking before he presses anything further. He pulls me into his lap, careful of my injured arm, and we get lost in each other until the car turns into the driveway for the house.

Instead of letting me get out, Derick carries me in his arms. He hasn't done that since he dragged me to the guest house after our wedding, but my feelings are so different now than they were then. If things had gone differently and I'd been seriously injured tonight, I wouldn't have any regrets.

Elliott is at the dining room table, instruments, gauze, and other things laid out on the table next to him. Growing up the way I did I'm familiar with the belief that we don't go to the hospital. We will work very hard to make sure no one knows what happened at the gala, and that means no one can know that I got shot.

Derick puts me in the chair across from Elliott, then kneels down next to me and holds my hand. We don't talk. No one talks. The tension is so high and the stress level is so thick we could be swimming in it.

I hiss when he cleans the wound, and squeeze Derick's hand tight.

"Talk to me," I beg him. "I don't care about what, just talk."

He nods, and thinks for a moment. "We didn't meet my grandparents, my mother's parents, until I was 6. Eifa had been with us since the day we were born, so we grew up speaking Welsh alongside English, and it was natural. It was also nice because our father didn't know it and it felt like we were communicating in code, keeping secrets from him. Not that he was around much." Derick's fingers trace patterns on the back of my hand, and it's the perfect distraction as Elliott prepares to do the first set of stitches.

"They'd come to see my mother, and we were temporarily banished until it was time to meet them. Things had been strained - that's a story for another time - and she was trying to keep distance between all of us. Of course, I eavesdropped and heard Gran complaining about how we were removed from our culture and our family, and it didn't matter who mother was married to, we had to know where we came from." He laughs at the memory of what comes next.

"Jack, small but fierce, immediately charges into the room, speaking perfect Welsh, and trying to defend our mother. It's a very aggressive language when spoken in anger. She was horrified, but it was the best thing that could have happened. It was the first thing that mended fences between them because it showed my grandparents that she hadn't forgotten where she came from. Even though it was Eifa who taught us mostly, our mother primarily spoke to us in Welsh as well. They were part of our lives until they died, then, and I think things would've been very different for Jack and I without them."

"He's told me some things…about your family."

Derick sighs and presses a kiss to my hand. Warmth spreads throughout my body but that could also be the medication Elliott is putting into me. He's started on the other set of stitches. The exit wound is uglier and bigger, he's messing around with it and I'm glad that I can't see and can't feel it. I know he's doing something but I can't feel it. My head is getting a little light at the thought.

"There are things that have been kept from Jack. He's my little brother…"

I squeeze his hand. "I understand. I've done the same."

"I'm going to give you something more long term for the pain now - it'll knock you out and help you sleep," Elliott interrupts us. "No training until I say so.

It takes all my control not to roll my eyes. There's lots of training I can do that won't bother my arm, I don't have to stop.

I feel the prick of the needle in my arm again, and the cool flood of the medication racing through my veins. Derick scoops me up again and carries me up the stairs. I think about protesting but my head is already feeling light and woozy. Plus, after all that happened tonight it's comforting to be this close to Derick. My heart races every time I think about what might have happened if I hadn't pushed him down.

My arm is a small price to pay for him being alive and unharmed.

When we get upstairs, he sets me gently on the bed and then unzips my dress. I'm a little embarrassed by the pasties and quickly rip them off and throw them on my bedside table. I'm completely naked, bloody and disheveled.

"Not the way I thought tonight would end," my voice is slurry and sleepy.

"Me neither." Derick kisses my shoulder and then maneuvers me so he can slide me under the covers. When he seems to feel that I am adequately tucked in, he kisses my forehead and lingers there for a long time.

"Never again, *lleidr bach*. Not ever. The sight of you bleeding in my arms will never be repeated."

The world is fading around me and getting fuzzy, but I manage to slur out: "Will you tell me what it means?"

The world is narrowing to a pinpoint and all I can see is his face as he looks down on me, with so much emotion in his expression that it puts a lump in my throat. How can he feel so much? How can he feel it for me?

"It means little thief."

My brain takes a long time to process that, getting slushier by the moment. "What did I steal?" I ask, and then giggle.

I don't think he's going to answer, and my eyes close. Just as I'm starting to drift off he answers me, and I don't think he knows I'm still conscious.

"My heart."

37

Derick

Alina sleeps and I sit with her. My phone has been buzzing with alerts and updates about the incident at the gala, as well as from our own staff about what actions we are taking. Jack decided to stay and smooth the ruffled feathers of the donors so they wouldn't suspect anything, and he stayed until the last guest left. No one knows a single bullet was fired.

The new perimeter sensors we had installed send another alert to my phone and I check the cameras - Jack is home. I kiss Alina on the temple and linger for a moment as the fear consumes me again. She was hurt because of me.

It's not that I was ignorant of the danger being with me put her in, or the fact that she had trained her whole life to protect others, but I honestly never believed we'd be in a situation like this. There was also the fact that I never even considered she would act to protect me rather than to protect herself.

She trained to protect her father and her sisters - they're her family, she loves them. Alina wasn't someone who dreamed of being a bodyguard and trained accordingly, it had been for a very specific and love-driven purpose. I was fairly certain Alina didn't love me, or if she did she wasn't consciously aware of it, but her first action when danger presented itself was to protect me.

It made my heart wrench in a hundred different directions. Awe that she would do that, hope that maybe she felt the same, and as always pride at who she was and that I was the one that got to have such a magnificent woman. I felt humbled that I got to love her.

But I also felt scared, angry, and irritated. She should know better than to ever risk herself for me - the near reality of losing her ate through my gut and I wanted to wake her up and shake her, making sure she truly believed me when I'd told her in the car that she needed to protect herself over me. Sure, Alina said the words, but that doesn't mean she believed them. I felt insane with the fear of something happening to her.

I brush my lips over her injured shoulder, vowing to myself that whoever did this would die by our hands. Hers or mine, it didn't matter, as long as they were punished.

As I make my way downstairs, I wish I'd taken a minute to change my clothes. I'm still in my bloodstained dress shirt, unbuttoned and destroyed. I have no idea what happened to my coat and don't really care. Alina's blood stains me and I hate knowing that.

I follow the sound of voices into the kitchen. Eifa is at the counter making food and coffee is brewing. Not a bad idea, since we'd likely be up all night hashing this out.

At the table in the kitchen are Andrew, Roe, Elliott, Saul, and Kade. Jack paces back and forth across the tiled space, his dress shoes clicking briskly, making his frustration audible. When he sees me he charges across the kitchen - his hair is a mess and his face is pale.

"Where is Lina?"

Jealousy rears for a second that he called her that - even if the rational part of my mind knows their close relationship is a good thing, I am not in a rational state of mind right now.

"Upstairs, resting. Elliott took care of her injuries, she's sleeping."

He nods and runs his hands through his hair, taking a few deep breaths. "What the fuck happened?"

For the answer to that question, I turn to the people who were there and who stayed behind to get answers. Kade and Andrew share a look. Kade wasn't even there but he's who gets called when shit goes down. I also know that he probably arrived at the warehouse shortly after we left to look into things.

"Whoever it was, Alina hurt them - her knife was on the ground with blood on it, so I'll be having it tested and see if we get a match. Otherwise, we…don't know anything. There were no threats made, no attempt to disrupt the party or cause a scene, it was simple and low key and that makes it more dangerous. It wasn't about attention, it was about getting to you." Kade looks frustrated. He rarely finds a problem he can't solve and this must really rankle. I'm disappointed we don't know more.

"Why escalate like this? We're getting out. That is a known thing at this point. What could someone gain by taking me out right now? Chaos wouldn't help."

"It might," Roe says. "Either because there'll be a change in leadership," he nods toward Jack, "or everything will be so vulnerable they can snatch it or burn it."

"There isn't a way to extricate ourselves faster that won't bring us attention from the cops and feds. This seems so…" I search for a word.

"Sloppy." Kade finishes for me.

"Yes. Like throwing darts blindfolded and hoping enough points land."

"So what do we do?" Jack sounds like he's barely got a rein on his anger, and it's another reason why I can't trust him. His emotions rule him too often and it's going to keep getting us into bigger and bigger messes.

"Keep going as we have been - selling off the businesses and making it all look as legitimate as possible. I've initiated some contracts, but we're looking at 6 weeks."

"That fucking ridiculous!" Jack explodes, and swipes at a glass on the counter and it smashes on the floor. "You know the cartel would take everything off your hands in a week at the most. You'd be out."

"And the city would be flooded with even more fucking drugs - there's more to consider than just us, Jack."

He doesn't notice that everyone but Kade quietly leaves the room, even Eifa. She gives me a soft, sad look before heading down the stairs to the staff area. We've had a lot of conversations where she's on Jack's side of things, encouraging me to let him do more, and to hear his voice on matters, but honestly he acts so ridiculous that I struggle.

"More to consider than Alina?" Jack gets in my face and the rage rushes through me. I have never been angry with my brother, but this is a low fucking blow.

"What about Alina?"

"She got hurt because of you and your thinking. I know she's a business arrangement that you're fucking but it's not fair to her."

I see red. Before I can calculate a response I'm grabbing his throat and shoving him against the counter, bending his body until he's pressed against the marble.

"Don't speak about her like that." I let him go and step back, shaken at my violent reaction. Jack holds his throat and glares at me as he takes a few ragged breaths.

"She deserves more than this." He growls at me.

"More than what Jack? Tell me what she deserves."

"She deserves to be loved! Not sold off in marriage for a fucking business merger like it's the middle fucking ages."

I get up in his face, looking down at someone who feels like a stranger. "Do you remember how I met her? That I was supposed to marry someone else and nearly blew the deal because I had to have her?"

Jack looks shamed, and can't keep eye contact with me.

"She is loved. I love her. I think I loved her from the first moment I saw her. I want to burn down this whole goddamn city to find out who did this and who hurt her, but she wouldn't want that."

"You're right," Jack gulps and nods, stepping back from me and deescalating the tension between us. "I'm sorry. We've gotten close and I feel like it's our fault she's hurt."

"It is our fault." I sigh, forgiving him. I put my hand on his shoulder and squeeze, showing him that I need him. "We did this."

"Let's figure out how to fix it." Jack steps back from me and leaves the room. When I look over at Kade, he's watching Jack with a strange expression on his face that I can't interpret. It's gone when he looks over at me.

"What now?" I ask, at a loss and still reeling from tonight. It's not my first attach, I've been in fights, and I've killed before, but the enemy coming at me those times wasn't unknown or anonymous. I knew who I was fighting so I had a strategy to fight them. The unknown of all of this, and that Alina got put in the middle of it, makes it hard for me to pull back and focus the way that I should. It's why I'm going to lean on Kade now and trust his judgment because he's going to be able to be rational where I can't.

"Jack is right we should step out of some things faster, to show you're serious about leaving it behind. But there are some places we need to be careful. Let me make some calls and start looking into things. For now, go to bed, get some fucking rest, and take care of your wife."

Kade stands up from the table and I stop him before he can head to the front door. "I don't say this enough, but thank you."

"I mean, you do pay me," he elbows me in the side.

"Yeah, but regardless. You're as much my brother as Jack."

217

Kade looks surprised, but nods. "Does that mean I'm going to get a nickname from Eifa?"

"You already have one - you're her *cariad*."

He frowns, waiting for me to tell him what it means.

"Sweetheart. Her love."

I'm shocked when Kade blushes, and nods. "I'll call you when I have something."

After he leaves, I check the security and make sure that the doors are locked and the alarms are armed. When I go upstairs, I crave to hold Alina in my arms but don't want to hurt her as she heals from her wound.

The medication has knocked her out, and she snores lightly. Her hair is still braided and up in the front like she had it for the gala, and there's still makeup on her face. First thing when she wakes up I'll take a shower with her, get her cleaned up and relaxed so that she can sleep and recover more. Elliott was going to pick up some pills so he didn't have to give her shots to help with the pain for another day or two.

I've already emailed Jonah to cancel everything for the week, citing a family emergency. He'll bug the hell out of me to know what that really means, and to try and convince me to come to at least a few meetings, but nothing is more important than this. I've been letting other people do the work, when it needs to be me. Even though I trust them, I have to do this myself.

38

Alina

I come back to the world slowly, as if coming up from underwater.

My phone buzzing is what woke me up.

The first thing I notice is that my body is stiff, like I've slept for too long in the same position. Then comes the pain, and I'm pulled back to full consciousness with blinding clarity. I sit up quickly, and then regret it because my head pounds. My arm is bandaged, and hasn't bled through, which is a good sign. I touch the skin around it and it's normal temperature and color, so no signs of infection.

The bed next to me is rumpled and cool, so if Derick did sleep with me last night he's already been awake for awhile. It's still early, not even 7 yet, and I doubt he got more than a few hours. We attempted to leave the gala shortly after 11, so I'd guess we got home around midnight. Paying attention to the time after getting shot hadn't been high on my list of priorities.

I turn my body so I can grab my phone. The message is from an unknown number and my stomach fills with dread.

See what happens when you stand at his side?

There's a photo attached - it's from last night. I'm on the ground just after Roe tackled me, and my bloody wound is obvious. Whoever is sending me these messages was there last night, and wasn't the shooter. I feel like throwing up, but I need to get it together and tell Derick and Kade.

I throw back the blankets and the gust of cold air reminds me that I'm nude. I almost never sleep naked - it makes me feel too vulnerable and unprepared - but it was probably the best option last night. When I stand up I wobble a bit, probably after effects of the pain meds, but make my way to my bathrobe. It seems like the easiest thing to get on right now that doesn't involve moving my arm much. The more I move, the less it hurts, and that's a good sign too.

I wrap myself up and slide on my slippers, and then quietly make my way downstairs. I hold on tight to the railing, feeling unsteady inside even though my steps are sure. The further down I go, the louder the voices get.

Even before I can make out the words, I know from the voices themselves that it's Jack and Derick fighting. Maybe they're finally having the knock down drag out that will clear the air for them, spurred on by the attempt on Derick's life last night.

Then I hear my name, and think it's probably not the case.

"Send Alina away?!" Derick yells. "What the fuck for?"

"You can't protect her. We can't protect her," Jack shouts back.

I'm sure they think I'm still passed out from the drugs and that they don't need to worry about the volume of their voices. There's no way in hell they'd be stupid enough to have a conversation like this about me where I could hear it. I decide to eavesdrop for a little longer before interrupting this testosterone display.

"I can protect her, and she can protect herself," Derick snarls back, and I am immediately filled with a flutter of emotion. I don't want to name it. It's scary as fuck to name it, but his defense of me feels good. It feels like he knows me.

"That's not good enough. This isn't her fight."

"She's my fucking wife, of course it's her fight. Everything I have is hers." Who knew eavesdropping could reveal so much? My heart is squeezing in my chest and I want to burst into the kitchen and kiss the shit out of Derick right now.

"Stop thinking with your heart and your dick," Jack hisses. "If you really loved her, you'd have her leave so you could focus."

There's so much in that sentence that sends me for a loop. They want to send me away - because I'm a distraction for Derick...because Jack thinks Derick loves me.

"Have you ever been in love, Jack?"

There's silence, and I'm taking that as a no. I'm holding my breath, waiting to hear what's going to come out of Derick's mouth. While he talks about the future and has hinted at having feelings for me, he' s never spoken this openly and honestly to me. Not that I blame him since I've shut down or run every time he brushes against the topic. There's freedom in hearing it like this, when he's not speaking to me, that maybe the next time he tries, I'll be in a place that I can listen.

"I trust Alina, and I know her. There is no way in hell she'd walk away from this, and I would never ask her to; even though I want to put her in a fucking bubble and keep her safe, I'd never disrespect her that way. That woman doesn't even know that she walks around carrying my heart with her, and I love her so fucking much I don't even care because I would do anything she asked of me, even having her stay when everything in me screams for her to run."

I'm stunned, and awed, and embarrassed that my first response is to tear up and start crying. Jack wasn't assuming that Derick loved me, he knew, and it's clear that discussing Derick's feelings for me has been an ongoing conversation.

Derick thinks he's in love with me. That's not giving Derick much credit, but I don't think either of us have ever been in love before so it's hard not to throw some doubt in there. It's true that Derick knows me - I've been resisting acknowledging that he knows me on an emotional level, not only a physical one. He knows my mind, and even if he doesn't realize it, he knows my heart.

I might be in love with my husband, and that's scarier than facing a man with a gun.

That's scarier than getting shot because I can heal from a bullet wound.

If he breaks my heart, I will never recover.

I take a deep breath and wipe the tears from my face, schooling myself to interrupt this conversation before I hear more things that will shatter my sanity and the self-enforced ignorance I've been hiding behind when it comes to Derick's feelings.

"I still think we should send her to Chicago. She can be with her family while we take care of business."

"We aren't sending her anywhere," Derick responds. "We aren't making decisions for her."

"Damn right you're not," I step into the kitchen then, and almost laugh when both Derick and Jack pale because they know they've been caught. Kade's at the table drinking coffee and when he sees me and my expression, he smothers a laugh and looks back down at whatever he was reading on his phone.

"I'm not going anywhere. I can help you." I put my hands on my hips and that's a mistake because pain shoots down my left arm. "Fuck." I cradle my injured arm and curl in on myself to soothe away the pain. Jack and Derick both run for me, and even Kade stands up from the table. I step away from all of them and put up my good hand.

"Let's get you back upstairs," Derick comes forward and puts his hand on my back, rubbing up and down and I relax under his touch. I give both Jack and Kade a stern look, but follow Derick's lead. I'll tell him about the message later - this needs to be handled first.

I don't say anything until we're definitely out of their earshot and up onto the second floor.

"I don't want to go."

"I know. Jack is scared and angry." Derick and I get up the other flight of stairs, and enter our bedroom, but he doesn't stop touching me. "Do you want to take a shower?"

"Yeah." That sounds incredible.

Derick takes my face in his hands, holding me there as he looks at me. How could I not see in his eyes that he loves me? It's in every line of his expression - a warmth and softness, and that he sees me like I'm a treasure. I'm special. I've never been that to anyone. To be honest, I've never let anyone get close enough to me that wasn't my family to be something special to them.

Instead, I get myself in a situation where I'm pushed into a life I hadn't planned for only to find that it might be the best thing that ever happened to me. I'm standing here with a fucking bullet hole in my arm, and I wouldn't trade it for anything if it means I get to be standing here, cherished by this man.

Fuck, my heart is in so much trouble.

"Let me take care of you," Derick purrs, his breath ghosting across my lips.

I lean in and kiss him. "Okay." I agree, and I think it's the most vulnerable thing I've ever done in my life. Since my mom died, I've never let anyone take care of me. Not even Anora. It became vital, after that loss, to be the one taking care of myself as well as everybody else.

I trust Derick to take care of me, and if that doesn't tell me that I love him...

He sits me down on the end of the bed and goes into the bathroom. I'm confused when he comes back out with my hairbrush, but then he stands in front of me, towering over me, and starts pulling pins out of my hair. Each one kind of hurts, but the relief of my hair being released also feels really damn good. I moan when the braids fall down around my face, the pressure on my head releasing.

Derick's getting hard, and I know because his dick is right in front of my face. Gently, he undoes each braid until my hair is a loose mess. When he digs in and massages my scalp, I can't help how my body reacts. I break out in goosebumps, and a whimper that is way too sexual escapes me before I can stop it. It feels so incredibly good.

I hold on to Derick's thighs as he brushes my hair, undoing the worst of the tangles.

Then he steps away and I feel bereft. I hear him turn on the shower, then I watch with interest as he steps out of the bathroom and takes off his clothes. We rarely shower together, and I'm a little disappointed it's under these circumstances. His cock is hard, and I want to touch him and pleasure him, but I know that right now he won't let me. He needs to take care of me to heal himself as much as I need him to physically take care of me because I can't do all of this on my own.

He offers me his hand and I stand. I watch, mesmerized, as he undoes the belt on my robe. I gasp when his hands dive inside, and he runs them up and down my sides, tracing the curve from the side of my breasts, down my waist, and then over my hips. It feels so good to be touched right now, like I'm extra sensitive to everything.

Carefully, he slides the robe off my shoulders, and frees my injured arm. Tears spring to my eyes when he leans forward and presses a kiss over it. The apology shines in his eyes but before he can speak it I put my hand over his mouth.

"Take care of me," I say softly. He nods, controlling his own emotions as we walk into the bathroom.

The shower is amazing in here, and I can't wait to get under it. There's plastic wrap on the counter, and I laugh as Derick grabs it and covers my bandages, wrapping me up like leftovers.

"Elliott will check you out later." He kisses my shoulder again and I swoon.

We step into the shower and he holds my hips and guides me into the spray. The hot water rushes down my back, immediately providing some relief for my tense and aching muscles. I lean my head back and get my hair wet, the final tension from sleeping in that hairdo leaving.

Derick turns me as he grabs my shampoo, and then starts lathering up my hair. It feels amazing - better than any time at the salon no matter how good they are.

"You should do this all the time," I murmur.

"If that's what you want, I will, *lleidr bach.*"

When he says it, I'm thrown back to the blurry memories of last night. I asked him what it meant and he told me - little thief. Then he'd told me I'd stolen his heart.

I turn around to rinse out the shampoo, and then let him proceed with my conditioner. Things get more dangerous when my body wash enters the picture. His big, warm hands running a loofah all over my body is too much. It's so fucking erotic to be washed by another person when you know it's more. He's not washing me, he's worshiping me. I can feel it in the way his hand follows behind the loofah, running over all of my skin, slow and careful.

When he gets on his knees to wash my legs, I look down and god, it's fucking beautiful. There is nothing sexier than Derick on his knees for me. My clit is pulsing with arousal. He teases me, trailing his fingers up my inner thigh and then sliding them along my slit. I moan, and throw back my head, letting the water cascade down my body.

"May I?" he asks, teasing my pussy lips again.

"God, yes, please," I respond, and take a step back so I'm leaning against the shower wall. I don't notice the cold, and barely feel the jolt of my shoulder. Derick puts his hand behind my knee and lifts, bending it to rest on the little corner outcropping of the shower.

I look down and watch as he moves between my legs, the water dripping down his gorgeous body, as his head moves toward my aching, pulsing center.

The first swipe of his tongue almost has me screaming, and my right hand dives into his hair, tugging and begging him to give me more. Derick teases my entrance with two fingers as he licks at my pussy lips, teasing me by not playing with my clit. I shudder as he presses his fingers inside, and clench around them, only a few strokes from coming already.

Derick moves his fingers in and out slowly, drawing out my pleasure with a bit of torture. His tongue pushes me apart and finds my clit, and he moves his tongue around it with firm, slow strokes. The fire building in my stomach is making my body tense up and shake and I already know this is going to be one of the best orgasms I've ever had. I roll my hips slowly, following his pace as I fuck his fingers back, and then I detonate. Derick presses his fingers deep inside and curves them, hitting my weak spot, and at the same time he sucks on my pussy. It's too much and not enough and I'm screaming his name, holding on to his head so I don't fall.

Even when I come down, he still laps at me softly, licking up my come and kissing my sensitive skin. When he stands up, I step to him, the water cascading over the both of us as I kiss him. I can't get enough of him right now, our mouths open and soft as our tongues chase one another.

He reaches behind me and turns off the water.

"I need more," I tell him between assaults on his mouth.

Derick picks me up, and I wrap my legs around him. We don't even bother with a towel and I don't give a shit if our bed gets wet. He lays me down gently before crawling over me. I can see the restraint he's exercising.

"Are you sure?" he asks.

"Yes." I shift so my left arm is comfortable, and then lift my hips to rub against his erection. "Be soft with me."

"Anything you want," he whispers over my mouth, and then takes his cock in his hand and presses inside me. I'm still so wet and needy that he slides in easily. I wrap my legs around him, hooking my feet together over his waist.

We move slowly against one another. It's a deep, grinding movement that I feel in my entire body. There's no rush, just us, and I cannot stop kissing him as we move together. I don't stop when I orgasm, I cry and moan into his mouth, not caring that it's hard to breathe because I can't imagine breathing is worth breaking our connection right now.

No one and nothing exists right now but me and him.

I'm working back up to coming again.

"Come with me," I whisper against his mouth. "Please come with me Brody."

He breaks our kiss and stares down into my eyes, never looking away as his movements become harder and more erratic. It's the thing that sends me over the edge - there's something about the way he moves as he's about to come that feels better than anything else.

"Brody," I moan, tears welling in my eyes at the intensity of the orgasm hitting me. My body moves, reacting to the pleasure and stealing all the air from my lungs.

"Allie," he whispers, before kissing me again and groaning into my mouth as he comes inside me.

He buries his face in my neck as we both catch our breath.

"*Ti yw fy nghariad i,*" he whispers to me. I might not know the literal translation, but I think I know what he said nonetheless.

39

Alina

It's Tuesday, and I am very bored with convalescing. I've been doing it for three days and I am miserable. Since the bullet went through the meat of my arm, it's healing well and I can move okay. Bumping it hurts like a bitch and I move slowly so that I don't piss anything off, but Elliott checks on me constantly to make sure I'm not overdoing it.

Monday I managed to get down to the gym and was unceremoniously rejected. I fought them until Roe threatened to tie me up with a jump rope and march me upstairs before tattling to Derick that I wasn't following orders for my care.

Traitor. He's supposed to be on my side.

It was after that incident that Elliott started checking on me. He shows up every four hours with ibuprofen, a bottle of water, and a snack. Eifa is stress baking desserts and if I keep eating like this without hitting the gym I'm going to lose my abs, and I worked really hard for them. The homemade cinnamon rolls might be worth it, though.

I've spent the day wandering from room to room, trying to find anything that will hold my interest. I spent most of Sunday sleeping, Monday I read a book after my gym incident, but today I can't sit still.

I'm not built for relaxing - nothing holds my interest.

Luckily, Jack arrives to save the day.

"Eifa made caramel corn and we're watching *Mindhunter*."

"Fine," I scrunch my nose but agree. We go to the living room and get ourselves situated. We sit in different spots than usual, since I need the arm rest to be on my left side. It's weird but necessary. Jack gets the show started and I get pulled in immediately. We both know our stuff about serial killers well enough that we can talk about the real things they put in the show, and about the origins of behavioral analysis.

"I thought about studying psychology," Jack tells me. "But those programs aren't really aimed at people who will go into my line of work, and it's not like I could've gone off to be an FBI agent."

"Why not? I mean, you weren't obligated to stay here or work at Venture. I know Derick tried really hard to give you freedom." Derick had also told me that Jack barely graduated college because he'd spent more time partying than studying. After everything that happened with the former maid, Jack had doubled down on living the young and crazy life. Still, Jack got his BS in Business Marketing. That's more than I could say - I had my high school diploma from my fancy private prep school and then damaged their statistics by not going to college.

Jack snorts. "Sure. My freedom."

"Come on - when has he ever pressured you to work at Venture? You could've done anything."

"Because he's the heir and I'm the spare."

My mouth falls open in shock. "I should hit you for talking about yourself that way. No one thinks that Jack. Would working at Venture make you happy? Is that what you want?"

Jack stares at the TV, not answering my question. I can see him thinking hard, his jaw working as he contemplates.

"I don't know. I've never had the chance. Venture was always

Derick's, and even when I asked him he gave me the clubs to run instead. Venture is our family's, but I've never really been part of it."

I feel sad for him, and wonder if this is the kind of thing that I could talk to Derick about without betraying Jack's confidence. I know that Derick has no idea Jack feels like this. I also understand why Jack wouldn't tell him. Derick is protective of Venture, but he also still sees his 27 year old brother as a little kid, the guy who broke an innocent woman, and as the dude who fucked around too much in college. That's not who Jack is anymore, but it's hard for him to see that.

With my younger sisters, Aster is a genius and graduated high school early, starting college at 16. She had her master's degree by 21. Aro - well Aro was always kind of adrift and her liberal arts degree was a good fit for her. Of my siblings, she's the one I still see as a little kid. Aro will always be the little girl who would hide away reading books, who has a romantic heart, and decided to learn how to fight with a sword and a bo staff because she read about them so often in fantasy novels. I get why Derick struggles to see Jack as he is instead of as he was because I've done the same thing.

"You really should try, Jack. Figure out what actually interests you at Venture. When you ask, you can be specific, and it'll show him you're taking it seriously."

"Sure, Lina," Jack reaches over and takes my right hand, squeezing it lightly. I expect him to let go, but he doesn't. I slowly move my hand away and then rub my hurt shoulder, trying to be subtle that I did not want him to hold my hand. Jack has been touchy-feely since I met him so I know it's just how he is, but it still makes me feel weird sometimes.

The other thing that's been eating at me comes to mind, and now it's my turn to stare intently at the TV while I talk.

"Why do you think I should leave?"

He goes so still and quiet for so long that I don't think he's going to answer my question.

"Derick needs to focus on the problem in front of him, and much as I love you sister-in-law, you are a distraction. He can't go scorched earth if he's feeling all mushy about his wife."

"He's not mushy," is the only thing I can think to say. "I don't want to abandon him, or you. Leaving would be doing that." I've had a lot of debates with myself about leaving - would it take stress off Derick if I wasn't here to look after? Even though I'm doing well, I'm not much good in a fight right now when I only have one good arm. What good am I really doing him being here?

"He wouldn't think of it that way - not if you talk about it."

We sit quiet again for a long time. The next episode of the show starts.

"I'll think about it."

"Thank you, Lina. I think it will keep both of you safer, if you're out of danger."

When I look over, he's watching me, and his eyes are full of sadness. Jack gives me a tight nod and then looks away. He swallows tightly, and I'm surprised he's so emotional about this. He must be more worried than he's letting on.

I get pulled back into the show, focusing on the hunt for a killer that they won't catch in the end. It mirrors what we've been experiencing lately. An enemy that we know is coming for us and despite throwing everything at it, we can't find them. We don't even know the source of their enmity because it's spread so wide. It feels personal, but honestly, even in the underworld most people respect Derick if they don't fear him. He's practical and willing to negotiate, he's protective of everyone until they're disloyal, and he has the patience to figure out the big picture. It's hard not to respect him.

He and Kade have crawled through their history for the last few years with a fine-tooth comb trying to find anyone that may hold a grudge, but even the few things they theorized about crumbled under scrutiny. Derick has been pulling the Claytons out of crime, and that's only worked to the benefit of others.

"Our mother died when I was 5. Derick was 8, and our father was useless. I saw him maybe once a week. All I had was Derick, Eifa, and our grandparents."

I don't say anything, wondering where he's going with all of this.

"But then life just kept kicking us in the ass. By the time I was 10, both our grandparents were gone. Our asshole father was dead just before Derick's 16th birthday. " Jack wipes his mouth, still watching the TV. "Money talks, so he got special guardianship of me. Until my 18th birthday, Derick made decisions about my life. I'm not complaining, exactly, it's just that he never fucking stopped. My brother never bothered to get to know me because he forgot he doesn't own me. I'm not a fucking pet."

"Jack," my voice is soft, and I feel so wrenched for both of these men. Derick because he cared so much about failing his brother that he never connected with him the way that he could have, and Jack because he hasn't pushed himself to step up and be in control of his own life.

"It doesn't matter, I'm not asking you to do anything," he puts his hand on my arm and I fight my instinct to pull it away. "I wanted you to understand why I'm frustrated with him. He's half parent, half brother, and he hasn't figured out that I don't need him to be a parent anymore."

"That might be true, but you'll always need someone looking out for you. You're lucky that it's family."

"Is that why you married Derick? Looking out for your family?"

The question hits me in a hard spot because I've been very careful to only brush against the subject of my feelings for Derick, even in my own mind. I'm afraid if I confront them head on I'll retreat because when it comes to emotional things, that's how I work. Even my sisters know better than to push me to talk about my feelings. I'll listen to them and help them dissect their own all day, but I don't contemplate my emotions. It causes a spiral I struggle to recover from. It's been that way since my mom died.

"Yes and no," I answer cautiously but honestly. "This deal was good for both our families, but there was also something about Derick and our chemistry that I couldn't resist. I still can't."

"Do you love him?" Jack's question is forceful, so I don't look at him and instead look down into my lap. I'm toying with my phone, wishing right now that it would light up with a text or a call so I could escape this conversation.

"Whether I do or not," my voice is firm, "that's a conversation for Derick and I."

There's silence again, and when I finally look up at Jack there's a weird expression of satisfaction on his face. I basically told him to mind his business, but he looks like I gave the answer that he was looking for. It's gotten weird tonight, I'm sore, and I'm tired.

"I should go to sleep," I stand up and grab my stuff, trying to move out of the room as fast as possible. Jack doesn't move to stop or follow me, and I feel relieved.

"You should go back to Chicago, Alina," Jack turns on the couch and watches me leave the room. "It's better for everyone if you aren't here."

That hurts.

40

Derick

Kade caught our shooter.

He put out word to anyone who does under the table medical treatment that they would be well-compensated for letting us know if they treated a stab wound, and within a few hours we got a call from a vet who does quick fixes for criminal types.

It took another hour for Kade to find him, incapacitate him, and now he's tied up in the very hard to find room inside the backroom of the biggest club we own, Violenza. It's an obvious title but most people don't know what I actually use this building for. The loud music covers the screams.

His name is Granger. He's skinny with dark hair, and looks like a junkie barely holding on to recovery. It doesn't take long to make him spill what he knows, except he doesn't know much of anything. It shouldn't be surprising considering how careful our adversary has been, but that doesn't make it any less annoying. Granger will bear the brunt of my annoyance.

Between Kade and I, he's got a few broken ribs and several broken fingers. I prefer pain that doesn't result in blood spatter - not unless I'm going for the final stroke.

I pick up a hammer off the table, and Granger's skinny face blanches. "How did this person find you?"

"I don't know!" he says immediately, his voice hoarse from screaming. "I got a call, the voice was masked, they transferred the money before I did the job. I went where I was supposed to, I saw you and I shot."

"What were your exact instructions?"

"Shoot Derick Clayton, don't harm anyone else. If anyone gets in the way, stand down."

"In the way?" I sneer. "Like my wife...who you shot?"

"I..." Granger's face pales, and I think he finally accepts that he's not leaving this room alive. I don't care that Alina is going to be fine in the long term, she should not have been harmed in the first place. This man spilled her blood. Took years off my life with the depth of fear he caused in me for her.

"Is there anything else I need to know? Think hard, Granger. If it's something good I'll make this quick."

"They called me after. I thought they'd want the money back but they told me to leave Seattle, that the attempt was enough, and I could keep the money."

He had been trying to pack up his shit when Kade caught him. Scrambling to fill a bag with the possessions that mattered to him and leave the city before we could find him. He was too late. Right now, he's taking his last breaths and then I'm going to tear apart his phone and his accounts to find any way I can to reveal my enemy.

"Thank you, Granger."

I take a step back and grab my gun from the table. Even with the club sounds, I still have a silencer on the end.

"You took the wrong deal."

"No, please, I didn't - I didn't mean to hurt her. It was just a job."

"So is this," I reply, and pull the trigger. The sharp dart of the bullet

235

sounds, and goes through his skull. Granger slumps forward, blood oozing down in a stream from the wound.

"I'll start ripping apart his phone and getting our people on it."

"I know. Get rid of the body. I'm going to stay home with Alina tomorrow."

"Yes, boss."

Kade and I exchange a look as I move to leave, communicating with one another on a mental level. We're both frustrated, we both know that we didn't get as much out of this conversation as we wanted, and that our time to rest will be brief because it's all coming to a head now. Saying I'm taking a break to be with Alina is also me telling him to take some downtime before we hit this hard again. We have to recharge, let our brains simmer with the information we have, and give it an opportunity to rearrange and change shape until maybe something makes sense.

None of this makes sense.

Fucking hell.

Andrew is waiting in the alley behind the club, and as soon as he sees me he starts the car. I don't climb in the back like usual, but go around and get in the passenger seat. We ride in silence for awhile, and it's a restorative kind of quiet. Andrew is a good person to be restful with.

After his family was killed, he had to go to inpatient treatment for awhile, and then he disappeared for a month to a retreat in Arizona. The violence that he's capable of never left him, but his ability to maintain control on his emotions and channel them for his own purposes is infinitely useful.

The thing is, while we've had threats and fights, they've all been petty squabbles by bit players trying to make their name by taking out the Claytons. We've never been in any kind of danger we couldn't overcome.

I've never had anything to lose before - not really.

Jack has always been physically capable of taking care of himself and no one has ever targeted or attacked him. When they come after us, they come after one of the businesses or they try and mess with me directly. Having my name on everything has always been a shield for Jack because why go after the prince when you can go straight for the king?

Now I have Alina. Even if she wasn't the target, she was the collateral damage. I could lose her. I could lose her on purpose or lose her to someone being careless. I am not willing to accept either one. Life is messy and unpredictable and there are a million ways that I could lose her to the normal fucking course of events, but this isn't normal. Our lives aren't normal while we are still tied to criminal activity. We're already rich assholes - being criminals puts too many extra targets on our backs.

I ask Andrew something that feels shitty and necessary all at once.

"Would you do it again, knowing that you'd lose them?"

"Yes." Andrew doesn't even hesitate.

I nod, swallowing hard. No matter what happens, how dark or how bad, I can't and won't regret anything that led me to Alina.

"Loving them and having them changed me profoundly, and losing them..." Andrew shakes his head. "It fucks with me every day. Breathing every day without them is work. But they are worth it. I'm still here because I have some purpose to serve. That's all that keeps me going."

I don't think he means serving me either. I never took Andrew as the spiritual type but the idea that he has a purpose to serve outside of himself is something I understand. I will do anything, fight anything, feel anything, if it means she's safe.

We don't say anything else and we don't need to. When we get to the house, I hold my hand out to Andrew.

"Thank you, my friend."

For a second Andrew stares at me in shock, but recovers himself and shakes my hand. While I always felt sympathy for him, I never understood, never even had an inkling, of what it takes for him to get through every day without his family. I have the barest hint of it now and I'm collapsing like a faulty house of cards in panic and emotions. Andrew might truly be the strongest man I know because he's living through his grief every day.

The house is quiet when I go inside, but it's Tuesday, so I check the TV room before heading upstairs. Jack is still on the couch, scrolling through his phone rather than watching the show on the screen.

"Hey," I get his attention.

He looks over the back of the couch at me, and I'm struck with a memory of little Jack doing the same thing. Only then, he was hiding in here. There had been a fight at school and he was waiting for our father to find him and discipline him. Dad hadn't given a shit. He'd thought the whole thing was amusing.

What I remember is what I said to him that day, after making him tell me about the fight. It was over something stupid, and Jack had lost his temper.

"Only fight when you know you're going to win, or when you're protecting someone else. Everything else is foolishness and pride." Jack had agreed with me, and while there had been other fights over the years, I'd always had his back when he told me his reasons. I'd been in plenty of scraps myself and learned that lesson the hard way.

There were only three years between us but sometimes it felt like three fucking decades.

"How's Alina?"

Jack sneers for a second. "You can go ask her yourself."

"I'm asking you," I sigh and come closer. "As her friend, and our brother, I need your perspective. Please."

His face softens with surprise. "Unsure and bored out of her mind."

Bored I knew, but there's not a lot I can do about that. "Unsure?"

"If she should stay, what her role in all of this is. I think she's going to go back to Chicago - with her family. Until either she's healed or this is done."

I don't want her to go. I hate the idea of her leaving. However, if it makes her feel safer and gives her a sense of purpose again, then maybe she should. Knowing that she'd be halfway across the country from me and not within reach…the idea of it feels horrible. I won't be able to see and feel for myself that she's okay. The reassurance I get from her presence, her strength, and her submission cannot be underestimated.

Still, her comfort and peace of mind matter too.

I won't bring it up unless she does.

"Thanks for being there, for both of us. I don't know what I'd do without you."

Jack frowns at that and turns back to the TV, effectively dismissing me. I want to say more, but I don't have it in me to fight with him again tonight. There's a huge gulf between us and I don't know how it got there, or how to fix it in a way that doesn't start with me screaming at him to grow the fuck up.

Instead, I let it all go and head to Alina.

She's already sleeping. It's fitful and twitchy sleep because she has to be on her back instead of on her side like she likes. Alina always sleeps on her left side, and I loved it because it meant that at any point in the night I could shift over and wrap myself around her, the big spoon holding her close. It also felt like an act of trust that even from night one, she felt safe putting her back to me.

I want to exhaust her.

I pull the blankets down slowly, and am delighted to find that she's sleeping in nothing but a t-shirt. It's bunched up around her stomach, exposing her pussy to me. She already has one leg bent up, doing half the work for me.

I step into the closet and quickly take off all my clothes. Alina is as I left her when I step back to the bed, and I lightly crawl up, shifting her legs until they're spread open and around my body.

Her pussy smells familiar and seductive, and I start with slow, wet laps of my tongue. It gets her shifting more, murmuring in her sleep but not waking up yet. With the point of my tongue I delve between her lips, taunting her clit with firmer strokes.

I know she's finally awake when her hand slips into my hair. Alina's nails tease my scalp and I groan at the sensation. It gets me every fucking time. Even though I know she's up and she's with me, I tease rather than satisfy. I want to get her worked up and ready for a pounding. I bring up my hand to spread her open more, and my tongue lightly works her clit over and over. Alina's hips are thrusting, seeking more from me, but I don't give it to her.

"Brody," she whines, tugging on my hair.

"Yes, Allie?" I say as I glance up, hiding my grin as I dive back into her.

"Either do it right or do something else," she growls at me. "I need you."

Her tone is as needy as the words, breathless and heated.

I back away from her pussy and move so that I can look at her. "You want me to fuck you, *lleidr bach?*"

She nods.

I keep teasing her, running a finger from her clit, down to her entrance, and back up in a light, lazy pace.

"Tell me how."

When she blushes, I grin, but wait.

"Get on top of me - kiss me when you slide inside me. Kiss me when I come." Her voice is so fucking quiet but her embarrassment makes it sexier.

"What else do you want."

"I like it when you spank me first. I like it when you soothe me with your mouth after, because it makes me want you so fucking bad." Her hips start moving as she turns herself on, talking about the things we do together. "I want you to hold me down so I can't move, and you fuck me until I'm screaming because it's too much and it's not enough."

"I can do that," I start kissing up her stomach, moving up her body.

"I want you to come inside me and keep fucking me until you come again."

I freeze. That's new. And fucking dirty.

I like it. "Mmm, dirty fucking girl," I grin up at her as she blushes.

I resume my path up her body with my mouth, pushing her t-shirt up even further. I tease the underside of her breast with my tongue before using it to attack her hard, dusky nipple. She moans, and then surprises me again.

Her good hand moves to touch her pussy. I watch, entranced, as she plays with herself while I suck at her nipples.

"You're earning that spanking right now, Allie. Did I say you could touch my pussy? Did I say anyone but me could give you pleasure?"

She doesn't answer, just moans, and I lift my body from hers.

"Roll over. Your ass needs a reminder that your pussy belongs to me."

41

Alina

I carefully move on to my stomach, not wanting any pain from my arm to interrupt the pleasure. If I thought being stressed about the danger coming at us would decrease our physical need for each other, I was mistaken. Derick touches me every chance he gets, like he's checking that I'm still there. Even when we sit down to eat, his hand is on my leg or his arm is resting on the back of my chair, fingers teasing my back and shoulder.

Now I lay down, my naked body vulnerable to Derick's ministrations.

"Who does that pussy belong to?" he growls, before giving my ass cheek a quick slap. He doesn't let me answer, slapping me twice more on the same cheek. It stings but I love it - I love the force and the way the pain radiates to the sensitive parts of my body, causing my pussy to overreact.

"It's yours." I moan into the blankets.

Derick goes to work on the other cheek before massaging them both, then licking at the hot, red skin of my ass cheeks and soothing the sting. He squeezes hard, then asks me: "Did I give you permission to pleasure that pussy?"

"No," I moan. He smacks one cheek and then the other, and my hips grind down into the mattress, my wetness soaking my thighs.

"Who pleasures your pussy, little thief?" He says it in English and it catches me off guard.

"My husband," I answer, grinding, desperate for him. "My husband pleasures my pussy."

"Fuck," he rasps, then I gasp when he sinks his teeth into my ass for just a second before moving to roll me over onto my back again.

Derick crawls over me and I wrap my good arm around his neck, and the other rests on his hip. His hot, hard cock rests on my stomach.

"Say it again."

For a second I'm confused, but then repeat the last thing I said. "My husband pleasures my pussy."

"Fucking right," he says before savagely capturing my mouth. I'm so distracted by the way that he's kissing me I'm blind to everything else. When he moves his cock to my entrance and slides inside me easily, I moan into his mouth. He doesn't stop. He's doing exactly what I asked him for. All I can do is hold on and enjoy the sensations as he gives me what I want. The pleasure is unceasing.

Even when I finally reach a peak and cry out, the pleasure barely dims, like the orgasm is stretching on and on into infinity. I move without finesse or thought, pressing for more of him. I want all of Derick, all that he'll give me.

He lets my lips go and lifts himself up, arranging our bodies so that he can grip my hips and look down at me. Derick's hips snap, fucking me hard, and his eyes are focused on my breasts bouncing with each thrust. I can't look away from his face - the dark intensity of his eyes and the hungry way he watches my body. Then he presses in deep and grinds my clit against his body, holding me so tight I can't move. It's too much and I'm too sensitive, but he doesn't stop moving even as I cry out and shudder with an orgasm.

I can feel my pussy squeezing around his cock, and his fingers dig in to my skin as he starts moving again. Each thrust is erratic, and I love the way he moves inside me as he starts to come.

When I think he'll stop, he doesn't. Instead, he moves so that's laying over me again and continues to thrust inside me with slow strokes that I feel every inch of. He's kissing me softly, tasting each part of my mouth with is tongue until I'm floating and desperate. It's such a tease to be touched softly after being fucked roughly, and my hips start moving up to meet him. It's a slow, grinding pace that builds and builds.

"Are you going to come again, Allie?" Our eyes are so close I almost can't see both of them. I'm staring into those dark wells and they are filled with the fires of a thousand sins. I love them. "Can you feel how wet it is, our come together? Don't you love the way your pussy slides on my cock when it's already fucking drenched?"

His words make me even more aroused, and I'm so close to coming again. Derick can tell and keeps saying filthy things to me.

"You love knowing that I've filled that pussy up already, don't you?" I can't speak, I can only nod, and his voice gets more strained as he gets closer to the edge with me. "You want me to fill you up again - a good little slut who loves my come."

"Fuck!" I scream as I tip over the edge, grinding against him, squeezing his cock and feeling like there's lightning in my veins. I can't stop crying out as pleasure radiates through my entire body, squeezing him with my inner walls as hard and as long as I can to draw out this incredible feeling.

As I start to come down, Derick kisses me softly. "Good fucking girl." Then he grips my hair, holding it tight at the nape so I can't move. His hips pound into me but I don't get far because he's keeping me there, and then he tightens up, groaning into my neck as he comes inside me again.

It's one of the hottest things that's ever happened to me. That will probably ever happen to me.

Derick whispers something against my throat before kissing my pulse point, but I'm beyond words and can't ask him what it was.

42

Alina

After talking to Jack last night, I sent out the SOS to my sisters. I needed to talk to all of them, at once, and get their perspective about what's been going on.

We didn't tell them that I got shot. It was kept quiet enough that it didn't even get back to my dad. I knew that as soon as they found out they'd demand that I come home. Or at least demand that some of our own staff come out here to protect me.

The thing is, Chicago isn't home anymore. Seattle isn't home either. Derick is home. The way I feel when I'm with him is home. It's like the parts of myself are blending together and becoming truer. The person I was before was focused on being a protector, working on my body and my awareness to keep other people safe. I didn't spend any time thinking about the rest of the world and how I could affect it - I only thought about how it affected me and my family.

Now I see how much I can impact things outside myself because Derick wants to impact the world. He trusts me to be both strong and fight for myself, but also shape what Venture and his other work is going to do. I genuinely believe that if I asked him to find me work at Venture, he'd do it in a heartbeat. I don't have to be his socialite trophy wife, although I do get a lot of satisfaction from the charity work and projects.

It makes me a little sad that he wouldn't as easily do the same for Jack, but that's a different history and series of complications.

Derick is down in his office, and I hide out on the big sectional in my room, looking out into the sky.

My phone rings with a video call from Anora.

"Hi." My voice is sad, but I'm happy to see all three of their faces squeezed in to the phone camera. Aro highlighted her hair, shades of blonde and lighter brown streaking through it and softening her look. Anora isn't wearing makeup, so I know she has no other plans for the day. Aster looks the same as always - I swear she hasn't changed since she was 16 even though she's 22.

Aster's eyes zero in on my shoulder. I've been wearing tank tops because material rubbing against the bandages drives me crazy. It's not painful but the sensation and the sound make my skin crawl.

"What the hell happened?" Her voice is low and threatening. Aster unleashed is not a further complication that we need right now.

"Um, I got shot."

They all simultaneously freak out and talk over each other, asking what happened, if I'm okay, who did it, and what we're doing about it.

"It happened last weekend - I'm fine. Just the meat. We've been having some...issues."

"I knew it," Aster snarls and steps away. I can see her pacing behind Anora and Aro's heads.

"What do you need?" Anora hones in on the real reason for the call.

"Advise? I guess?" I sigh and close my eyes, pulling my thoughts together. "Someone is going after Derick - this happened because I pushed him out of the way."

"You idiot!" Aster yells.

"The thing is, Jack suggested that I leave. With my injury I am more vulnerable and he accused me of being a distraction - that Derick will be able to focus and fix things if he's not worried about me."

Anora and Aro both frown, and even Aster stops pacing.

"Jack said that?" Aster still sounds furious and I don't know how to calm them down. I can't say it's nothing because it's not - and they are allowed to be worried about me.

"Should I leave?"

They exchange looks, and beats pass with no response. Finally, Anora speaks.

"Did you fall?"

I swallow around the lump that forms in my throat. I can't answer, so I nod.

"Did he?"

I nod again.

"If you feel vulnerable, you probably are. If someone takes you or hurts you, they could leverage a lot out of him. It's not the worst idea." It's Aro that answers. Like me, she likes to consider the angles, and she's cautious when she's paying attention.

"But if I'm not here and something happens…" my voice cracks. I've cried more since knowing Derick than I ever have in my life. It's like he unlocked a door on my emotions I hadn't even known existed.

"That's a risk you take, to maybe keep him safe." Anora looks at me with sympathy and I look away. "I think you won't know until you talk to him."

She's right, of course. "I will. I should. I'll text you - let you know what's going on."

"We'll be here - whether you come home or not," Aro reassures me. Aster still looks grumpy and suspicious in the background but that's kind of what she's like all the time. I wave to them, and end the call.

I walk through the bathroom and into our bedroom. I'm surprised to find Derick sitting on the end of the bed, staring at nothing and lost in thought. Fleetwood Mac is playing on the turntable. He looks up when I walk into the room, and something in my expression makes him look resigned.

"Should I go?" I whisper.

Derick holds out his hand to me and I take it. He pulls me between his knees, and I rest my hands on his shoulders. I need to feel him right now because this conversation is going to suck, however it ends up. If he doesn't agree to it, I won't go. It has to be his choice or it will feel like I'm running.

"Did Jack tell you to go?"

"Yes." I take a deep breath. "I'm vulnerable right now. I don't want anyone to use me against you, or have your focus split because you're worried about me."

"I'll be worried about you anyway," his smile is sad.

"Will you be less worried if I'm in Illinois?"

Derick looks away from me and he's silent for a long time. I shift my hands so that I'm trailing one of them along his nape, running my nails along the sensitive place where his hairline ends. He shivers and then wraps his arms around my thighs and presses his face into my stomach. We stand like that a long time, giving each other comfort because we both know the answer to that question.

"I want you safe," he says into my belly, and I can feel his warm breath through my t-shirt. I take his face in my hands and tilt it up so that he's looking at me.

"This isn't me leaving. I am not leaving you."

Derick swallows heavily and nods. "I know."

43

Them

The ride to the airport is quiet. Derick and Alina sit close, all four of their hands wrapped together during the entirety of the ride. Both of them are trying to think of what to say but can't come up with anything that feels right for this moment.

You don't say I love you for the first time because you think you're going to die, or you're never going to see each other again. That makes the situation seem hopeless, and will forever taint one of the most important things they'll ever say to one another.

Derick doesn't believe Alina loves him, and doesn't think she's ready to hear him say it. Saying it right before she gets on a plane because he's put her life in danger seems like a recipe for disaster.

Alina feels that Derick won't believe her. He'll think she's saying it because she's about to get on a plane and leave him in danger. That she'll be saying it because it's what he wants to hear. No matter how sincere, he'll always doubt if it's the truth. It's not the right time.

Instead they hold on to being in the presence of the other, soaking up the way they feel together. Both are lost in their thoughts and memories of time with the other person, reliving moments in their minds.

Despite what he said, Derick does feel like she's leaving. Not that Alina is abandoning him, but that he hasn't kept the promises that he made to her so of course she's going back home. Derick didn't keep up his half of the vows, and she has every right to walk away from him. Maybe when he fixes this, he'll find a way to deserve her again. If he comes out the other side, he plans to do exactly what he said he'd do if she left: chase her down, bring her back. Alina belongs to him, and he belongs to her. Even if this is the right thing to do, she's leaving, leaving him, and it hurts.

Alina wants to stay. The thought circles relentlessly in her head that leaving is the wrong thing to do. They are better together - Derick needs someone watching his back. It's not that he doesn't have Kade, Jack, the other guards - it's that she sees what they don't. Alina is afraid that going now leaves him blind in one eye. She wants to stay. If they go down, they go down together. That's what those vows amounted to, right?

As they pull up to the drop off area at SeaTac, both of them tense. Derick feels sick and Alina's stomach swoops like she's just gone down the hill of a roller coaster. This feels wrong. Every instinct they both have is screaming at them not to do this, but their minds are overruling everything else. Logic is ignoring instinct because how could this possibly be a bad choice?

They stand on the sidewalk as Andrew unloads her suitcase. It's small, and that's symbolic of her belief that she won't be gone long and she won't need much. Either Derick will resolve this, or she'll be healed enough to come back and help. That's the only two ways she will allow this situation to end.

Derick stares at Alina, drinking in every tiny detail about her appearance right this moment. The next time he sees her will be through a phone screen, and it's not the same.

Her dark hair is pulled back in a low tail, a few pieces of hair slipping out around her face. There are dark circles under her eyes from the lack of sleep, and he's sure he has a matching set of them. She's pale, and it eats at him seeing how the stress of this is eating at her. She's wearing black leggings and and oversize white sweatshirt. It looks cozy. The kind of thing he'd want her to wear if they were going to sit on the couch and do nothing, or take a nap together in their bed.

Alina looks at him looking at her, the sadness in his usually pleasant face. She has seen beneath his mask and doesn't know how he ever managed to hide from her. To the world, Derick is a business man - charming, generous, authoritative, decisive. To the underworld, he's still charming and it makes his deadly side all the more terrifying to know that he can take you down with a smile. To Alina, he's a deep well of emotions. Derick is protective, demanding, and still humble. She knows what really makes him laugh and what music he listens to for each mood, and the way he takes a long time to wake up every morning.

She knows him in a way no one else ever will, and they both know it.

Derick brought out a side of Alina she never thought she'd be capable of, or even bother to experience. She found a place where it was safe to be soft.

They've changed each other.

They haven't spent a night apart since the day they were married. 4 months of nights and neither can imagine being alone again.

Alina dives at Derick, wrapping her good arm around his neck and burying her face there, doing everything she can to hold back the tears. He's stunned for a moment and then holds her in return, pressing her close and appreciating her nearness.

Alina slides back and moves her mouth over his, kissing him softly. Derick doesn't let that stand, sliding one hand up her back until his hand is firmly entrenched in her hair. Then he tilts her head and devours her - spreading open her lips with his tongue, tasting her like it's the last time he ever will, because it might be.

They kiss until he feels moisture on his lips, and then he breaks away and looks up at the sky for rain.

It isn't rain.

Alina's tears drip down her cheeks, and dripped across their lips. Without saying anything, he wipes them away.

"Call me when you land. Text me whenever you want." *Come home,* he adds silently.

"I will. Get this done, be safe." *Hurry up so I can come back to you,* she thinks.

They take a step back from each other. Alina grabs her suitcase and wheels it into the airport, looking back so often that she bumps into people which isn't like her at all. When the doors close around her, she focuses on what's in front of her.

Derick stays until he sees her leave the counter and head toward security.

Then Derick directs Andrew to drive him to Venture - there's work to do before going home.

44

Alina

Somehow, I sleep on the flight. I fall asleep before we even takeoff and wake up when my stomach swoops from our decreasing altitude. Weirdly, I think I felt safe. Sometimes being in public is the best way to disappear. It didn't hurt that I was flying first class either, and had the space to stretch out.

This still feels like the wrong decision. My internal response every time someone brought up me leaving had been: no, absolutely not. Even Derick seemed reluctant when he agreed I should go. I can't tell if I'm being selfish because I don't want to go, or if there's something my senses are aware of that I am not. My arm is healing well, and in desperation I could still fight through the hurt, but I'd be slower. That's what would get me killed, and that would ruin Derick. I know that.

I slide off my wedding ring and look at the inside where he had them etch "Brody." I run the tip of my finger over it, feeling the fine little lines in the platinum. Life would be so much easier if we were really them - Allie and Brody. I put the ring back on my finger, considering how easily and quickly I got used to it when I never wore jewelry before. I'd feel naked without it.

The plane lands, and we all go through the motions of getting up, stretching, getting our things, and shuffling down the aisle. I give the flight attendants a perfunctory smile, and head up the gangway and into O'Hare.

What I don't expect to see is Aster waiting for me in the seating area.

I walk straight to her, confused, and also a little scared to ask how she got past security.

"I bought a cheap ticket, dumb ass," she answers like she could read my mind and waves a boarding pass in my face. "Come on, let's talk."

I follow her through the concourse until we get to a gate at the end that's mostly empty.

"I got you a ticket back to Seattle. It boards in an hour."

My mouth opens and closes but nothing comes out for a minute. "Why?"

Aster frowns like all of this is obvious and I'm being obtuse on purpose. "Coming here was the wrong thing to do. You need to go back."

I can only stare, and I feel like I'm having an out of body experience. "Why do you think that? I know why I think that but I want to know why you do." Aster and I get along but aren't usually on the same page about things. We look in different directions for solutions. Hers usually involves things that are illegal and/or violent. Mine are protective and defensive, careful. She'd rather go balls to the wall and hope it figures itself out.

"You don't run from a fight, Lina. This is against your nature, and that never works out for anyone." Aster scrunches up her curls in their messy ponytail. "I know that you're hurt and it changes how you fight - I get that, I do - but you will regret it for the rest of your life if something happens. You will always wonder if you being there could've tipped the balance and changed things."

"You're right. You're absolutely right." I yank her to me and hug her.

Aster gets stiff for a moment and doesn't hug me back, but she relaxes against me and that's basically a hug from her.

"I know. I'm a genius, remember?" She gives me a small smile. "If you need me, I'll be ready. I've got a friend who can help if I need it."

"A friend, huh?" I raise an eyebrow at her, and I'm even more shocked when she blushes slightly.

"Yeah, something like that. Things haven't been entirely perfect here either."

My face falls. "What? Why haven't any of you - or dad - said anything?"

"We knew what was going on with you and didn't want to add to your burdens. Plus, it's not a threat or anything like that. Someone has been messing with Designation. I'm on it. Dad's on it. My friend is on it."

"What does your friend do, exactly?"

Aster's face gets very serious. "He makes problems go away."

I'm worried about her now, worried about my family too, but she's right - they aren't facing the overt threats that Derick has been over the last few months. A hacker can only get so far when someone like Aster is protecting their system. She's so damn smart, and this "friend" has got to be pretty impressive if she considers them to be helpful rather than a burden.

Aster explains what's been going on since just after I left. There have been all kinds of digital attacks on Designation, trying to get to the base code for all of our security programs. It would be like a master key to anyone who uses our software. She's leading a small team within Designation to account for it, but whoever is doing it is determined and well-funded. Aster tells me about her team in detail, but kind of glosses over what's going on with the guy dad hired. She slips one time and refers to him as Freelancer, and I hope that's his job description and not a name, because dad's fucking crazy if he hired that psycho.

But I don't push Aster because that's the easiest way to get her to shut down.

The time passes quickly, and then she's walking me back to my gate. We bump fists.

"Thanks for coming through, baby sister."

"Ew, don't call me that. But any time, to the rest of it."

She throws me a wave over her shoulder as she walks off. I watch for a moment, and listen for them to call my boarding group. This was the most expensive waste of travel of my life, but Aster was right.

If I didn't go back, I'd regret it.

45

Derick

I'm heading home from the office and Jack calls me when we're not far from the house. My mind has been going over and over how it will feel to be there without Alina. I lived in that house for years without her, but it won't be the same now that she's gone. The emptiness will be larger somehow.

"Derick - something- get here -"

There are loud noises and what sounds like gunshots behind him. The phone cuts off.

"Fuck - Andrew, faster." Andrew puts the pedal to the floor, maneuvering the curves of the road with the ease of long familiarity. I tell him what I heard, and we strategize as we get closer.

The new gate I had installed is busted open, one side hanging off it's hinges like they used a charge to get in. I'm pissed as hell because none of the perimeter sensors went off, and I should've gotten a notification if someone tampered with the gate. We drive up slowly. The clearing where the house sits is empty - there are no cars, or signs of other people.

The front door is wide open.

There's a body in the foyer - I can't see who it is but they're wearing dark pants and a white shirt, which makes me fear that it's Saul or David.

Andrew turns the SUV, and we both slide out with our guns ready.

I hear shouting from in the house, and we start to move toward it.

Then, before we can do anything, two large men come from the shadows on either side of the door. I hear shots but don't feel them, and something hits me in the head.

As everything starts to go black, I think to myself that I'm glad Alina is gone - and safe.

46

Alina

When I land back at SeaTac, I call Derick. There's no answer, but I don't think much of it. I send him a text telling him to call me when he can. Then I rent a car because I really need the time to clear my head and figure out how to explain to Derick why I came back.

The drive helps, even though the weather is rainy and the roads are a little slippery. It gives me something to focus on. If I'd called for a car, or even tried to get one of the staff to come get me, that would've been way too much free time to overthink and start to panic. Hell, by the time someone would've gotten to the airport to pick me up I might've bought a third ticket back to O'Hare.

Derick will be glad I'm back, even if it also makes him anxious. I fully believe that. We're stronger together, and I'm his partner. In everything. He's made that abundantly clear since the day he brought me here. I've been a part of decisions, been given control of things, and my word has as much weight with our people as his. This place, this city, this work - it's *ours*. It's everything I never knew I wanted.

The drive makes me face the denial I've been engaging in for awhile now.

I love him. Jumping in front of a bullet for him should have made that obvious to me, but even then I wanted to believe that it was me falling back on the training I've ingrained in myself. That's not true though. Even had I been entirely untrained, the second I saw that gun aimed at him I would've done whatever it took to save him.

That's why I'm back. I love Derick, and we need to protect each other.

He's my Brody - the man who let me see a secret side of himself the first time we met, and I'm his Allie - a woman who lets go and goes after what she wants. We had so much in common from those first conversations even when we were hiding what seemed like big important things at the time. In the end, when we couldn't talk about our surface reality we had to dig deeper and expose what was underneath. Our jobs didn't matter, the wealth we both lived with every day, those were trappings that while they had an influence, didn't make us who we are at the core.

We are adults who'd grown up with the loss of parents, the responsibility for our siblings, the desire to make sure we made a world that was better for them. We are both people who often felt trapped or stifled and seek open spaces and rainy skies.

All of these thoughts leave my head when I see the gate to the house.

I'm unarmed because I was getting on a plane, and I've never felt more vulnerable in my life. As I pull into the driveway, I can see Derick's SUV. It's unharmed, so I pull up behind it and make my way out of the car.

This is so stupid, but I have no choice. I have to find out what's going on.

I open the driver's door of the SUV. Andrew's usual piece is gone - but the middle compartment has a knife. I lean in further and check the glove compartment, but it's empty. There's nothing in the backseat.

Holding the knife and prepared to attack, I step up to the front door.

Andrew is laying next to the entryway, hidden from sight until I was right next to him. There's a bush that he's basically shoved under, and I bend down to check on him. When I touch his throat, his eyes snap open.

"Andrew!" My hands flutter as I try and figure out how to help his wounds. His breathing is shallow and so slow that I didn't notice it at first.

There's blood in his mouth, and he opens it but no sound comes out. Andrew is looking at me desperately, trying to tell me something. I lean closer, hoping that will help.

"Jack...Jack..." he rasps, and my gut clenches. "Jack and Derick."

I turn to look at him and his body starts to spasm, struggling and shaking as he fails to draw in a breath. I don't know what to do and I'm fairly certain there's nothing I can do. I take his hand and hold it tight until his body goes limp. His light eyes stare at nothing, and I hope that there's a world after this one and he's with his family. Tears burn my eyes but I pull myself together and step into the house.

Saul is lying on the ground in the foyer. A pool of blood is formed around his head, and there's a small bullet hole in his temple. My eyes close for a second, mourning him. There's no one else around, and I don't hear the sounds of anyone in the house.

I step over his body and head toward the kitchen.

When I peek my head around to look, there's a screech, and a kitchen knife comes flying at my face. I dodge it, dipping back into the dining room as it clatters to the floor.

"Eifa?" I call, hoping that she's alright.

"Alina?" The sound of her voice fills me with relief. She comes around the corner. "What are you doing here?"

"I came back."

"Oh thank god," she hugs me, and I can feel her shaking.

"What the hell happened?"

Eifa takes a deep breath. "Men showed up, they attacked. I hid in the pantry and they never even looked for me. That's where Derick always told me to hide." She presses both hands to her mouth, holding in the panic that wants to escape. "I didn't help. I didn't do anything. I just listened while they were killed."

I put my arm around her and pull her to me. She's tinier than her personality makes her seem. "You did what you were told. All you would've done otherwise is get yourself killed and you wouldn't be here to tell me what happened." Eifa nods. "I need to look around and see if anyone else is here. Do you want to stay, or do you want to come with me?"

"I'll come with you."

"Are you sure? These are your friends. We're going to see things, Eifa, that you won't be able to forget."

"I know," she nods, then grabs another knife from the butcher block. When I step further into the kitchen, I know she's already seen the worst - David is dead up against the wall. A hole in his forehead, and blood spatter like grotesque art.

If I was going to attack our house, and I knew the details of it, my first stop upon getting inside would be going to neutralize the security staff. They were all downstairs, so that's where we go.

In the gym, Louis and Riley are dead on the mats. Whoever came through was a good shot and kept it quiet until the last minute. Riley was caught off guard and his body is face down next to the leg press. Louis was clearly trying to dodge behind the weight racks. He was hit twice in the chest, with a follow up shot to his head.

It's bloody and sad, and we keep going down the hall to the bedrooms. I check each room, constantly checking behind us as we go. There are more rooms than there are staff, so the first few are empty.

Then we find Sean dead in his bed. He never woke up or knew what was coming for him.

We stop outside the next room. "This is Elliott's," Eifa whispers, her strong voice shaking.

I open the door.

It's chaos inside. The bed is tipped over, as is the dresser, and there are bullet holes in the wall and a broken lamp. I don't see a body though, and hold out hope that Elliott made it out.

"Elliott?" Eifa says his name. We both hear a slight grunt. I follow the noise to the closet, and when I open the door Elliott raises a gun. I step back and hold up my hands, and his collapses into his lap.

His stomach is a mess of blood. From what I can see, he's been shot at least two times. He also put up a hell of a fight.

"Where is Derick? Where is Jack?" He rasps. I shake my head and his eyes close in distress. In his mind, he probably believes that he's failed them. "Everyone else?"

"You and Eifa are the only ones I've found so far." I turn to her. "Stay with him, call for help." I hand her my phone. "I'll be back."

"Ma'am, you can't," Elliott tries but I shake my head at him and leave the room.

When I enter the next bedroom, a soft cry leaves me without my permission. It's Roe's room. He's hanging from the door handle of his closet, slumped against the door but hovering over the floor.

I move closer because his face is red, rather than blue, and I swear when I made a noise I saw him move. When I reach out to touch him, his skin is still warm. Then I check his pulse and it's there - there but faint. Quickly, I cut the tie that holds him to the door, and he drops with a thump. I remove it from around his neck and move him down to a flat position.

Before I can push oxygen into his lungs, he coughs and opens his eyes.

"Fucking hell," his voice is like gravel, and I help him sit up. "What happened?"

"Bad shit," I answer him. "We got attacked."

"Fuck." He tries to get up and wavers, crashing into his dresser as he recovers.

"How are you - how are you alive?" Not that I'm not grateful, and it looked like an incomplete attempt at strangulation, but most people don't have a tolerance for being deprived of oxygen for that long. From the looks of things and what Eifa said, it's been a couple hours since the attack occurred.

To my surprise, Roe turns deep red. "Uh, my girlfriend and I - when we - I like to be," he gestures to his neck, "ya know. During sex. Sometimes I even pass out. So I have a tolerance for that."

"Well your sex life just saved your life. Get your shit we need to check upstairs. Elliott's hurt and needs help."

Roe gets his gun, gives me his back up, and then grabs his own knife. We go through the rest of the floor - the only other room that usually has an occupant belongs to Jack's guard, Remo, and it doesn't look like he was here when the attack came.

We check on Eifa and Elliott before heading upstairs. We check each room but the floor plan is so open that it's obvious whoever they are, they are gone.

"Was Derick home?" I ask.

"No, he was still at Venture last I remember. He was wrapping some things up so he could take the time off."

"The car is here," my voice is soft, and defeated. This is bad.

We go through the upper floors, and then cross to the back of the house to go through Jack's wing. He keeps the door to it locked most of the time, and it still is now. That's a good sign.

Roe kicks open the door, and we enter a living room area. It's empty except for furniture, as is the bathroom. We enter Jack's bedroom, and a chill goes through me.

It's empty too. Completely blank.

Nothing personal, only a few clothes in the closet, and a bed that isn't even made up to be slept in. There's nothing that would indicate that anyone lives here - not even a computer. I'm not sure why that freaks me out so much, but it does. Like Jack has been telling us he lives here but actually lives an entirely different life.

For a second I stand still and let everything fall into place in my mind.

"I'm going to get my phone - you stay here. You're in charge, and if anyone asks - I was never here. You woke up, you found Eifa and Elliott, you have no idea what happened."

"What are you going to do?"

"I'm going to find Derick. I have a bad feeling…" I shake my head. "I have this handled. I need you to take care of this so I don't have to, okay?"

"Yes, ma'am."

Roe and I head back downstairs. I get my phone from Eifa and as I walk upstairs, I call Kade. We only ever text because a call means all hell has broken loose and it's an emergency. I'd hoped I'd never have to call.

"What happened?" He answers. "Aren't you in Chicago?"

"I came back. Is Derick with you?"

There's a long, dark pause. "No."

"Someone attacked the house." I relay everything that I saw when I got back as I get into my car, and what I saw in Jack's room. "I think - I think Jack has something to do with this." I can't even believe I'm saying that out loud. He's my friend, my brother, and he and Derick have done so much for each other. I can't believe that Jack would intentionally endanger his brother.

"I need you to meet me," Kade says and tells me an address. I put it into the car's GPS and start driving. As I go, an ambulance and police cars race by me, and I'm glad that the people I'm leaving behind in the house will be taken care of while I take care of their boss.

Kade and I start making a plan - Kade knows some people who consider themselves Jack's allies, and might know where he is. If he really did orchestrate this, he isn't going to go anywhere obvious. We both think it's a good sign that Derick isn't at the house. It means he's a captive because they want or need something from him.

When I hang up with Kade, I call Aster.

"You need me already?" She jokes.

"Someone took Derick," my voice cracks with her in a way that I won't let it when I'm talking to Kade. I'm holding everything inside of me as tightly as I can because we need to move fast.

"I need you to track his phone, and Jack's too." I give her the number even though I'm sure she could probably find it as fast as I could tell it to her.

"Both are turned off, but if anything even flashes for a second I'll catch it and I'll tell you." She hangs up and I'm grateful I don't have to say anything else.

I get into the city and the address Kade gave me. It's an apartment complex. As soon as I park, he's out the front door and motioning for me to follow.

"I know where Remo is. Whatever Jack is doing, Remo isn't with him."

"That's odd. They seem close."

"I know - so it might be a misdirect. However this comes out, Jack wants to be on top. I think he wants Venture."

"Why?" We get in Kade's car and he takes off, driving with speed and confidence.

"He talks about it all the fucking time and Derick never picked up on it. Jack's been restless for years. I didn't feel like it was my place to say anything and I never suspected Jack would do anything like this."

"He killed - they killed everyone, Kade. Elliott might not make it and Roe survived by accident. He knew these people well and they're dead because of him."

"Derick might be dead, too, Alina."

"Don't you fucking say that," I snap at him. "I won't believe that. We can't believe that or this will all go to shit. He is alive, and we're going to find him."

Kade's face is grim, but he nods.

We stop outside a strip club, of course. Kade checks that I'm still armed, and then I follow him around the back of the building to the staff entrance. The few girls in the dressing room don't even bat an eye as we walk through and continue getting ready for their time in the spotlight.

One of the bouncers is standing by the entrance to the back. Kade speaks to him quietly, passes him some cash, and the guy points to one of the VIP rooms. We trek across the floor and the lights and music are a little disorienting.

I take a breath and go to that place inside myself that exists when I'm working. When I have to turn off my emotions and be a weapon.

Before Kade can open the door, I step in front of him and do it myself.

There's a stripper on her knees in front of Remo, his cock in her mouth. She freezes when we enter and I have my gun trained on Remo before he's aware enough to grab his own. Kade closes the door behind us. The room is small, but we all fit.

"Put his dick away," I tell the stripper. "I'm not going to hurt you."

She does as I say, putting his increasingly limp penis inside his boxers and then zipping up his pants. Remo is glaring at me, and it's the most emotion I've ever seen on his sharp, pale face. I motion with my head for the stripper to move over by Kade. He's still blocking the door.

I step closer and keep the gun aimed at Remo's forehead.

"Where is Jack?"

"How the fuck should I know?"

Remo is overconfident because he hasn't even noticed that my other hand is holding a knife. I dart forward and slash his chest. Through the cut in his shirt, a thin line appears and starts bleeding. It isn't very deep, but it's going to sting like a motherfucker.

"What the hell bitch?"

He starts to rise up and I slash at him again, this time from behind his right ear down to his clavicle. Remo arches away, falling back on the dirty velvet couch and clutching at his neck.

"Where is Jack?"

"Not fucking here." Remo spits on the floor at my feet.

I take a few steps closer and lower the gun. Once again, Remo is getting overconfident. This time, I crack him across the face with the barrel of the gun. He collapses on the couch, blood spilling from a wound on his cheek and dripping from his nose. I grab him by the throat and push him down. He squirms, but I'm bigger than Remo and right now I have the advantage.

"Remo," I say very quietly. "You can die quickly, or you can die painfully."

He turns his head to meet my eyes, and I stare back at him. Horror starts to dawn in them that I'm absolutely fucking serious. Remo is going to die in this room, whether he tells me where Jack is or not. He's not our only chance, but I can't believe that Remo didn't help him pull this shit off. The way Remo's behaving confirmed my suspicions, and I don't have time to process how that makes me feel, nor do I want to. I want to find Derick.

"I don't know," he whines, nearly crying as he accepts what's about to happen to him. "He was working with some guy he called Mr. Romeo, and talking about Tate at Violenza helping him out."

"Good boy," I hiss at him. "What were you supposed to do today?"

"Stay here, and if anyone asked, Jack was with me."

"That's what I thought."

I pull the cushion from the back of the couch, put it over Remo's head, and pull the trigger. The cushion stifles the sound, and I feel Remo's body slump under me. When I turn, Kade is talking quietly to the stripper and handing her a card.

As we walk through the club again, he texts someone on his phone. This will be cleaned up, and it's probably not the first mess Kade has had to handle.

"Tate's at Violenza already," Kade tells me as we head back to his car. "I told him to meet me in the back. There's a room at Violenza for wet work."

Kade and I don't say anything as we drive to the other side of town. Violenza is in a more upscale club district, and I know from all the time we've spent pouring over its information trying to find a leak that it's incredibly successful. There's lines at the door every day of the weekend, the VIP is always reserved, and the liquor sales alone could give anyone the room to live comfortably in Seattle, which is fucking expensive.

Tate's been questioned about the issues we've been having at the clubs. Either he's an incredible liar, or we were asking him the wrong questions. Maybe he wasn't part of whoever was ripping off the Claytons, but that doesn't mean he's not part of Jack's plan, whatever that may be. Tate's ambitious. He's a good bar manager, he's there every night, and he always likes to talk about how he won't fuck the staff because he doesn't want to make things complicated. That doesn't mean he hasn't been caught fucking a guest or two in return for free drinks or access to the VIP area though. There have been complaints about Tate in the past and Jack brushed over them.

Now I think that's happened for a reason.

Tate's standing at the back door when we arrive. He looks nervous, which is a new look for him. I don't even wait to get inside the club before I wrap my hand around his throat, shove him into the wall, and press my knife to the underside of his chin. I can feel him swallow and the way it pushes against the blade. It's so sharp that when he does, it digs into the skin a little. A thin line of blood drips down, and he whimpers when he feels it.

"Where is Jack?"

Tate holds up his hands. "I don't know what he's doing!"

"I didn't ask that, Tate," I snarl. "I asked where he is."

"There are rooms over Cartref - he had me take some things from the back room over there."

"Didn't that concern you?" Kade comes up next to me, and Tate looks at him with hope. As if Kade is going to be more reasonable than me. The man has been vibrating with tension since the second we got in the car - if anything, I'm the reasonable one.

"It's not my place to ask questions."

"It's your place to report when something feels fucked up." Kade says.

"Tate, you knew what he was up to, didn't you?" My voice is sickly sweet.

"I knew that he was pissed at Derick, but - he wouldn't - his own brother - it's a play to get control, right?"

I tsk at him and shake my head. "You betrayed Derick. There's only one thing I can do about that."

Tate opens his mouth to protest but I slide the knife forward. It parts his skin easily and with a firm push, goes through his Adam's apple and windpipe. I yank it to the side, tearing through the artery. Tate sputters as blood gushes from his mouth and the wound, covering my arms as he slides away and falls to the ground.

"Can you clean up that mess too?" I ask Kade.

He stares at Tate with hate and fury, and I feel it too. I bend down and clean off my hands and the knife using Tate's shirt.

"No problem."

My phone rings - it's Aster.

"What do you have?" I ask.

"A location on Jack's phone." She names an address and it's right where we were headed. Cartref.

"We suspected as much."

"There are six other cell signals at that location. There might be more people than that, but there are at least six."

"Thanks, Aster. Is Jack's phone still on?"

"Yeah."

"Good, thanks." I hang up and think, then dial Jack's number.

47

Alina

There's music playing in the background when he answers. "Hey, Lina." His voice is so casual and relaxed, as if he has no idea what's happened to everyone who populated his life. As if he didn't orchestrate the murder of everyone who cared about him.

"Jack, oh my god," I put a crack in my voice, filling it with panic. Jack's muffled voice tells someone to turn off the music, and then I hear shuffling before he answers me.

"What's the matter? Are you okay?" His concern sounds so genuine that for a second I almost entertain doubt that he did all of this, but the evidence is right in front of my eyes, staining the alley with blood.

"I can't get a hold of Derick." I let the real fear that I won't find him or see him again out into this conversation. Jack has him somewhere, and I have to find him. "I've called and texted and he hasn't replied, the calls go to voicemail - I'm scared that something has happened."

There's a long pause, and then Jack says in a soft, sad voice, "Alina…"

"What?" I prompt him.

"There's an event tonight. Cat is hosting."

Anger explodes inside my chest and if I could I would reach through the phone and kill Jack right now. He's trying to make me believe that the second I leave town, Derick would be unfaithful to me. That his brother would run back to a mistress he was so entirely done with. What an asshole.

"What are you saying?" I make it sound like I'm crying because I need Jack to believe it's working.

"Derick went to the event and probably turned off his phone so he wouldn't have to explain to you where he is. I've been suspicious…" Jack is trying to sound sympathetic. "I know you both said he cut things off, but I think that was for show."

"How could he do this to me?" I shriek. "I have to come home, Jack."

"No!" Jack shouts and then backtracks a little. "You're still in danger. When this is done you can do what you need to, come back here, or stay there - don't come back now."

"He's my husband," I whisper.

"He's a shit husband," Jack snaps. "A shit brother. He doesn't deserve you or me. This mess will clean itself up and then we can all figure it out. You and me can figure it out." His voice gets soft and my skin crawls. I know what he's implying there and it takes me a few moments to get my vitriol under control.

"Okay. Call me later?"

"Of course, Lina. I love you."

I gag, and don't say anything back to that. I hang up the phone, letting him think that I'm devastated. Jack has clearly had a long time to plan this, and not only how he was going to hurt Derick but how he was going to try and cover it up. This isn't just to kill his brother, he's also trying to get me.

When I turn to Kade he's watching me with disgust, having overheard the conversation I had with Jack.

"That motherfucker is going to die."

"Yes," I agree. "Let's go."

"I think we need more people - I know some guys - "

"No," I cut him off. "You and I can handle this. Jack has no idea we know, and thinks everyone is dead. If I hadn't come home..." I shake my head, holding on to the fact that I did. That I was meant to. "We know where he is. We arm up, we go in small and fast. Okay?"

"Yes, ma'am." Kade agrees.

We drove back to Kade's apartment and once inside, I was surprised by how cozy it was. Everything was shades of brown and green, and he had way more plants that I would ever have believed. Kade is a full-on plant dad.

He also uses the second bedroom to store a fuckton of weapons, so there's a lot of layers to my husband's best friend.

Kade gives me his 1911 that already has a silencer attached, and we both load up with ammo. I also put knives everywhere I can because if anyone touches me I want to make sure they meet the pointy end of the nearest one I can grab. We have to be stealthy, but covering a man's mouth and slicing his throat is quieter even than a silencer. I'm out for blood today and I'm going to get it.

Then we're driving to Cartref.

Derick and I have only been back there a few times. Not to the club, but to look at the rest of the building. It's mostly undeveloped space and we were deciding what to do with it. Cartref is exclusive but doing well, and we had just started the process of looking into turning the open floors into a hotel or apartments. It would draw further clientele to the club. I had been really excited to work on it with him, and develop our own empire together and above board.

The good news is, I know the building well. I've looked at it's blueprints and I know the points of entry and general layouts.

If I was Jack, I'd keep Derick in the back of the second floor. The second floor has the least amount of windows, and they're all high and skinny. No one can see in, and no one can use them to get in or out. Even if Derick could find a way to escape, he'd have a hard time getting out of there. It's a warren of hallways from when it used to be office space. Visibility is complete shit.

Kade and I park and walk up to the building. There's no one at the backdoor and I am struck by Jack's ridiculous arrogance. He's not even worried that his plan didn't work.

I pull open the door and it leads directly to the stairs. Again, there's no one.

I glance back at Kade and we nod. The plan is to go upstairs, take out who we can as fast as we can, and find Derick.

The steps are concrete so they don't make any noise, and right inside the door is the first guard we've seen. Following my plan, I wrap my hand over his mouth, pull him into the hall as my foot hits the back of his left knee, and when he drops to the ground in front of me I pull my knife across his throat. I hold him as he fights his fate, and when he becomes dead weight in my hand, I let him fall.

Kade is staring at me, but then looks into the hallway. I indicate with my head that I'm going to go left - it'll lead me around to the back of the floor where they most likely are holed up.

Without waiting for him to agree, I charge into the darkness.

Everything sharpens around me, and the adrenaline is making all of my senses go on alert. I can hear my own breathing inside my body, and feel the thump of my heart.

I know I'm going in the right direction because around the corner is another guard - I don't pull him back. This time, I go for his head, stabbing him through the temple and pulling him around to my side of the corner as he falls.

Just as I get him there, another man comes out of the room at the end of the hall.

"Jason?" He calls out, not giving a fuck about being quiet. "Jason?"

I hear his footsteps getting closer, and when he turns the corner the space between his eyes is level with my gun. His eyes cross, focusing on the barrel of the silencer the same moment that I pull the trigger. He slumps down, his already dead friend's body muffling the fall.

It's now or never for me - I move down the hallway past closed doors until I get to the one the last man exited from. It's an old break room. One of their guys is sitting at the table, playing fucking solitaire. Fury threatens to overtake me but I don't want Jack alerted that we're here yet.

He kidnapped his brother, murdered everyone who cared about him and took care of him, and then has the audacity to use completely shit thugs and bodyguards to get away with it. Jack's confidence is his downfall. These guys wouldn't keep their mouths shut. Even if this had gone mostly to Jack's plan, within a month someone would be talking. I can't see Jack having the wherewithal to think to kill everyone that helped him just to keep it a secret. He probably believes they're afraid of him, when it's that he's probably overpaying them.

The shot makes a soft, high sound as I pull the trigger and shoot the guard in the back of the head. Blood spatters over his cards and the table, and he slumps forward. Dead without even knowing he had a reason to be careful.

As I get to the other corner, I hear soft footsteps. I put my back against the wall and turn when they get close.

Kade and I are gun to gun, and both lower them when we see who it is.

"I got 4."

"2," he answers me. "Didn't see anyone else."

"Me neither."

We both turn to look at the door to the main office - it's the biggest room on the floor, and there's a line of light coming from the bottom of the door. If it's not Jack and Derick, it's someone who might know where they are. The security might have been shit but they weren't here for no reason.

Silently, we signal to one another what our plan is. With a firm nod, it's now or never.

Kade kicks open the door and I swing my arms around, gun first going through the door.

I see everything in the room in sharp, quick succession. Derick is bloodied and tied to a chair, Jack is standing next to him holding a knife, and another guard is in the room.

The guard starts to raise his gun toward us, but he's too slow and my aim is too good. He's down with one to the head and two to the chest. The body thumps to the ground, and Jack turns to us with his mouth agape.

The confusion and fury on his face turns to shock when he takes me in. Then the motherfucker smiles at me.

Derick tries to say something but his mouth is gagged, and he fights whatever is binding him to the chair.

Jack assesses the situation quick enough that he goes behind Derick and holds the knife to his neck. If I try to shoot, Jack might kill him. Jack can fight but he's also unpredictable and I don't know if I could take him out faster than he could fatally harm Derick.

I lower the gun, and wait to see what Jack will do. Kade follows suit beside me.

48

Derick

The throbbing pain in my head wakes me up. My left eye doesn't want to open because it's stuck together with blood, and my joints are throbbing from how tightly I'm bound to the chair I'm in.

I'm not sure what I expect to see when I finally have both eyes opened and focused, but it isn't my brother.

He's sitting in a chair across from me as if we're having a normal business meeting. Jack is in a suit as usual, clean and reserved. It's the look on his face that's new to me. The absolute hatred in the way that he's sneering and the coldness in his eyes. It's like I'm looking at someone I don't know, and have possibly never known.

Based on the light coming through the small, high windows I've been unconscious for hours. Whoever hit me really knocked me good, and I probably have a concussion on top of everything else. The body in the foyer flashes through my head and terror clenches in my gut that I failed to protect the people who live in my house.

When Jack leans forward, I snap back to attention, fighting through the pain of feeling my pulse pounding in my skull.

"Welcome back." His voice is lower than I've ever heard it and I wonder how long this has been festering in his mind, and how long has he been putting on a show in front of me. In front of everyone.

"What have you done, Jack?" My tongue is dry and my voice barely comes out, but he hears me. I know because his smirk gets bigger. The more conscious I get, the more details I take in. Unless I'm very wrong, we're in one of the floors above Cartref. Smart move to bring me here - we own the property and no one could hear whatever happens over the noise of the club.

"What I had to, Derick. Or should I call you Brody like Alina does?"

At least I know that Alina is okay. She isn't here, I know she got on the plane and I know she landed safely in Chicago. Allie is far away from whatever the fuck is about to happen to me, and smart enough to stay away when it's over. That's the only relief I have, because unless a miracle occurs I doubt I'm getting out of this alive.

Doesn't mean I'm going to make it easy for Jack though. Whatever he wants from me I'll fight him until he has no choice but to kill me. I can tell from the look of expectation on his face that he wants me to keep asking questions, so I don't.

I lean back in the chair I'm tied to, adjusting my position as best I can to appear relaxed. Nothing pisses Jack off more than feeling undermined and I will not let him believe for a second that I'm afraid of him, or that I respect him. This fucking stranger wearing my brother's appearance.

After the silence stretches out, Jack huffs and stands up, walking closer. His hands are in his pockets, and he's full of insolent swagger.

"I've been planning this for a long time. Originally, it was going to be an accident involving you and your bride so that the only person left to take over everything was me, but then Alina happened."

The way he says her name fills me with revulsion. Its a caress from his mouth. About a month ago, Kade tried to tell me that he thought Jack's feelings for Alina were more than brotherly and I'd laughed. Now I see that he was right. The act of saying her name changed his face and his voice, there's agony there and it's disconcerting.

"Then it was about getting her as much as it was about getting rid of you. I'd sweep in and take care of her until she had no choice but to be with me, because how could she even think of being with anyone else? I'd have the means to take care of her."

Jack turns to me then, fury on his face. When he leans close I can feel spit as he fumes at me.

"Then you fucked it all by changing your will."

Even though I probably should have, I didn't tell anyone I'd met with my attorney and modified my estate. Not even Alina, definitely not Jack. No one knew I'd done that. I doubt my attorney would violate confidentiality for Jack, so he must have been monitoring me in some way. Jack had never been very technologically advanced, but I could easily see him throwing his money around until he got what he needed.

With that thought, a lot of things click in to place. The sabotage and attacks, the theft...all of those things were Jack. It's no wonder we couldn't figure out who our enemy was - they were operating from the inside. They were one of the people investigating what was happening. It never would have occurred to me in a million years that he would betray me like this. I would never have looked into him because there had never been a reason not to trust my brother.

I was so fucking naive.

"I had to accelerate my plans after that because I couldn't have her becoming anymore attached to you or I'd never get her, not when you'd left everything to her."

My will had been updated right after I'd made the marriage agreement with Don Sorrelle between myself and Anora. The plan then had been in the event of my death, Anora would get a majority percentage of my liquid assets, but everything else would go to Jack. My controlling interest in Venture, all of my properties, anything else that was in my name and belonged to me. Everything would go to Jack.

Then, I'd been making a business alliance. The business was the center of my thought when I'd made those changes because there was no way I was ever going to let Venture go outside the family. It had been my plan to change it again in the event that we had children.

Except I hadn't planned on Alina. When things started getting dicey, I knew that I needed to protect her and I knew that I could trust her to carry on the legacies that I had expanded on and created for myself. I changed my will. Everything went to Alina. Everything I had and owned went to her. There were no provisions for Jack because he had his own money from his own trust, and his interests in Venture. I wouldn't need to make sure he was taken care of - our father had already done that.

"What does that matter?" I finally ask. I want to understand how we got to this point. I don't think I'll get the answer to that question, so I at least want to understand what's happening right now.

"Venture should be mine!" He screams it in my face and I can smell alcohol on his breath. That makes him even more dangerous - his emotions are high and he's not sober.

"That is OUR family business that you have KEPT ME OUT OF!" Jack is pacing now, yelling toward me as if this is a rant he's been holding in for a long time. "I came to you and asked to work at Venture and you told me no, then put me in charge of all these clubs like your fucking thug brother. I'm always seen as less than you - you run Venture, you're so fucking special, while your brother is a playboy who runs clubs. You never let me be part of what belongs to me too - Venture isn't only yours!"

It hits me like a blow. How could I have been so fucking blind? And would it really have changed anything?

Jack came to me a year out of college and asked to work at Venture.

He couldn't tell me what he wanted to do or was interested in, so I thought he was coming to me with his handout for a paycheck without doing any work. He didn't know much about Venture or how he could add to it, and I didn't want him to think that he could get something without earning it. I knew that he'd thrown a lot of parties in college and had quite the reputation - it was a better fit for him to take over running the clubs. It was a huge responsibility and a massive amount of trust.

But I never talked about it that way to him - I never made him understand or feel how important his job was. He's also not wrong that people treated him as less than me because of what he did, looking down their noses at him because he didn't do something corporate and respectable. Jack made more money for us in a weekend than some of those fuckers made in a month, but I never told him that I valued him and that I saw what he did as an asset. He thought I was hiding him away when I was really trying to use his skills to all of our benefit.

If he'd come back to ask me again about Venture, maybe it would've come out. Instead, his anger simmered over years and now he's a goddamn monster who wants to kill me and take my wife. What the fuck has my life turned into?

"You're right, I'm sorry."

Jack stops pacing and looks at me, incredulous. "You think that changes anything?"

"No. I'm still sorry. I thought I was doing the right thing."

"Oh you always do, responsible Derick, takes care of everything."

Jack picks up a gun off the small table in the room, raises it up, and swings it at my face.

Blackness comes after the pain.

Night has fallen the next time I wake up, and there are construction lights aimed right at my face like a bad police interrogation.

Jack and a man I don't know are talking quietly, and I only catch a few words like "cartel" and "message." I have no idea if that means he's working with the cartel to get rid of me, or he's going to try and make it look like they're the ones who took me out. I try and focus on their mouths to get more, but it doesn't help and there is definitely blood in my eye fucking with my vision.

While they are occupied, I test the zip ties holding me to the chair. They are so tight I'm surprised I still have feeling in my extremities, and the chair is metal and ancient so it's built like a tank and there's no breaking it to get out. I am well and truly fucked. If Jack and his henchman got everyone at the house, it'll be at least a day before Kade figures out that anything is wrong.

Alina was supposed to call when she landed - if I haven't answered her in hours, will she get worried enough to try and find me?

Jack notices I'm awake and gets down on his haunches in front of me. He has a pleased smile on his face.

"Alina called while you were out."

I fidget and strain against the ties.

"I told her you were with Cat, and that I didn't think you'd ever given up your trampy little mistress. Gotta lay the groundwork now, bro." He slaps me hard on the shoulder.

"Fuck you. She'll never believe that."

"Her tears sounded pretty sincere."

My stomach drops and I hope that she didn't believe it, that she wouldn't believe that of me. I would never betray her like that and I would never compromise us. I thought we were on the same page but I also know how delicate things are. If I'm out of reach and someone she trusts, like Jack, is filling her head with lies...I might die with her believing this crap.

The other man comes toward me with a length of cloth and when I figure out he's going to try and gag me, I fight as hard as I can, straining away and gnashing my teeth at him. It gets to the point where I knock over the chair, and the asshole puts a knee to my chest until I can't fight back because I'm out of oxygen.

When they sit me back up, I can barely make a sound and Jack has my knife in his hand.

"We're going to do this slowly, big brother."

Jack comes closer, puts his hand on my right shoulder, and then begins to push the knife into my skin, right in the soft gap that leads to the joint, milometers at a time. It burns like nothing I've ever felt in my life and I'm screaming in agony against the gag. I'm not even trying to hold back because there's no point. Stoicism would get me nothing, and if he wants to make me hurt - I hope the visions of it haunt him for the rest of his fucking life.

"Now that I've got you sore and vulnerable, what should we talk about, hm?" Jack taps the tip of the bloody knife against his chin as he contemplates.

"Maybe you can tell me what Alina likes in bed. How does our little queen like to be pleasured? Does she like it when you get rough with her when she sucks dick? Have you tapped her in that fine ass yet? I bet it's tight as fuck," he laughs. I fight and pull trying to get to him, seeing red and acting irrational. Blood drips down my arm and floods into my hand. It makes the zip tie slippery, but not enough for me to get out - not yet.

Jack comes back to me and in a much faster move, he pushes the knife through my left deltoid.

"That's for not having the decency to get shot. You let her take a bullet for you, you pussyass bitch." Jack backhands me, and the chair tips over. The guard puts me back upright, and I glare at them both.

At that moment, the door to the room bursts inward, and in comes Alina and Kade.

For a long second, I think my head has been hit harder than I thought and I'm hallucinating. They both have guns aimed and with zero hesitation and absolute calm on her face, Alina kills the guard. The sight of her so confident and powerful fills me with a weird combination of relief and lust. I think I'd have to be dead not to feel lust at the sight of her, even when I'm bleeding from two stab wounds.

Jack moves around me, yanks back my hair and holds the knife to my throat with enough pressure to nick the skin. The gag pulls on my mouth and at this angle it's hard to breathe, and hard to see. He's shielding himself with my body.

After a moment, Jack straightens up and lets my head go. The knife stays pressed to my throat. I can see now that Kade and Alina have both lowered their guns.

"What are you doing, Jack?" Alina's voice is soft, and her mouth pulls down. It might seem like care and sympathy on the surface, but her eyes look angry. There's fire there.

"Setting us free, Allie."

She flinches at the name, but puts her hands up in surrender. "From what? Tell me why you're doing this."

"Don't you see how he controls you? The same way he controls me. What we want doesn't matter to him. Did you want to get married, Alina? Did you want to become some rich society wife who runs charities and looks good on his arm?"

Alina shakes her head. "No."

My heart races in my chest, and my stomach falls. Was she unhappy and I missed it, the same way I missed what was going on with Jack? Had I been so blinded by what I wanted that I didn't see I was letting her down?

"We can be free, and I'll take care of you. I've already done so much for you - trying to warn you away, making you see who Derick really is - I'd never let anyone hurt you or talk badly about you. I killed Niles for you!"

Alina's mouth drops open. "You killed Niles?"

"I couldn't let him get away with talking to you the way that he did. Trust me. Let me finish this. It's all ready to make him look like a victim of his own crimes, and then everything is ours. Venture, the clubs, the money - it can be me and you, together, Alina. Running it all the way we want. In charge, not serving somebody else's dream."

"I don't know if I want that, Jack." Her voice is so sad it breaks my heart.

I feel Jack stiffen behind me and the knife slips down a little.

"Then I can let you go. Leave, right now. Pretend like you never saw this and you know nothing. Go home to your sisters and your father and it'll be like none of this ever happened. If I can't have you, I don't want to hurt you."

"Jack…" her whole demeanor softens as she looks at him. This is the offer she's going to take. I can't believe it but I also can't deny what I'm seeing. Alina was so unhappy she's willing to let me die to get away from the life we've been living.

"What the fuck Alina?" Kade roars. She turns on him and fires. He slams back into the floor, and he's not moving.

I roar behind the gag, having watched the brother of my heart get shot by the love of my life. The knife cuts into me, blood seeping along my neck and down to my chest.

Alina comes closer, her gun loose at her side. She reaches out her hand toward Jack, beckoning him to her. I want to close my eyes so I don't have to see this, but I'd rather die knowing the truth than hang on to a lie.

Jack steps away from me, letting the knife fall to the floor as he comes to her. Even from my angle I can see the joy on his face as she opens her arms to him. Then he steps into the circle of them - she has one arm around his waist and the other rests on his hip.

Except then his body bows, and a strangled noise comes from him.

Alina pushes him away, and he sags down to the ground. Now I can see the knife in his chest, pushed up and under his ribs, right into his heart. Jack falls down, and looks from me to her as a burst of blood spews from his mouth. She gets on her knees and holds his hand as he coughs, then his body tightens up, and his eyes go flat.

Then she's running to me, untying the gag and kissing me. I kiss her back, the fear that I would never taste her again rushing through me.

Kade sits up, groaning and holding his chest and lifting his shirt to look at the bullet embedded in his Kevlar vest. "That fucking hurt."

Alina stops kissing me and for some reason, we all start laughing. The release of tension now that the danger is over combined with the ongoing adrenaline rush has all of us near hysteria.

She grabs my knife off the floor and cuts the zip ties at my wrists and ankles. The return of full blood flow hurts like a motherfucker, and I groan as I feel it. I collapse forward and Alina kneels in front of me, holding my face. When I look up there are tears in her eyes.

"I'm sorry. I'm sorry - I had to do it. I had to," the tears spill over and down her cheeks. "Do you forgive me?"

"Of course I do." I wrap my hands around her wrists, even though my hold is weak. "There was no other choice." We kiss again, and I get lost when her lips part mine and our tongues touch, desperate and gentle.

Kade clears his throat. "You need medical attention, boss. Not to mention, we need to clean this up and get the fuck out of here."

"Can it be handled?" I ask.

"I can get it taken care of, but it's going to cost a lot."

"Whatever it takes."

"We've got plenty of bodies on our hands today. No offense boss, but I think I'd rather take on you than her."

Alina grins at Kade and then helps me out of the chair. The wound to my deltoid isn't as bad, so she puts that arm around her shoulders and keeps me steady as we walk out. We're going to have matching scars now. It's slow going, but eventually they get me in the back of the car.

Kade is making calls and driving us to a safe house outside the city. A doctor will meet us there - someone who can be paid off and stay discreet, and he'll let me know what can't be fixed. Alina fills me in on everything that happened since she turned around and flew back. I'm relieved to hear that Eifa is safe; she's technically the only blood relative I have left now. We couldn't hide that someone broke into the house, but we'll find a way to explain that too.

"Why did you come back?" Our hands are linked, like the ride to the airport, and she keeps letting go to run her hand through my hair or down my face, as if she's checking that I'm okay over and over.

"I needed to be with you. Danger be damned, we belong together."

I reach up and touch her chin so she looks down into my eyes. "I thought he had you. I thought you were going to walk away."

Alina curls herself over me and touches her lips to mine - its upside down but it's adorable, and when she releases them we're still so close our noses are touching. I can't see anything but her - she fills my vision. It's like that all the time in my mind, and now my reality too.

"Never. Never ever. I love you."

The feeling that washes over me when she says it is beyond words or description. It's like I'm experiencing the first deep breath I've ever taken in my life. Everything that's happened has been worth it if it gets us here. If it gets her to see.

"I love you, too." I say to her, and lift my head to kiss her again. "I think I have from the first moment I saw you."

Alina laughs. "I started to love you when you took off your shoes at our wedding."

"Only started?"

"Can't you just be happy that I love you now?"

I laugh, and then sober. "Say it again."

Everything about her softens and leans into me. Her golden eyes are glowing when they meet mine, and I can see everything I've ever wanted in them. "I love you, Brody."

"I love you, Allie."

Epilogue

Kade cleaned up their mess. Bodies disappeared, bodies were staged to draw attention elsewhere. It was believable that Jack and Tate killed each other in a dispute over the club. It surprised no one that Derick immediately sold Violenza and never looked back; that he sold most of his clubs under the guise of grief over his brother.

There was real grief. Both their hearts broke for the person they thought they knew. They grieved the relationship that never was, and the lies that they believed. The healing that took place was of their minds and hearts as much as their bodies.

Derick got lucky - neither knife wound was as bad as it could have been, and he carefully followed the concussion protocol the doctor gave him to a full recovery in just over a month. Derick will carry the scars of his mistakes for the rest of his life, and it made him examine some of his relationships differently. He started working harder to not make assumptions, and hear people out. It made him a better boss, and a better partner.

Alina helped all of them mourn, including herself. They took care of their friends according to their wishes, took care of the families and the people they left behind as much as they could, and then they shut down the house in the woods.

Elliott made it through surgery, and Derick paid him a generous retirement settlement to live out his days in peace.

They rented a penthouse in downtown Seattle as well as apartments in the same building for the security staff. It felt safer to be in the middle of the chaos of the city rather than isolated out in the mountains. Someday they'll move back, when they've recovered from the ghosts that occupy the house for now. Someday when they have new lives to shine out over the old.

After Derick was declared recovered, they immediately went on a honeymoon. They deserved to get away and be themselves - to be Allie and Brody as well as Alina and Derick. To celebrate their marriage honestly, as people in love. Whether they knew it or not at the time they said their vows, it was a love match and it always would be.

They chose Hawaii because it has three of the rainiest places in the world. They traveled around all of the islands for nearly two weeks, but both agreed that Big Bog was the best place. They could stand in the misty rain all day, then find their way to the big open sky of the islands. They could breathe and forget about the things that stressed them even if it was stress from things they cared about.

Everything was perfect. They were happy, and they were ready to go home and start pursuing their future together.

The day after they got back from their trip, Aster called.

The Sorrelle compound had been attacked. Don didn't make it.

The who, the why, and the how...that's someone else's story.

Playlist

No Lie - Sean Paul, Dua Lipa

Chemicals - The Vamps

Trouble's Coming - Royal Blood

Beggin' - Maneskin

Where the Dark Things Are - Kerli

murder party - NOT THE MAIN CHARACTERS

Buzz - Halestorm

Like You Love Me - Luna Vexa

As Long As I Have You - Dove Cameron

Acknowledgments

This would not have been possible without the intense and humbling support of my family. My husband, who will try anything I ask to make sure it's physically possible, who gave me space and grace to work, and the unwavering belief that I could do this. My parents, who dear god I hope never read this (or if they do they skip the spicy parts,) who knew I wanted to tell stories for as long as I've been reading them (which is a long time.) Big thanks as always to my mother-in-law for raising my husband, and for doing enthusiastic support and promotion.

Annie, my BFFL, for beta reading and honesty. Viktoriah and Jenn for beta reads, excitement, and genuinely helpful feedback. I trust you more than you'll ever know.

My fellow readers on booktok - I'm excited to be doing this because of you.

Thanks to the many indie romance authors I met during my obsessive romance reading journey who made me feel like this was possible and reminded me that we're colleagues, not competitors. I will support you always and appreciate the way you've supported me.

Special thanks to Sophie Lark. Possibly the most badass woman I know. Your belief was the tipping point for me to get my act together. Thank you. Also to her husband Ry, for consulting on random questions.

About the Author

Ash lives in the Midwest with her husband, two girls, a dog, and a cat. She reads during every spare moment. She hopes that her characters go in new directions with terrifying, strong women who go feral for their men, and that sometimes the men are the damsels in distress who need saving. Connect on Instagram and Tiktok at @totalsassreads

You can connect with me on:

🌐 http://www.ashleymackauthor.com

🐦 http://www.twitter.com/ashmacwrites

Subscribe to my newsletter:

✉ http://www.ashleymackauthor.com/contact

Also by Ashley Mack

The Sorrelle sisters are still finding love, and are part of a bigger world of crime, intrigue, and passion.

Look at Me: a Senses novella
Want to know if Derick's right hand man ever finds his match? Read Kade's unexpected love story! Releasing September 1, 2022.

Sign up for my mailing list and receive the FULL novella for FREE!

The Taste of You
By day, Aster Sorrelle leads a programming team at Designation, trying to protect her family's business from outside attacks. When someone threatens Designation, her father puts a man on her tail who discovers all of her secrets and what she gets up to at night.

Freelancer is an assassin and bodyguard for hire. Aster begins as a job and quickly turns into an obsession. When stalking her from the shadows turns into something more, he'll have to decide if keeping his secrets will bring them closer, or tear them apart.

Coming October 2022, pre-order now!